HANGDOG II
Rebirth

Book Two of the Hangdog Trilogy
By: Tylie Vaughan Eaves

Vertū Publishing, 2019
A Component of Vertū Marketing, LLC

VERTŪ PUBLISHING
A Component of Vertū Marketing LLC
www.vertu-marketing.com

Ordering Information:
Quantity sales. Special discounts are available on quantity purchases by corporations, associations, and others. For details, contact the publisher at the address above.
Orders by U.S. trade bookstores and wholesalers.
Please contact: Tel: (866) 779-0795.

Printed in the United States of America
ISBN 978-0692176702

Acknowledgements

Firstly, and as always, all my thanks and praise be to God – for everything.

Thank you to my husband, Wade Eaves, who is my "idea fairy," for his blunt honesty, support, and God-honoring perspective. Thanks to my boys, for being as excited about my career as I am – You are my happy place. As always, huge thanks to Deborah Vaughan, my editor extraordinaire (who also happens to be my mother) without whom I would no doubt produce the most grammatically erred work in the history of Christendom. And finally, the biggest, loudest, most substantial thank you to my readers – You have made this journey more rewarding than I could have ever imagined.

Hangdog II – Rebirth

PART ONE

CHAPTER ONE

Valerie tore through the top drawer of Eli's bedside table, tossing notes, small medical supplies, pens and folders onto the floor behind her. Throughout her married life, and certainly during the twenty years she'd been the mother of twin boys, she'd spent a large part of her time putting things away. Tearing things out of a drawer and tossing them onto the floor was in direct opposition to every domestic protocol she'd set for herself. But then again, watching one of those twins wake from a two-year coma was anything but typical, and Valerie couldn't contain her joy, much less maintain her composure. "I put that list of emergency contact numbers in here ages ago!" she said excitedly.

She worked feverishly, at a loss as to what should happen now. Behind her, her sweet, still-in-awe husband Joe was slowly, delicately bringing Eli up to speed on everything that had happened since he'd fallen victim to a horrific car accident on graduation night. A crash that had resulted in a brain injury so severe that he'd slipped into a coma. Joe struggled to find the words to explain to his son that he'd been asleep for more than two years. No matter how many times Joe told him, Eli could not believe so much time had passed. Wherever he had been inside his own head, it had become as real to him as the physical world — maybe more so. Beyond the passing of time, Eli found it almost impossible to believe that the crash had been his own brother's fault — that his twin had been arrested for reckless driving, vehicular assault and underage consumption, and that he'd been in court, lost his football scholarship and had somehow decided to join the Marines. It was too much to take in. Though Eli remained calm throughout the conversation, Joe and Val knew there would be a thousand more questions before the entire story was told.

"And you're saying Beau is in Afghanistan right now, as in, right this minute? Beau McKnight, my brother, Beau?" Eli asked, with a tone of disbelief in his voice. "No way," Eli shook his head in astonishment. "No way is the never-serious, everything-is-hilarious Beau McKnight an actual Marine! I just can't believe it!" Eli breathed deeply, taking in his reality. "I feel like I'm in a movie or something. This is so surreal." Joe looked on, a mixture of both joy and sorrow welling inside him. Eli's face, as he fought to process the mountains of information he'd just absorbed, was like that of a little boy. Joe saw him as a pre-schooler again, a small child facing a big world.

Julia sat in Eli's desk chair, the chair he'd used every night for as long as anyone could remember to do school projects and homework, and more recently, to send his friends instant messages and browse the internet. If Eli had noticed her presence, he hadn't said so. She remained in a stunned silence. She couldn't help but feel out of place, as if she were eavesdropping on moments she shouldn't be. How would Eli react when he learned that not only had his brother joined the Marines, but he'd also fallen rapidly back into a relationship with the girl who broke his heart in middle school, causing him to swear off committed relationships completely? Not only that, but how would he manage to process the reality that he was going to be an uncle, and that the middle-school heartbreaker now lived in his home and had a room down the hall? She felt her heart pounding in her chest, she was justifiably nervous, and yet, she was also excited. Her spirit soared every time she thought about Beau. She tried to imagine his excitement, to picture his reaction when he heard the news, but she couldn't. She thought about all the hours he'd spent in guilt, angry with himself and with the world, and she did her best to imagine a future with the full-of-life, joyful Beau they'd all remembered from before the accident. When would he call? The suspense surged inside her. She knew she should be focused on Eli, but all she could think about was Beau.

Joe tried in vain to remember every detail of every event that had happened since the accident. Eli was running over with questions. Joe took in every word Eli said, the shape of his face, the movement of his mouth as he spoke — his son was back! It seemed dreamlike, but somehow right at the same time. Eli's expression and tone were the perfect display of peaceful. He asked question after question, but he didn't become agitated or even flustered. The look on his face was peculiar, but in a way that put both Joe and Val at ease. He moved his arms and legs, making every effort to connect with his body again. At one point, he tried to push up in his bed, but lacked the muscular strength to support himself. Joe reached out and helped him, and instead of frustration, Eli looked into his father's eyes and said, "Do we still have a gym membership?" Joe's eyes grew wet with tears as he laughed at his son. But, he was shouting on the inside. He wanted to run the streets and yell from the rooftops, but tonight, he opted to bask in the beautiful, melodic tones of his son's voice — in that moment, for Joe, not even the greatest of symphonies could compare to the sweetness of Eli's voice.

"I found it!" Valerie shouted. She hadn't stopped crying since Eli opened his eyes. She half laughed and half cried every word. She opened the folder she'd received from the hospital discharge staff the day they brought Eli home and finally found a list of numbers to contact in the event of an emergency or urgent need. "Where's my phone?" She was buzzing. She couldn't think straight. Under her breath, she kept saying, "God is so good. He's so good. God is so good," over and over again. The emotion was almost too much for her to bear, and now she had to pull it together long enough to do the job she'd been doing for always — running the world, at least as far as it pertained to the McKnight house. Her hands were shaking when Joe reached out to give her the phone. He grabbed her delicate fingers and squeezed them. They made eye contact through the bleariness of tears and Joe smiled. Valerie's heart swelled with an excitement she'd not felt in so long she'd forgotten what it was like. Life had changed suddenly yet again, only this time, doors were opening instead of closing.

Val's hands were trembling as she dialed the number from Eli's discharge papers. She had no idea what she'd say when the line connected. Joe and Eli stopped talking to listen. Eli's face expressed his intrinsic desire to understand his newly emerging reality. "Hello? Hi, yes," Valerie spoke quickly, excitedly. "This is Valerie McKnight. My son is a patient of Dr.

Davies." After a pause, "Oh, I see. Yes, I understand. Well, I do think this qualifies as an emergency, so yes, please put me through." Joe could hear the quiver of excitement in his wife's voice. He couldn't help but smile. Life had just taken a very sudden and very joyous turn, and it swelled his spirit to see the spark in Valerie's eyes.

Joe laid a hand on Eli's forearm and patted him lightly. It felt strangely tiny under his big fingers. The two listened intently as Valerie waited on the line. Finally, she continued, "Yes, hello! Dr. Davies? Oh my goodness, yes, yes, it's Valerie McKnight. I'm so sorry to wake you, but Eli is awake and we don't know what to do! No, no, he's awake. Yes, totally awake! He's moving and talking and awake! Eli is awake!" There was another pause, fraught with uncertainty. "No, not at all. He seems perfectly lucid. He's talking. Yes, talking! Yes! No. Yes. He's moving, yes! He's weak of course, but he, yes, he can move. He really can!" Joe's heart was pounding with anticipation. Val paused again, this time for what felt like ages. "Yes, sir. I understand. Yes. We'll be ready. No, no. We want to do it right now. As soon as you want. Thank you! Yes! Thank you! We'll be ready." She pushed the call end button on the cordless phone she held in her shaking fingers.

"Well? What did he say?" Joe asked emphatically.

"They're sending a transport, an ambulance. They want to get him under observation right away! We should be ready to go within the hour!" Valerie turned to Julia, who was now standing behind her, keeping a distance, but very much engaged in the situation. Both hands still covered her mouth.

Julia didn't wait for Val to speak before asking, "What should I do?"

"Well, we need to get in touch with Beau, and Ivy, and well, everybody. But I don't know where to start!" She laughed. She was too excited and too emotional to think clearly.

"Why don't I stay here? You all go to the hospital, and I'll try to get in touch with Beau. I think I have to call the Red Cross or something."

Val inhaled sharply, "Okay. I'll go ahead and call my mom and Joe's mom and have them call everyone else. And then we'll try to reach Ivy." She looked at Eli with an expression that signaled her reluctance to speak. It was time to tell him that his long-time girlfriend, the girl he'd fallen madly in love with, the girl he planned to spend his life with, had entered the mission field while he slept and had been serving in Zimbabwe for nearly a year. She paused for a moment. Eli sat quietly, a slight smile on his face. He seemed so calm, so peaceful. "She's going to be so upset she's not here," Val said. She then tried to gently explain Ivy's agony over the decision she'd made to leave and how she'd been by his side every day prior to that decision, caring for him, talking to him and holding his hand.

Eli's peaceful demeanor didn't change. He seemed disconnected from any stress, and completely unaware of the passage of time. He took in his mother's words and finally spoke, "She won't be upset, Mom. Especially not if I'm the one who calls her," Eli smiled broadly.

"Oh," Val laughed, "good point. I guess you *should* be the one to call, huh?" She started to cry as she walked over to Eli's bedside. She put her hands on his shoulders and kissed his forehead and then wrapped her arms around him, kissing his cheeks and squeezing his frail frame. "I'm... I don't even have words. I just love you so much! We've missed you so much!" She wiped the tears from her cheeks before reminding herself, "Oh! I need to get dressed. But, I don't want to leave the room!" She laughed again and reached out for Joe's hand.

"Well, I ain't leavin' the room," he responded, eyes wide beneath raised eyebrows.

"We'll tag team, okay? I'll go and then you go?" As Val spoke, she nodded her head, showing her approval of her own idea.

"Deal."

Julia stood frozen in place. She knew she was too unfamiliar to run to Eli and hug him, but she had been living in the house long enough to have grown attached to him, even as he slept. She felt awkward. This wasn't the first time she'd felt awkward since reuniting with Beau in what felt like an urgent whirlwind, but it was certainly one of the most dramatic. Eli must have sensed her uncertainty, because within seconds he looked at her and said, "Um, I think we probably have some catching up to do." He recognized her face. He knew who she was, but she felt like a stranger at the same time. She definitely wasn't the girl he remembered from middle school, and seeing her now, standing in his room in the middle of the night as if she belonged there, was surreal.

Julia chuckled, "That's an understatement." Joe laughed in response. Eli produced a chuckle too, albeit an awkward one. "We'll have plenty of time for that later, though. I'm going to go back to my room and let you all talk." She walked over to his bedside slowly. She hesitantly put a hand on his shoulder. She didn't know if she should hug him or shake his hand, or what. After all, she'd been sleeping down the hall from him for a while now. She'd helped his mother move him and shave his face, and though she felt connected to him, he didn't know her at all. "I'm so grateful." She smiled at him and Eli knew it was genuine. Eli smiled back at her and she made her way out the door.

"Her *room*?" Eli raised his eyebrows at his father and cocked his head in an expression that showed his perplexity.

Joe sat in the chair by Eli's bed and laughed to himself, "Um, yeah — about that… " he began.

~

Ivy was slow to answer when the phone on her hip began to vibrate. She was well into her morning routine and it was her turn to volunteer at the village school. At first, she thought she might ignore the call, but something in her spirit told her she should answer. She tore herself away from the daily soccer game and reached into her pocket. When she pulled out her phone to see a U.S. country code followed by the McKnight's home number, she felt her heart sink. It was the middle of the night at home. Something major had to be going on. Her heart began to beat faster and she could feel a queasiness in her stomach. Her hands grew clammy. Val usually only called once every couple weeks, in the evening. Why would she be calling now?

She quickly hit the call button and held the phone to her ear. "Hello?" she said, with both urgency and mild panic in her voice.

There was a pause, "Hey there, beautiful," she heard a calming voice say on the other end of the line. Her mouth fell open as the breath caught in her chest. It sounded like Eli. But, it couldn't be, could it? But she would know Eli's voice anywhere. His cadence and tone were unique to him alone, despite the similarities between him and his brother. She stood in stunned silence for longer than Eli could handle, "Are you there?"

"I... I... I'm here." She paused again, her heart racing, her hands shaking, her knees beginning to buckle beneath her, and she placed the fingers of her free hand over her eyes as she began to weep silently, "Eli? Is it... is it really you?" The tears flowed freely now. She was powerless to stop them.

Eli could hear the tears in her voice. He could make out the sound of her staggered breaths catching in her chest. "Yep, it's really me," he smiled when he spoke. She could hear his joy and the clarity of his words. As her knees wobbled, her head began to swim a little.

"I... I don't know what to say. I need to sit down." Through her tears, she slowly shifted her bodyweight into a seated position, right in the dirt. She crossed her legs beneath her and let the tears come. She didn't speak right away, the only sounds emitting from her body were a combination of sobs and labored inhales.

"It's okay," Eli said. "Please don't cry."

One of Ivy's fellow missionaries noticed her posture and jogged over to check on her. After all, she was supposed to be working and it wasn't in her character to leave the children to play without her, not without a really good reason. As he approached, he noticed her tears. She looked up and made eye contact with him, but he couldn't get a definitive read on her expression. It seemed happy and heartbroken all at once. He didn't ask. Instead, he gave her a reassuring look and turned toward the kids, immediately taking her place and seamlessly integrating himself into the game. Ivy nodded into the phone, but still couldn't form words. Instead, she began to laugh through her tears — a deep, yet somehow fragile, laugh.

"How are you?" Eli asked the question as casually as he could manage, as though he hadn't just awakened from a two-year coma.

"How am I?" Ivy asked, shock abounding from her lips. "I'm… good. I'm actually really good." Her words were hesitant. Was it right to admit she'd been happy? She paused for a moment, trying to gather her wits. As she began to come to her senses, wonderment filled her being and excitement began to stir inside her. She began to teeter between feelings of shock and giddiness. "How long have you been awake?" she asked. Eli could tell by her voice that her emotions were on a wide swinging pendulum.

"About an hour, I think," Eli said.

"Oh, Eli, I… I'm so, so sorry I wasn't there. I should have been there." Ivy wiped her eyes. She felt a pang of guilt.

"No, you shouldn't. You definitely shouldn't have been here. I'm so proud of you Ivy! Mom told me how well you're doing. I'm so happy for you!" Eli's response was gentle and caring. He missed her. He selfishly wanted her to be there by his side. But, he really *was* proud of her. And he certainly couldn't begrudge her the experience, nor could he rightly expect her to put her whole life on hold to sit by his bedside.

Ivy smiled through her still-flowing tears. After all he'd been through, how was it possible that he'd feel pride for a decision she'd made that took her away from him? How could he be okay with a choice that didn't include him? She took a deep breath and finally spoke, "How do you feel?"

"Well-rested," he chuckled, "and really, really skinny. I've never been a runt before. I don't think I like it," Eli laughed at his own words. Ivy smiled and shook her head. Her shoulders shrugged as she scoffed. It was as if she were dreaming. She half expected to wake up at any second. Only Eli she thought. "No really, I feel great," he said. "Mom and Dad have been filling me in on what happened. It doesn't seem real."

"*This* doesn't seem real!" Ivy responded. "I'm expecting to wake up from a dream at any second!" She heard Eli chuckle. "I've thought about this day for so long," she said. "I don't know how to act. I don't know what to say. I've missed you so much." Her heart pounded in her chest. She felt tension behind her eyes and she couldn't seem to stop crying.

"Tell me about Zimbabwe," Eli said. He wanted to interject a little normalcy into their conversation, though there was nothing *normal* about what they were going through. Ivy tried to tell Eli all about her mission team and her duties, and their goals, but she kept coming back to questions for him, about him, about what would happen next. He did his best to answer them, but he didn't have many answers. He smiled as he spoke, "At this point, you know more about what's happening than I do! I've been asleep for two years, remember?" At that moment, all he knew was he would be in the hospital under observation for a few days and then probably start rehab, but even that was uncertain.

After a few more minutes, when Eli could hear the medical transport team coming in downstairs, he took a breath, trying to process what it must be like for Ivy to have been without him for two years, to be living in another country, and he wondered if she'd distanced herself from him. Their conversation had been strange, both familiar and somehow new at the same time. Had she moved on? Had she changed her mind? Finally, he spoke up, "They're here to transport me to Houston." He held a long, fat pause, loaded with uncertainty. "So, for me, it feels like we've only been apart for a little while, a few hours maybe, I was only gone a little while." He inhaled again, "What I'm trying to say is, for me, nothing has changed. With us, I mean. But for you it's been a long time, a really long time, and I wouldn't blame you if... Well, so, do you... are you... do you?"

Ivy cut him off, her stomach flipping, her heart pounding and her eyes sobbing all at the same time, "Do I still love you?"

Eli took a deep breath, "Um. Well, right. Do you?" He was as nervous and sweaty-palmed as he had been the night they last spoke, a night that was as fresh in his mind as it was when he kissed her goodnight for the last time. A night he now feared had become a distant memory for her.

"As much as ever, maybe even more," Ivy smiled as the words rolled off her tongue. She had waited to hear Eli's sweet voice for more than two years. She had struggled to keep hope alive, to keep believing for a miracle, and now, on the other end of the line, was an actual, real life miracle — and he wanted to know if she still loved him. She loved Zimbabwe. She loved her work, but she loved Eli McKnight more, at least she had at one time. Somehow, before Zimbabwe, even as he slept, their bond had become solidified. She knew, in some ways, they were both different people now and that they'd probably have to relearn how to be together. She could hear change in his voice, and as she looked around, she could feel the change within herself. But, she also knew that she *needed* to be with Eli. Through the phone, in the background, she could hear voices and hustle and bustle. "I'll see you soon," she said.

"I can't wait," Eli responded, his heart pounding as his fears eased and a different kind of adrenaline began to course through his veins.

"I love you," Ivy spoke the words in a whisper, as if she were reassuring herself as much as she was reassuring him.

"I love you, too." Eli's smile was broad when he heard the click on the other end of the line.

Ivy immediately ran to her ministry partner and asked him to cover for her. She gave him a brief explanation of the miracle she'd just experienced, but she was focused on only one thing. As she dialed her mom's number, her mind was once again filled with hazy visions of a future she thought she'd never see. She didn't know what the coming days would bring or how she'd make it work. She didn't know what her team leaders would say or if she had the funds to cover travel expenses, but she didn't care — she was going home!

~

Valerie couldn't help but notice that the medical transport to Houston seemed to be much shorter than it had during the few trips she'd taken to and from the hospital throughout Eli's initial stay. This time around, the journey was actually enjoyable. Riding in the ambulance with an alert, talking Eli made the trip feel like a party. At the hospital, word had already spread and news of Eli's arrival was buzzing through every nurse's station. Everyone knew his story, many had been part of his treatment in some way or another, and, if they were being truthful, none of them thought they'd ever see him alive again, much less awake.

~

Dr. Davies' sleep deprivation was no match for the exhilaration he felt as he poured a cup of coffee for the drive to the hospital. He was in awe. It had been so long. Truth be told, the day they'd given Val and Joe the approval to take Eli home, he hadn't expected him to live two months, let alone two years. He'd been Eli's neurologist ever since, and nothing in his scans pointed to a day like today — nothing. Davies was so excited that he woke his wife to tell her what was happening. He never woke her when he was on call. She had grown accustomed to rising to an empty bed, either finding him away from home or asleep on the sofa having returned from the hospital at some ungodly hour with the need to watch TV and wind down. She had heard her husband mention Eli before. She remembered how much this case had impacted him and how he'd spent sleepless nights, unable to understand why Eli hadn't recovered as he had first expected, and unable to accept that his health had declined so rapidly after that initial surgery. Over time though, as Dr. Davies continued to care for other patients, they'd both put Eli largely out of their minds — out of sight, out of mind, as they say. Now, her husband was lit up like a Christmas tree. He'd never had someone remain in a coma for so long and live to tell the tale. She watched as the scientist in him burst into action, but she also noted a sense of wonderment she'd rarely seen over the years, a wonderment no scientific explanation would be able to extinguish.

CHAPTER TWO

Julia laid down on what had become her bed, her mind reeling with this new development, with the miracle happening down the hall, and with the reality that her entire life had changed so much, so quickly. She'd now become part of someone else's family and it felt both comforting and unsettling at the same time. She struggled to formulate a logical plan for getting in touch with Beau, partly because she was sleep deprived and partly because she was feeling a bit nauseated. She'd grown accustomed to a moderate amount of morning sickness, but she was rarely awake at two o'clock in the morning, and it certainly didn't sit well on her stomach.

She reached for the small plate of saltine crackers on her nightstand. All the mommy forums and pregnancy blogs named nearby crackers as a winner in the battle against morning sickness. Julia loathed the texture of dry saltines, so, as her face involuntarily signaled her disgust, she instinctively reached for the customary bottle of water by her bedside, hoping to quench her desperate desire to rinse away the thick, pasty feeling from her mouth. As much as she hated that feeling, she had to admit, she always felt a little better after a few crackers. She hadn't yet decided if her relief was due to the crackers themselves or to the placebo effect of simply taking action to help herself.

She rubbed her face with her hands and laid back against her pillow. Maybe it would help if she slept a little while longer. She might be able to think more clearly if she was better rested. She rolled onto her side and allowed her mind to drift to Val's reaction, or even Beau's reaction, if they ever found out she had even considered more sleep at a time like this. With those thoughts in her mind, she'd never be able to fall asleep anyway, so she pushed herself up and sat on the edge of the bed, willing herself to think. She slowly stood up and walked over to the desk, where she pulled open a drawer and retrieved a folder with the USMC crest emblazoned on the front. She flipped the folder open and began rifling through the mountain of papers Beau had given her before he left. She knew there was a list of contact numbers in there somewhere.

When she found the numbers, she made a mental note of the time. "Nobody is going to answer a phone at this time of night," she thought. She sat down at the desk and flipped open her laptop. Within a few minutes, she booted up and constructed an urgent message for Beau that read, <IF YOU'RE ONLINE, OR WHEN YOU GET ONLINE, CALL ME RIGHT AWAY! IT DOESN'T MATTER WHAT TIME, PLEASE CALL! IT'S SERIOUS!> After reading it back, she was afraid that it sounded like she had bad news, and she definitely didn't want to give Beau that impression. She added a smiley face emoji and a few Xs and Os for good measure. She debated about whether or not she should just put the news out there, but thought better of it. This was too huge to hear about through a text.

Next, she grabbed her phone and began pressing numbers — starting with the first command contact number on the list. After a few rings, the call went to voicemail. "Naturally," she thought. She left a voice message with her name and number and a brief explanation of her need — an explanation that omitted the details and instead described some urgent medical news that needed to be relayed. She left the same message on the Family Readiness line and then found herself locked in a sleep-deprived, internal battle about whether or not this situation was serious enough to warrant a call to the Red Cross. The paperwork in her folder made it very clear that the Red Cross Emergency Communication line was reserved for explicit emergency contact needs only. Was this an emergency? No, not technically. At least, not so far as the Red Cross or the United States Marine Corps was concerned.

Julia looked at the clock again, ultimately deciding that she would let her previous calls brew for a few more hours, until the world was awake enough to check voicemail. She reckoned that she would call the Red Cross *only* if her other efforts proved fruitless. "Now what?" she asked herself. She sat back down on the bed and sent a group text to Val and Joe, <LEFT AN INSTANT MESSAGE FOR BEAU, CALLED THE COMMAND AND FAMILY READINESS AND LEFT VOICEMAILS. I WILL LET YOU KNOW WHAT I HEAR.> She sat on the edge of her bed, staring at her phone, smiling slightly, and imagining Beau's reaction to the news. She pictured Beau's face and felt the pang of heartache caused by the distance between them. She missed him more than she thought she ever could.

Even as she became lost in the thoughts of her heart, she remained at a loss as to what her next steps should be. Was there something else she should do? After a few moments, she returned her phone to its charger and decided her next step would be more sleep. She turned off the bedside lamp and nestled down, pulling the blanket up around her. She closed her eyes and allowed the joy of the night to rock her into a peaceful sleep.

~

Julia jolted awake to the sounds of an unfamiliar ring. Her mind struggled to make the transition from sleep to wakefulness as she threw her body out of bed in a panic. On the third ring, she recognized the tone as the house phone and slapped around on the desk in the darkness to retrieve the handheld. She squinted as she hit the green, glowing talk button. "Hello?" she answered, with a tone of hesitation and uncertainty. It was still too early in the morning for a ringing phone to be perceived as anything less than startling.

"Hello, ma'am. My name is Cpl. Ballantine with the United States Marine Corps… "

Julia cut Ballantine off, still in a half stupor from being jolted awake. "Oh, thank goodness, you must be calling about my message!"

Cpl. Ballantine was silent for a long beat. "Um, no ma'am, I'm sorry," she paused, "a message?"

Julia could hear the confusion in the corporal's voice and decided she was better off letting her do the talking. "I'm sorry, never mind. You were saying?"

The corporal shook off her uncertainty and returned to her mission, "I'm calling from Headquarters Marine Corps in Arlington and I'm trying to get in contact with Joseph or Valerie McKnight."

"Oh. Um, well, they're not here," Julia said. "But I'm Beau's girlfriend. Maybe I can help?"

"I'm sorry ma'am, but I can't give you any information. I am required to speak to the Marine's next of kin. I have those names listed as his parents, Joseph and Valerie."

"Oh, I see," Julia said, mildly dejected. She wasn't family and she knew it, but she wanted to scream, "I'm pregnant with his child, lady — isn't that kin enough for you people?" She sighed to check herself. "Well, they are at the hospital. I can give you their cell numbers..."

The corporal paused again. Hearing that Mr. and Mrs. McKnight were at the hospital took her aback. She furrowed her brow, "Um, no, thank you... that won't be necessary. I have those numbers listed here, as well. Thank you for your time."

"Oh, okay. No problem," Julia responded, despondent. She tried not to take it personally, but she was confused. She expected someone to call *her* back. She was, after all, the person who left the messages. How hard could it possibly be to get a message to Beau? It didn't make sense.

"Have a good day ma'am."

"You too," Julia softened her tone, but not her attitude. After hanging up the phone, she began to wonder why the Marine Corps would call the McKnight house line when she'd left her cell number as the callback contact on every voicemail, and since she was the caller, why wouldn't they be allowed to talk to her? She stewed over the idea that, because she and Beau didn't share a last name, she wasn't considered a viable point of contact where the military was concerned — regardless of her efforts to reach him or her status as his girlfriend. She knew the rules and regulations. She knew it shouldn't bother her so much, but it did.

~

Laughter filled Eli's room as he joked with his nurses and his parents. The entire neurology wing was filled with a renewed sense of purpose, having now witnessed a real-life miracle. And Eli, they now knew without a doubt, Eli was something special. Just a few minutes in the room with him had given everyone extra pep in their steps.

Dr. Davies arrived and immediately visited Eli. As he walked into the room, Val spoke up, "Dr. Davies! Hello!" As she spoke, Joe reached his right hand out toward Dr. Davies, who took it in a handshake. He smiled and made eye contact with Joe and Val briefly. He was still smiling as he urgently turned toward the bed where Eli was sitting up, watching the scene unfold. As Davies stepped toward him, Eli reached out his hand, extending his now-slim arm toward the man his father had told him saved his life that first night and whose work kept him alive for many nights thereafter. He also knew Dr. Davies was the man who had predicted he would never wake up. Davies took his hand and squeezed it. His face was a testament to his astonishment. He couldn't hide his surprise. Dr. Davies took it all in. Eli seemed to be perfectly lucid and displayed no residual neurological effects from a two-year coma — impossible!

"Nice to meet you," Eli said.

"And you as well, young man." A broad smile spread across Davies' face. "How are you feeling?"

"Like I could really do with a few push ups and maybe a meatball sub," Eli smiled back.

"He's been talking about food since he woke up, but I didn't know what to do with the feeding tube and all. So there he sits, still talking about food!" Valerie laughed.

"Some things never change," Joe chimed in as he placed his arm around Val's waist, the first embrace they had shared since witnessing their miracle. Val allowed herself to feel the warmth of Joe's arm against her body. If it were possible to feel more joyful than she did in this moment, she didn't know how.

Davies laughed out loud, "Well, he'll need a small procedure to remove the tube, nothing serious, but we're not quite there yet." He gestured to a nearby nurse, "Let's get him some formula pushed through that tube to tide him over and then we'll order some scans. I can't promise you when those will take place, but we'll get to them as fast as we can. After that, we can formulate a plan for the next few days, okay? I promise, we'll get you to meatball subs as soon as we can. Okay?"

"Sounds good to me," Eli smiled as the nurse began to move around the room.

"I've got some phone calls to make. There's a whole team of experts who aren't going to believe what I'm seeing right now, son." Dr. Davies put a hand on Eli's shoulder, "I also want to have a nice, long conversation with you later."

"I'll be here," Eli answered.

"Before I go and let you all get some rest, do you have any questions for me?" Davies looked around the room, from face to face, deliberately.

Eli had seen his father yawn at least ten times since arriving at the hospital. Somehow, knowing that sleep would eventually be expected of him, too, caused a fear to rise up in his gut. "I'm going to be honest Dr. Davies. Since I woke up, I've known everything was going to be okay, really, I have, but I've seen this guy yawning his head off," he gestured toward his father, making a funny face to mask his concern. "But knowing everything is going to be okay hasn't stopped the nagging fear I've had about going to sleep for the night. I mean, I don't feel sleepy yet, but I know it's coming and, well, am I okay to sleep? Because, I'm having doubts."

Dr. Davies smiled again, "A fair question, young man. Yes, you are absolutely okay to go to sleep. Healthy sleep is actually very different from coma sleep. Healthy sleep starts and finishes in cycles of completely normal electrical activity. Coma sleep isn't really sleep and typically doesn't involve those electrical cycles. So, you should definitely sleep when the sensation hits you. In fact, you may feel tired sooner than you think because your body isn't used to all this activity, so you're burning calories at a different rate and will need to recharge your battery as a result."

"That makes sense," Eli answered. "Thank you." He smiled, and he was appreciative, but hearing the doctor's words still didn't erase his feelings of vulnerability.

Dr. Davies turned to Val and Joe, he was smiling and shaking his head as he put his hands into the pockets of his khaki pants, his lab coat held at bay by his forearms. He looked at the beaming parents, nodded and simply said, "Congratulations. It's remarkable." He looked down toward his feet and smiled, shaking his head again as he made his way to the door.

Eli's nurse trailed behind him. "I'll be right back with that formula," she said, as she let the door close behind her.

"I'm not so sure I like the idea of having formula for breakfast, unless it's got a mashed up meatball sub in it," Eli said, displaying the same straight-faced sense of humor they remembered. Joe and Valerie laughed, probably more than they would have any other time, but the literal impossibility of the moment made every joke that much funnier and every smile that much sweeter.

Val turned toward the TV and glanced toward Eli. "Let's see if there's anything good on! Your Uncle Pete is on his way with Nana and Pop and you'll probably have tons of visitors in the next few days. Hopefully, Julia has been able to get a message to your brother." She was so excited she couldn't contain her tears. "I'm literally busting over with gratitude. Could God possibly be any better?" She smiled toward Joe.

"I still can't believe Beau is in the Marines, and that he's going to be a dad. I mean, Beau? A father?" Eli said, shaking his head. "I'm really going to need you to start at the beginning with that story."

Valerie glanced at Joe. She didn't want to burden Eli with more information. It was too soon. "I promise we'll tell you all about that, and everything else you want to know, but for now, I'd like to just enjoy this moment, okay?" She walked to Eli's bedside and he instinctively wiggled over, making room for her. She sat down next to him and kicked off her shoes, raising her feet onto the bed. She laid her arm over her baby boy's shoulder and said, "Besides, they'll be here with your Enfamil in a minute." She paused, smirking and looking at Eli out of the corner of her eye, waiting for his reaction.

"Enfamil?" Eli asked in a dramatic and surprised tone, feigning concern. Valerie burst into laughter and Joe chimed in.

From across the room, Valerie heard Joe say, "Today is a very, very good day," and she nodded, thinking to herself that the word *good* to describe this day might just be the understatement of the century.

CHAPTER THREE

Eli was somewhat transfixed by ESPN, but at the same time, peppering his parents with questions about every detail of the past two years. Valerie buzzed around the room, adjusting things, trying to make the room feel more homey and using her cellphone to snap as many pictures and videos of Eli as the memory would allow. It wouldn't be long before social media would take their miracle to the masses. Joe's face was frozen in a permanent half-grin as he watched his wife transform before his eyes. He began to see flickers of the woman she'd been before Eli's accident — flickers he hadn't known he'd missed until they began to resurface. He'd forgotten that she used to hum while she performed household chores. When the sound of her humming softly fell on his ears, he found himself falling in love with her all over again.

Valerie reached into Eli's bag and pulled out his Bible. It had been on his bedside table, unopened, for far too long. She looked at its slightly worn cover and gently ran her thumb across the edges of what appeared to be well-studied pages. She placed the Bible on the rolling table by his bed and patted it lightly. Eli glanced in her direction and smiled. He wasn't sure what to say, but felt he needed to say something. He paused to think for just a second before saying, "Mom, it was peaceful."

"What?" Valerie questioned. "What do you mean? What was peaceful?"

"I mean, to me, it didn't feel like I was gone very long, but I remember it was so, so peaceful. I just knew everything would be okay." Eli looked first at his mom and then his dad. Joe's forehead was crinkled.

"I just thought you should know, I was never afraid. It wasn't scary." By this time, Valerie had crossed the room and was sitting on Eli's bed. Joe was leaning forward with his elbows on his knees.

"What do you mean, 'gone'? Gone where, son?" Joe asked.

"I'm not sure exactly. Maybe nowhere, but maybe somewhere between here and Heaven. I wasn't alone, though. I know that. I just remember feeling so peaceful and light, like weightless."

Valerie and Joe were speechless. They stared at each other. "You weren't alone? Who was there?" Valerie asked.

"I'm not sure. I just knew someone was there with me. I felt safe and loved. I knew everything was going to be okay and I felt like I was floating." Eli's face was serene. The peace he recalled in his mind was clearly evident in his expression.

Joe moved to the other side of Eli's bed, opposite from his wife. "Did you see anything? What else do you remember?"

Eli closed his eyes, "It was sparkly, or maybe glittery somehow. It was dark, but there was light at the same time, coming from somewhere I couldn't see. I can't really describe it. I just automatically knew that everything was going to be okay." His parents stared at him, and at each other, in stunned silence. Eli smiled, "It's not brain damage. I'm not crazy. I promise," he laughed to himself and glanced over at his Bible, "but I'm not afraid of dying anymore either."

Joe and Val were speechless. How does a person respond to that? Though it wasn't one of those profound, tunnel-of-light, visiting-the-beyond, message-from-the-Creator experiences they'd heard about before, it definitely held merit and, for them, was made all the more legitimate because of who Eli was and who he had been before all this.

As quickly as he'd brought it up, Eli abruptly changed the subject. "I realize this doesn't fit the moment at all, but I just have to say, my position on catheters is not favorable." Val and Joe were jerked from their existential stupor in an instant. Joe made a face and immediately burst into laughter. After a few seconds, Valerie began to laugh, too. She'd almost forgotten what it was like to live in a world where Eli's sense of humor made everything more fun, even catheterization.

~

Valerie's phone began dancing as it vibrated on the windowsill. She knew that Pete was on his way with her parents and that Ivy was probably already packing. She knew Julia was safe at home, trying to reach Beau, and she knew Eli was safe with her. She picked up her phone, glancing at the screen. She almost didn't answer because she didn't recognize the number. But, it crossed her mind that the night's events were anything but typical, so she knew that it could literally be anyone and decided she should answer, "Hello?"

"Hello, ma'am. My name is Cpl. Ballantine. I'm calling from Headquarters for the United States Marine Corps on a secured line. I'm trying to reach a Mrs. Valerie or Mr. Joe McKnight."

Automatically assuming, as had Julia, that the kind woman on the other end of the line was responsible for communicating with Beau, she responded with a resounding, "Oh, good!"

Cpl. Ballantine paused. What had she missed? "Uh, yes ma'am, are you Valerie McKnight?"

"Yes, I am!" Val answered eagerly. In the back of her mind, she expected to be connected with Beau at any minute. She could feel the excitement welling up inside her.

"Ma'am, are you mother to Private First Class Jonathan Beau McKnight?"

"Yes, ma'am!"

"Mrs. McKnight, regretfully, I am calling to inform you that Pfc. McKnight has been wounded in action."

"What?" Valerie screamed into the phone. She couldn't believe what she was hearing. Her ears began to ring, making the corporal's words even harder to process. Her body failed her as her mind was thrashed from the highest high to the lowest low in a matter of moments.

"Yes, ma'am. Pfc. McKnight was wounded in action when his convoy fell under attack at an undisclosed location. At that time, he was stabilized at a forward aid station and now he's being treated at Bagram Air Base in Afghanistan."

"Treated how?" By this time Valerie was frantic, and Joe came running to her side. "Hold on, I'm going to put you on speaker so my husband can hear."

"Pfc. McKnight is being treated for shrapnel wounds to his right arm, shoulder and neck. He's currently stable, but in serious condition. Tomorrow, he will be transported to the Landstuhl Regional Medical Center in Germany for additional surgical intervention." The corporal continued talking, relaying information about travel and also relaying what little information she'd been able to get from the hospital liaison at Bagram.

Valerie felt her knees buckling beneath her, she could barely hear Eli's voice when he said, "Mom?" She felt a cold sweat form over her body. She could hear the muffled voice of her husband, getting the notification official's contact information, she heard the words travel and airfare and then she felt her body sinking to the cold, tile floor.

~

When she came to, Valerie was surrounded by nurses and had a cold washcloth on her forehead. Someone had folded a pillow and placed it beneath her feet. She raised her hand to her head to feel the washcloth, blinking hard. How long had she been out?

"There she is," she heard the sweet voice of Eli's nurse. As Val tried to sit up, the nurse said, "Take it slowly. Get your bearings before you move."

Joe was kneeling next to her, "Honey?" He reached for her hand and her elbow at the same time, helping her as she maneuvered her body. "How about that chair?" he asked and looked at the nurse inquisitively.

The nurse nodded and removed the pillow from beneath Val's feet. "How long have I been down here?" Valerie asked with a bit of a groan.

"Not long," Eli answered. He was nearly dangling off his bed, his heartrate monitor beeping at a rate none of them had ever heard before.

"Eli almost dove off the bed for you," Joe smiled as he spoke, more to calm his own nerves than anything else, "but he went for the call button instead."

"Well, my mind was willing, but my body basically gave up before it started." Eli looked at his dad. Joe could see the concern in his eyes.

"Joe, what else did she say about Beau?" Valerie asked. By this time she was sitting upright in the recliner. The nurse stood close by, holding the washcloth to Val's head as she reached down to extend the footrest. Joe still held tightly to her hand and elbow, as if she might fall right out of the chair.

"Well, first, let me say this — he's going to be fine. He's going to be just fine. It's my turn to speak faith, okay?" He paused, "Look over there." He pointed at Eli. Valerie's eyes filled with tears as Eli looked back at her with unmistakable love in his eyes. "Faith did that. God did that. So I believe, no, I *know* that Beau will come through this, and the next time we're all together, it will be to celebrate. I know it." Silent tears streamed down Valerie's face. She didn't bother to wipe her cheeks. Even the nurse, who hadn't left Valerie's side, had tears in her eyes. "He's going to be just fine? Right? We agree, right Val?" Val nodded, her heart swelling with renewed love for the man she'd leaned on for more than twenty years. "Now that we've established he's going to be fine, and we know he'll be alright, we can call Cpl. Ballantine back once we've decided which of us will fly to Germany."

"You should both go," Eli told them without hesitation. He had spoken the words almost before Joe had finished speaking. There was intense resolve in his voice. "I am okay. Beau needs you, and you need each other. You should both go."

Valerie wiped her cheeks with her fingers and sat up in her chair. She'd been trying to carry enough faith for everyone for so long that hearing Joe pick up the mantle with such fervor gave her a sense of security she couldn't describe. She squeezed his hand, realizing in that instant that he seemed completely calm. He wasn't anxious and he'd been there to lift her up when she needed it. Valerie knew she should say something, but the words wouldn't come. As she sat, trying to regain her senses, her brother Pete came bounding through the door, followed closely by her mother.

"Eli!" Pete shouted. "You have no idea how good this is. It's... it's just so, so good." He wrapped his arms around Eli. Eli lifted his right arm over Pete's shoulder and propped himself up with the other. He laughed a little as Pete hugged him tightly. When his grandmother began pulling at Pete's shirt, signifying that it was her turn, Eli could see tears in Pete's eyes — something he'd never seen before. The Pete Eli knew had never been serious a day in his life and was really just a big kid at heart. Pete turned toward Joe and Valerie, who were still seated, hand-in-hand. The nurse continued to blot Valerie's forehead. "Well, good grief, for a happy person, you sure look sick. What's all this about?" he chuckled at his own joke, but immediately regretted it when Joe and Val looked at each other with an expression that told a story he knew he didn't want to hear.

CHAPTER FOUR

Ivy had a hard time trusting her own reality. Though she had dreamed of, prayed for, and believed in the day Eli would wake up and come back to her, she simply couldn't wrap her head around the fact that she was about to board a plane and fly thousands of miles back to a life she'd forced herself to forget. But even as she was thinking of Eli, her mind reluctantly flashed to an image of Mark.

Mark had served with her in Zimbabwe for eight months now. During the last six, they'd grown close — too close. Working with him side-by-side, all day, every day had allowed her to get to know Mark in a way she'd never gotten to know Eli, because that chance had been violently ripped away from her. As they'd gotten to know each other, Ivy had told Mark all about Eli, and he seemed genuinely sympathetic, but that didn't stop him from pursuing her, from expressing his feelings for her and from falling for her — a feeling he'd expressed quickly, despite her unwillingness to return his love.

For six months, he'd made no secret of his affections for her. For six months, he'd made no secret of his desire to build a relationship with her. And for five months, Ivy had let herself care for him, too. They both knew their relationship would be frowned upon by mission leadership, so they tried to keep it to themselves — but, somehow, everyone knew! When she'd finally admitted to Mark that she had feelings for him, at first, the guilt had been overwhelming. She had wrestled with her own feelings of shame and self-loathing for weeks, before finally rationalizing her choice to entertain Mark's affections. She told herself she and Eli weren't married, that they weren't even engaged, and that he'd been asleep for so long he may not even remember her when he woke up. She buried her love for him way down deep inside herself and allowed her growing feelings for Mark to consume her days.

Her mind was a tangled knot. What would she say to Eli? Would she tell him about Mark? Would she admit she had feelings for someone else? Would her affection for Mark fade away completely the minute she saw Eli? She had no idea. Her mind volleyed back and forth between Eli and Mark. She closed her eyes and did her best to remember Eli for who he had been two years ago. But she didn't have to reach very far to conjure images of Mark. He was sweet and caring, handsome and had a desire to serve, *plus* he had a heart for missions. Up until Eli's call, she'd let go of her feelings of resistance and guilt and she'd allowed her heart to open up to him and the possibility of love with someone other than Eli. But now, faced with her own truth and the fact that she'd already, by her own words, reassured Eli of a love she didn't even know she still had, the repressive hand of guilt had returned in full force. As she waited to board her plane, no matter how hard she tried to focus on her gratitude, she also found herself feeling shame. She tried in vain to push Mark from her mind, even as she indulged in her worry that Eli might not be the same person he was before the accident.

So much time had passed. She'd grown and matured in ways she never expected, all while Eli slept. Was it wrong for her to think of him as a man? Was he a man? Was he still eighteen inside? If he was, how long might she be waiting for him to catch up to her? Did she even want him to? Even if she saw him and fell in love with him all over again, she wasn't sure she could patiently accept the fact that being with Eli might mean waiting even longer to get the things she wanted out of life. What would life with Eli be like now? What about life with Mark? She thought about Mark's tenderness when she left, the sweet kiss he'd given her during their goodbye before she made her way through the airport, and the wisdom and bravery it took for him to admit that her trip *had* to happen in order for *them* to happen.

When she realized where her mind was taking her, she stopped herself, taking her thoughts captive, "What are you doing? Eli is awake! That's what matters." She silently thanked God for His miracle and chastised herself for allowing her mind to be anything but grateful. She shook the thoughts of self from her mind and began to focus on the goodness of God.

While sitting and waiting at her gate to board a plane for the long journey home, she imagines seeing her mother and father, who should be waiting for her at the airport when she finally arrives in Houston after thirty hours and four airlines from the moment she leaves Zimbabwe. She had the option to spread her travel out over a number of days, but she wanted, she *needed*, to get there as fast as possible. The extra expense had nearly drained her account, but the money and the exhaustion would be well worth the effort when she finally got to hug her mom and dad and lay her eyes on an actual, real-life miracle.

Her parents had allowed the passing months over the last year to drive their thoughts farther and farther away from the McKnight family. Ivy knew that her parents — though her mom would deny it to her dying day — had spent that time hoping she'd just move on, away from Eli and the pain of all that waiting, as well as the uncertainty of pining for a future that may never come to fruition. Had Ivy told them about Mark, they likely would have been happy about it.

She loved her parents, so much. They'd always wanted the best for her, provided her with everything she'd ever needed and often everything she wanted, but they'd also expressed disappointment in her decision to delay college and stay in the mission field for an extended period and in her willingness to remain committed to a young man they believed would never again be "right." It simply wasn't the life they'd envisioned for their little girl, their princess. Despite knowing all that, Ivy knew their intentions were rooted in love. She couldn't wait to hug them. She couldn't wait to see their faces, in person, and tell them how she'd missed them. Though she'd found herself unexpectedly fulfilled in Zimbabwe, and unexpectedly caring for someone who wasn't Eli, it hadn't stopped her from missing her family and friends, and it certainly hadn't stopped her from believing in the day Eli would wake up — even while so many people were telling her to let him go.

The first time she'd made this trip, she was with her mission team. She felt secure in a group, but now, she was traveling solo and she'd be lying to herself if she said she wasn't intimidated. She'd told herself a thousand times that fear doesn't come from God, so again she closed her eyes and spoke a silent prayer for safety, asking God to send His angels to protect her flight and to give the pilots supernatural guidance. With butterflies in her stomach and guilt in her heart, she breathed deeply in an attempt to muffle the anxiety she felt about flying alone, seeing her family, and, most of all, seeing Eli again and facing the reality that he didn't really know her anymore. If she did choose Eli, they'd almost be starting again. She loved him. This had never changed. She believed it never would. But, she also had to face the truth. What if the love she felt now wasn't the kind she felt before the accident? She wasn't the same person she had been when they were last together.

~

At the hospital, every word Joe and Valerie spoke was thick with uncertainty. The entire McKnight family was experiencing a strange blend of emotions. On one hand, they were excited, overjoyed and grateful to have Eli back. On the other hand, they were anxiety-ridden, tentative, nervous and downright scared about what might be happening with Beau on the other side of the world. Joe and Valerie stood shoulder to shoulder in every discussion, clinging to their resolve that they would remain faithful, and that Beau was going to come through his ordeal unscathed.

"How could it be possible for one day to hold so much good and so much bad at the same time?" Valerie shook her head, sighing to calm herself.

"I don't think we should see it that way, Val," Pete spoke up. "We know Beau's alive and stable. That's a blessing all by itself. Whatever happened, he survived it, and we already know he's a fighter. Right now, this minute, we should be focusing on the good parts of this news, not the bad. It's just like you said when Eli got hurt, 'There's always, always, a reason to rejoice.'"

"Exactly," Joe said. "I can't believe I'm saying this, but Pete's right." He slapped Pete's back.

"Now that was funny." Eli laughed and then turned a serious look toward his mother, "He's going to be okay, you know. He really is. We all are."

Valerie fell onto the vinyl chair in the corner of the room. She wanted to go to Beau, but she also wanted to stay by Eli's side. She couldn't bear the thought of leaving him so soon after getting him back. Eli remained adamant that she go.

"Mom, you need to go. Please?" Eli looked at her pleadingly. His plea stopped everyone in their tracks. "You need to go."

Val stood facing her son, her head down. She raised her eyes to meet his and when she saw his face, there was no more debate. She knew she had to go. Something inside her made any other option feel impossible. "I'm going," she said. She looked Eli in the eye, seeing a wisdom in his young eyes that she'd never noticed before. She walked over and took his head in her arms and said softly, "I'm going." The mood in the room felt strange, almost surreal somehow. The quiet was palpable.

"Well, that settles it then," Pete spoke up. "I'm calling work. Mom and I will take shifts. Eli won't be alone, I promise Val."

Joe walked over to his wife, "I was willing to go it alone, but I'm really glad I'm not." He put his arms around her and held her.

"I'm going to book a hotel room like last time. Did they give you any idea how long we'd be here?" Pete had sprung into action. While everyone else in the family had seen this side of Sweet Pete before, Eli was new to the experience. His facial expression displayed an obvious combination of disbelief and appreciation.

Joe made eye contact with Eli and shrugged, shaking his head, as if to say, "I know, me too."

"They haven't said anything about that yet. Dr. Davies was planning to schedule scans and tests for tomorrow — or, well, I guess that's today, but that's literally all we know right now," Valerie answered Pete. "Are you all sure about this?" She looked at her mom.

"I'm not going anywhere," Val's mom said and moved across the room to where her daughter stood. She was also tall and slender, and the two of them together were a real-life picture of timeless beauty — not perfection, just true beauty — the kind that started from the inside and made its way out.

"Well, except maybe the vending machine, right Nana? Because, when this tube comes out, we're putting that little change purse of yours to good use." Eli's expression was serious, but his tone was light.

Everyone laughed, Pete most of all. "Man, I've missed you, kid," he said, as he rubbed his chin with his right hand, shaking his head.

"You better pump the brakes on that, son," Joe spoke up. "Stick to the doctor's orders before you go implicating your grandmother in a hospital vending-machine heist. They may not let you go straight from formula to processed food."

"Good point. You're absolutely right, Dad," Eli spoke in a droll voice while simultaneously winking hard in his grandmother's direction. She smirked silently, but reached into her handbag to retrieve her change purse, which she shook noisily in front of Joe's face. This time, there was no straight face for Eli, he laughed a deep, joyful belly laugh — a sound that brought tears to the eyes of everyone else in the room as they laughed with him.

Val and Joe walked together to Eli's bedside. Knowing they'd be in a flurry of chaos and travel for the next several days, they decided they should discuss what the coming days might look like for all of them. Joe reiterated the fact that Eli was over eighteen and legally had the right to sign paperwork and make decisions about his own care, a realization that startled not only Eli, but Valerie too. He made sure everyone knew that Eli was still covered by their insurance policy and that the hospital already had their information, but he decided to write it all down just in case. They talked about communication, medical procedures, medical choices and financial decisions.

Val knew that having a plan and a process gave Joe a sense of control, even when they had none, so she continued to nod as he spoke. As laid back as he was, a sense of order made him feel calm — something they both needed at the moment.

Though she knew she should be listening to the conversation, her thoughts were consumed with breaking the news about Beau to Julia. Over and over in her head, she thought about how she would broach the subject. Her heart ached at the idea of it. Julia seemed emotionally fragile. She seemed to be walking in a season of uncertainty, everyone around her felt it — and now *this*. But as Val ran a loving hand over Eli's head and watched Joe lean in to hug him, she realized how strong they'd become — how strong she'd become. She realized that Satan had been trying to tear down their family for months and months, and he'd failed. They were still standing. They were still fighting, and they had no intentions of giving up now!

CHAPTER FIVE

On the drive home, Valerie kept asking, "How can this possibly be happening?" She didn't know if she was asking Joe, asking herself, or asking God. She sighed and then sighed again. "I can't help but feel defensive. None of this feels coincidental. It's almost like it's personal. This feels personal to me, Joe. In fact, I'm a little angry right now." She pressed her lips together and shook her head slightly.

"You know what I think?" Joe glanced at her and then back at the road, reaching his right hand across the console to take hers. "I think it doesn't matter either way. Even if it's an attack from Hell itself, we will still win. We're supposed to resist Satan, right? And we already know that God *is* good. We have just witnessed a miracle. We will win this battle because of Him. Don't let it stifle your faith, Val."

Somehow, witnessing the miracle of Eli's recovery had ignited Joe's faith in a way Valerie had never seen, not in all their years of marriage. Since they'd learned about Beau, he had reassured her time and time again, and she genuinely believed him — she believed in his faith and it spurred her own. For months on end, Val felt like she had been carrying all the faith for the whole family, now it felt as though she and Joe were sharing that duty. Today, he had become a hero to her, a spiritual leader. Valerie felt as much relief as she did appreciation. She squeezed Joe's fingers in her own, "You're right. We can't let Satan win."

"I can't remember the chapter or book, but I remember that verse you posted up on the wall in Eli's hospital room after the accident. You know, the one that says that if we agree in faith on earth, anything we ask will be done by the Father. Well, we agree that Beau is coming through this thing whole and complete. We already know he's stable and alive, so we have nothing to be anxious about." As Joe turned into the driveway and glanced at his wife's face, a face that looked pained and hesitant, he added, "Nothing!" He leaned over and kissed Val's cheek as he pulled the keys from the ignition. He chose not to tell her that the words he spoke didn't match the emotions he felt on the inside. He didn't tell her that he was using words of faith to beat back a heart of fear. He didn't need to.

"Right, nothing to be anxious about," Valerie repeated, "nothing except walking through those doors and telling Julia." Val responded with a deep breath, which she blew out through pursed lips. Joe gave her a close-lipped smile and patted her shoulder before turning to unlock the front door to their home. He held it open for Val to walk through and then he followed her across the threshold. Val took a deep breath, knowing that somewhere inside Julia was waiting, completely clueless and probably checking her computer every five minutes for a message from Beau.

"I need to go to the bank and get our passports from the safe deposit box," Joe said, as he stood in the doorway, propping the door with his left arm.

"Well, it's not Bora Bora, but we'll make it work, won't we?" Valerie asked. She made a face as she put her purse on the table by the front door. "But, Joe, do you have to do it now? Right now?" Neither of them expected Julia to take the news well. Val couldn't put her finger on why, but in her spirit, she knew Julia was emotionally brittle. Everything had happened so quickly between her and Beau, and though she *did* seem to truly love him, she also seemed overwhelmed by life. It was easy for Val to understand why. In the months since she'd reconnected with Beau, she'd gone from single to committed, she'd gotten pregnant, seen her unborn child's father leave for deployment, moved away from her lifestyle and her partying roommates into, essentially, a stranger's house, and even changed jobs so she wouldn't have to work as many late nights. She was struggling to keep up with her school schedule because of morning sickness and she seemed to think she was supposed to be able to do everything perfectly, and all by herself. Because Julia didn't have a relationship with Jesus, or faith of any kind really, beyond her occasional church attendance with the McKnights, Val knew that nothing she could say would bring comfort. Without the help of God, Julia would crumble, and, in her spirit, Val knew it.

"Well, I guess I don't have to go right this minute, but I'm supposed to call Cpl. Ballantine back in thirty minutes to get more help with booking our flights and stuff. What if we need them to book flights?" Joe asked.

"She might ask if we have them, but I highly doubt she's going to need them." Val gave him a look that told him she knew what he was up to. "I know you don't want to be here for this, but I need you, okay?"

Joe took a deep breath, resigned, "Alright, alright," he said.

All the way home, Val had gone over the scenario in her mind. What would she even say? She took a few steps into the house and called out, "Julia? Are you home?"

Joe and Val heard a door open upstairs and saw Julia, who was dressed in a sweatshirt and shorts, appear behind the open banister on the second floor.

"Hi!" she said. "How's Eli? What did the doctor say? Did you get to talk to Beau? A lady from the Marines called, but wouldn't talk to me because I'm not related. She was going to call you." She peppered Val with questions. "I didn't think you'd be back so soon. I was going to drive over later."

"Why don't you come downstairs for a minute?" Val asked. "I need some coffee. We can talk in the kitchen." Val wasn't sure how to ease into the conversation. At a time when she should, by all rights, be a mess herself, she was concerned about Julia's reaction.

Julia turned to make her way down the stairs. "Okay," she said.

Valerie made her way toward the kitchen, buying a little time to decide once and for all how she was going to tell Julia about Beau. "Do you want something to drink?" She turned back to Julia, who was moving toward the breakfast bar.

"Um. Some orange juice would be great, but I'll get it." She rose from her place at the kitchen island and walked over to the cabinet containing the juice glasses. After pouring a glass, she walked back to the island and sat down. She was yawning when Val finished making her coffee.

"Are you tired?" Val asked, already knowing the answer.

"Only all the time," Julia replied, her tone of voice soft but slightly sarcastic.

"It'll get better," Val reassured her, still trying to buy some time. When she was finally seated next to Julia, she spoke up, "So, the Marine Corps Headquarters called while we were at the hospital."

"Oh, good, what did they say?" Julia took a sip of her juice.

"Well, it… it wasn't what we expected." She cleared her throat and then continued, "They weren't calling us back. They were calling to give us some news about Beau." She reached out a hand and rested it on Julia's forearm.

"What do you mean?" Julia gave Val a confused look, her brow furrowed.

"Well, they were calling to tell us that Beau has been wounded in action."

"What?" Julia shrieked. "What do you mean 'wounded'? Wounded how? Is he okay?" Tears began to form in her eyes and her breathing became fast and shallow.

Joe, who had been standing in the doorway, walked across the room and stood behind Val. Val covered her mouth with her hand as Joe stepped in, "We know he's alive, stable and on his way to the military hospital in Germany for some surgery." He put his hands on Val's shoulders. "Val and I have already been making travel arrangements with the help of the Marine Corps. We should fly out tomorrow sometime."

"I want to go, too. Please, please?" Julia pleaded through sobs and strident gasps. "I need to go, I really need to! Do you think they will let me? Do you?" Julia's words came out in short bursts, punctuated by choppy breaths.

"Ah, uh, I'm not sure. We don't know how it all works yet. I don't know what they do with airfare or anything yet. But I'll find out, I promise," Joe tried to sound reassuring, but he could tell his words did little to calm Julia's nerves.

"Is he going to die?" Julia asked, her voice coming out in a whisper. She started gasping for breath. She was hyperventilating.

Val stood next to her, placing a hand on her back. "You have to breathe, honey. Slow down and breathe," she pleaded.

Julia was doubled over, gasping for air. She began to wretch. Val looked at Joe, silently asking what she should do. Joe knew that, inside, Val was struggling, too. But he fiercely admired how she nurtured those around her, no matter what the circumstances and despite her own need for nurturing. She'd always had that quality, and this moment proved no exception. "Let's get her to the couch, Joe."

Joe and Val flanked Julia and lifted her to her feet. It wasn't until they were moving toward the door to the great room that Val noticed something that caused her to stumble slightly. There was a small spot of blood on the stool! But before she could even gasp, Julia cried out, grabbing her stomach and doubling over again. Without asking, Joe immediately picked her up in his arms and carried her the rest of the way to the sofa.

Julia still couldn't catch her breath, but managed to tell Val, "It hurts," as she struggled to get air into her lungs and at the same time hold her stomach, drawing her knees to her chest.

"Should we take her to the hospital?" Joe seemed frazzled. His voice was urgent as he looked to Val for answers. She could see in his face that he was maxed out emotionally — what else could possibly go wrong?

"I think we should call 9-1-1," Val said. "They could at least treat her on the way." She didn't know what to do either. At this point, she was just reacting. It was as if they were plugging holes in a dam with nothing more than their fingers and toes — they were stretched to the maximum, and one more leak might just do them in.

"We're still going to win, right Joe?" Val asked, even as she urged him to call emergency responders.

Joe could only nod his 'yes' as he pulled his phone from his back pocket, dialed the number and waited for a dispatcher to answer. As he handled the call, Val was encouraging Julia to calm down, to lay back and relax.

But Julia was sobbing and gasping, more concerned now for the baby than for herself. As she lay there on the sofa, her mind was a tangle of emotion and pain. She was afraid — afraid for Beau, for their baby, for herself and afraid of what the future would hold. She had carried that fear of the future from the moment she fell for Beau again. She had tried to keep her fear at bay, but in this moment, it surrounded her like a wet blanket. It stuck to every inch of her.

Joe remained on the phone with the dispatcher until the rescue workers arrived. He was waiting outside when the ambulance pulled up.

"She's in the great room!" Val heard him calling from the door.

"In here!" she echoed. "She's calmed down a bit, but she's still hurting and she's… she's… "

"It's okay, ma'am." One of the EMS workers gave Valerie a calming look. Val took a deep breath. As the EMS team surrounded Julia, they began asking her rapid-fire questions. Joe and Valerie backed away and moved closer to each other. Val reached for Joe's hand and then looked at him, numbly. The look on her face told Joe that she was overwhelmed. He felt exactly the same way, but he squeezed her hand reassuringly.

At Julia's request, Val asked the EMS personnel if she could ride in the ambulance with her. At first, the emergency workers seemed hesitant to agree, but when Julia pleaded with them, with tears flowing from her young, beautiful eyes, they agreed.

Joe arranged to meet them and said, "I will see you there. Text me where they take her so I can find you. It's going to be okay." He kissed Val quickly before she climbed into the back of the ambulance. As they pulled away, the practicality of his mind took over. Julia was without insurance. He put a hand to his head, knowing that the expense could be overwhelming. He walked over to his recliner and fell into it, "Lord? I don't even know what to pray." As he sat there, breathing in and breathing out, he suddenly felt a wave of peace come over him. He didn't know how they'd get through it all. He didn't know what they'd lose along the way. He didn't know how it would all work out, but somehow he knew it *would*. Somehow, in his heart, he knew it would all work out — eventually.

CHAPTER SIX

Beau began to stir beneath the weight of warm hospital blankets as the effects of his anesthesia wore off. He had muttered the name "Gabriel" over and over in his sleep since before he arrived at Landstuhl, and even now he repeated the word again and again as hazy, sporadic visions of IVs, bandages, blood and unfamiliar faces crashed in his mind like waves against the shore. Some of the nurses and staff at Landstuhl had chosen their own explanation for *Gabriel* — they preferred to believe Beau had met an angel. They were both wrong and right. Beau hadn't met a messenger from God, but he had met a Navy Corpsman by the name of Juan Gabriel, a guardian angel of a different kind — the combat medic kind.

In his mind, Beau carried visions of a uniform, covered in blood, his blood, bearing the name Gabriel across the chest.

Beau had a vague recollection of Gabriel shouting instructions as they rushed him into a small tented hospital. As his mind recalled the image of surgical scissors tearing through his shirt, his brain jolted him into wakefulness. He fought to open his eyes, but it felt as though they were glued shut. He felt a surge of panic course through his veins as his memory registered his last wakeful moments. He tried to lift his hands to his face, but they, too, refused to move. He could hear beeping and muffled voices. He was uncomfortable, but he wasn't in pain. In fact, he felt a little drunk. He began to get agitated as he struggled to move. He growled as he tried to lift his arms, and then cried out as pain shot through his right shoulder and into his head.

He heard footsteps and an opening door, then he heard a soothing voice, "You're okay."

Beau cut the voice off short, "Why can't I move? Why can't I see?" The alarm and hostility in his voice was apparent.

"You're just waking up from surgery. You're restrained because you became combative. I'll remove your restraints now, but you should know your right arm is bandaged and splinted. Please try to keep it still." The voice was even, calm and clearly female.

Beau struggled to wrap his head around what had happened to him. His memories of Gabriel and the tent hospital were split into shards, trying to remember was like trying to watch a movie in the pieces of a broken mirror. The last thing he remembered clearly was hearing Andy's voice as he called out to God. He remembered his own fear and pain, but his most vivid memory was that of Andy Mack's voice. "What happened?"

"You were wounded in an attack. You lost quite a bit of blood. We had to take you into surgery to remove shrapnel." The nurse worked to remove Beau's restraints. "Please try to lay still. Don't try to get up. I'm going to put a little button in your hand. Do you feel that? Like a joy stick. This is connected to your morphine pump. You can push this little button if you begin to feel pain."

"Where am I? Am I blind? Why can't I open my eyes?" Being released from the confines of his restraints did little to calm Beau's agitation.

"You're at Landstuhl Regional Medical Center in Germany," the nurse answered. "And no, you're not blind. But you have been under for quite a while and they probably had to tape your eyes closed to protect them from drying out. It's a common practice around here." Beau could hear a smile in her voice. "I'll check with your doctor to see if it's okay to remove them. I don't think it will be a problem." She adjusted the blankets around him, checked his vital signs and moved toward the door. "How about some food?"

Beau tried to shrug, but only one shoulder moved, "I guess." Beau could hear the door click shut behind her and let out a sigh. He laid his head back on his pillow and cursed under his breath.

"Food's actually not bad here." Beau was startled by the presence of someone else in the room. He jumped and then groaned in pain as the strain of his movements resulted in a hot poker-like sensation in his neck.

"Who are you?" Beau demanded, defensively.

"I could ask you the same thing, bro. I was here first. I had a private room until they rolled your grouchy self in here." Beau heard the curtain to his right fly open, then he heard an audible gasp. Covering his lips with his fist, Antonne Young sucked in a breath through his teeth and continued, "Shoot, son. My bad. You look like you got a thousand good reasons to be grouchy."

Beau wanted to turn his head toward the invasive voice, but he couldn't move. He wanted to say something in return, but he couldn't think of anything to say, so he said nothing at all.

"I'm Antonne. Er, Young, Spc. Antonne Young, but everybody calls me Pipes. What's your name?" Antonne's voice sounded genuinely likeable, but Beau still considered not answering. After a long pause, he finally spoke up.

"McKnight. Pfc. Beau McKnight," he answered begrudgingly.

"Bet you got a nickname, too, don't ya?" Antonne continued.

"Why would you assume that?"

"Well, you're a Marine ain't ya? Seems like all Marines get other names. I'm Army. I told you my nickname, and believe me, Pipes is not as cool as it sounds. In fact, it's kinda horrible as a name when you know what it means," Antonne continued to prod Beau for information.

"How long have you been here?" Beau asked.

"Long enough. Why?"

"Because you seem way too eager to talk to strangers," Beau told him as he rested his head back against his hospital bed. Beau heard Antonne's laugh forming in his throat, but he hadn't been joking.

"I guess so, brother. I guess so," Antonne agreed. He paused for a minute, "They call me Pipes because I apparently have skinny legs. One of the females in our unit said my legs looked like black pipe cleaners hanging out the bottom of my PT shorts and I've been Pipes ever since." Beau couldn't see him, but he could almost feel Antonne shaking his head at his own words. He tried to stifle his smirk. "What's worse is that I'm here 'cause I basically shattered my leg fast-roping into

Kandahar, and we weren't even that far off the ground. I mean, some of the guys just jumped. I've had two surgeries already and they said I might need another one. If that don't just add insult to injury, I don't know what does."

This time, Beau actually cracked a smile. 'Ol Pipes had a tone and delivery that made everything sound comedic. "Hangdog," Beau finally admitted. "They call me Hangdog, on account of the fact that I've been in a bad mood since they met me."

"Dang. And I thought Pipes was bad," Antonne chuckled to himself.

Finally, the door opened again and Beau heard his nurse's voice, "Let's get those bandages off your eyes, shall we?"

"Finally!" Beau exclaimed, as he heard her coming toward him.

~

Later, as his surgically administered medication wore off, Beau found himself in immense pain. He pressed repeatedly on his morphine button, but the pain in his neck and shoulder continued without reprieve. Antonne continued to chatter on, happy to have someone to talk to — even if that person was in so much pain he barely heard a word that had been spoken. Beau's food tray sat, untouched, on his rolling bedside table. Antonne fought the urge to ask for his uneaten pie.

When the nurse entered the room, she walked to Antonne's bedside and placed a small plastic cup on his bedside table. She retrieved his water and then handed the small cup to Antonne. Without a word, as if the practice had become so routine no instructions were required, Antonne threw back the little cup like a shot, swallowing all the pills in one gulp. The nurse checked Antonne's pulse and respirations and then turned to Beau. She looked at his IV bag and his blood pressure monitor, and then turned to look at him. She could see the distress on his face. She checked his bandages and lifted the lid to his tray, "Have you eaten anything?" Beau turned his eyes away from her, grimacing in pain, and said nothing.

"He ain't touched nothin' and I really want that pie," Antonne answered in Beau's stead. The nurse looked at Beau, then at Antonne, and then back at Beau, expecting a reaction — a nod, a shrug, something. When she got no response, she reached to the corner of his tray, lifted the small plate of coconut cream pie, adjusted the plastic wrap on top and began to walk in Antonne's direction.

"Don't give him my pie!" Beau growled. "He hasn't shut up for the last three hours. He can't have my pie!" The nurse jumped, startled. She couldn't tell if Beau was legitimately angry, or if he was joking. She returned the pie to his tray.

"What's your problem?" Antonne yelled back instantly. He pulled the small pillow from under his left arm and reared back to throw it at Beau's head, but, remembering the severity of his wounds and seeing his black and blue jawline, he redirected his aim and hurled the pillow onto Beau's lap instead.

"You're my problem!" Beau shot back, as pain-born sweat began beading on his crinkled brow. "Every nerve in my body is on fire and even the sound of your breathing is loud!" he snapped.

"Can ya'll do anything about this boy's attitude? I mean, he's pushin' that morphine pump like he's playing Pac-Man and still he's just layin' over there breathing all heavy, groanin' and acting like a big baby." Antonne directed his question to the nurse, laying on the sarcasm, but he was looking at Beau from the corner of his eye.

Beau leaned his head back. He started to yell a retort, but a sharp pain shot through his collarbone and up the right side of his head, so he winced in pain, gritting his teeth instead.

The nurse stepped toward the head of his bed. "You're hurting pretty bad, huh?" She laid her hand on Beau's left shoulder, trying to make sure he heard her words, "I'm going to talk to the doctor. We'll try to get you something more for pain, okay?" She turned to leave, but paused and looked back at Antonne, who was awkwardly adjusting his body under the skeletal traction device that held his casted leg in an elevated position. "Do you really want more pie?" she asked.

"Yes ma'am, I absolutely do."

"Okay, I'll see what I can do." She smiled in his direction and then said again, "I'll be right back."

As soon as the door shut behind her, Antonne turned to Beau and snipped with a half-joking tone, "Why you gotta be like that? All mean and nasty? I mean, I know you hurtin' but your problem ain't gotta be everybody else's problem too."

Beau didn't speak and, instead, closed his eyes. As he laid there, agonizing, he began to reason that he genuinely deserved the pain he was feeling. His brother may never wake up, may never have a life, all because of the choices he'd made. And yet, now that he was feeling some of the pain he believed he deserved — the very pain he thought he wanted the day he signed his contract with the Marine Corps — he was actively trying to stop it. He let his morphine pump fall from his fingers as intense feelings of cowardice and guilt mingled with his physical pain.

As his nerve endings fired jolt after jolt of electrically charged agony through his body, he forced himself to feel them, as if they were lashes from a whip. The pain was overwhelming. He knew he didn't have the strength to turn down the pain medication his nurse would bring. He knew he didn't have the strength to leave that morphine pump dangling beside his bed. And the realization of that truth magnified his guilt. Though he tried to fight it, tears of frustration and self-hatred began to form in his eyes. He pressed his eyelids together and gritted his teeth to stifle a sob.

When the door to the room opened again, Beau's nurse entered with another small cup and a piece of pie. She walked the pie to Antonne, who made short work of tearing the plastic wrap off and then sighing with pleasure at the taste of the pie as he forked the first bite into his mouth. She turned to Beau and reached out her arm, signaling him to hold out his hand for the contents. He almost refused, but his will was weakened by pain, so he reached his left hand toward her. "It's a pain pill and a muscle relaxer to help you sleep. The doctor on duty said they'd probably increase your morphine dose, but wanted to confer with your surgical team and anesthesiologist first, so he's giving you this in the meantime. You should be feeling better in a few short minutes. I'd really like you to eat something before you fall asleep, so I'm going to heat your food in the microwave in the nurse's breakroom, okay?" Beau simply nodded, so far as his bandages would allow, and popped the pills into his mouth. His nurse lifted a cup of water to his lips, holding the bent straw in her fingers, and he swallowed the medicine immediately, desperate for relief. She walked around the bed and lifted Beau's entrée off his bedside table. "I'll be right back," she smiled. Beau nodded again.

Antonne spoke up, "Thanks for the pie! And, uh, thanks for the drugs, for him I mean. Hopefully, they'll make him more tolerable!" He laughed at his own statement and shoved another bite of pie into his mouth.

The nurse smiled broadly as she exited the room. "Buzz if you need anything," she said in a pleasant-sounding voice as she turned to Beau. "I'll be right back with your dinner."

CHAPTER SEVEN

Julia was finally under a doctor's care in the ER. A dose of IV medication had stopped the signs of premature labor, but both Julia and Val still feared for her baby. Val was fighting impatience as they waited on the doctor to come in with news — any news. As she rocked back and forth in her chair, she began to marvel at the fact that she was currently sitting in an ER exam room at one hospital, while both of her sons were being treated at two other hospitals. She assumed, probably rightly, that she was the only mother in the world who had two sons in two different hospitals and an unborn grandchild in a third. She rubbed her face with her hands and took a deep breath, put her elbows on her knees, and rested her forehead in her hands.

When the door to the tiny exam room opened, Val immediately jumped to her feet, more out of impatience and her eagerness to get to her boys than anything else, a truth she had trouble acknowledging within herself and would certainly never admit out loud.

"Sorry for the wait, ladies," the doctor said as he walked past Val and stood by Julia. "Your vitals are good, the contractions have stopped and I think everything is going to be okay. But, I ordered a sonogram, just to be safe. The tech should be here any minute. Once that's done, and you're cleared, I will discharge you. You do need to make an appointment with your obstetrician right away, and I want you on bedrest in the meantime.

"What?" Julia asked, the sound of panic in her voice. She pushed herself up with her arms. "Bedrest? But, I want to go to Beau! What about Germany? What about Beau?" She began to become mildly frantic again.

"Shh... Shh... It's okay. Lie down. It's going to be okay," Val tried to calm Julia down. The doctor had heard the whole story when they first arrived, and Julia had made her desires abundantly clear. Val brushed Julia's hair off her forehead with a gentle touch.

"I'm sorry. I can't, in good conscious, allow you to return to normal activity until you've been cleared by your obstetrician. It's for your safety, and for the safety of your baby." Even though the ER doctor was sympathetic, the tone of his voice made it clear that his decision was not only final, but one that had been made without emotion. He was doing his job and doing it well, keeping his medically-related priorities in order.

Valerie had no intention of pressing the issue. "Thank you, doctor," Val said. "Julia, honey, it's going to be fine. You need to do what's best for yourself and for the baby."

"But... but..." Julia started to object again, but as she opened her mouth, the door opened and the ultrasound tech stuck her head in.

"Are you ready for me?" she asked.

"We are," the doctor answered before turning again to Julia. "Once the sonogram is done, I'll do my best to get you out of here as fast as I can." He held the door open as the tech backed through the door with her machine.

"Thank you," Val responded.

The ultrasound tech went about the process of getting her machinery set up. Once she was done, she walked over to the switch on the wall and turned out the overhead fluorescent lights, leaving on only one pot light over the bed. "I have the gel heater on, but it might still be a tad cold." The tech lifted Julia's sweatshirt over her small tummy and tucked a paper sheet into the top of her shorts. She pulled the wand from its holder and smeared the end with clear gel. Julia jumped just a little as the tech pressed the wand to her belly. "Sorry," the tech said. "I was afraid it might still be a little cold."

"It's okay," Julia said, as she stared eagerly at the screen, hungry for signs of life. Val moved quickly to the head of the bed, pulling the chair over to sit on the arm so she could see better. She grabbed Julia's hand and squeezed it as tears filled her eyes. She wasn't sure if her tears were the result of fear or excitement. Julia was breathing heavily, glued to the screen. Val could feel her own heart pounding as she followed suit.

The tech moved the wand around for what seemed like an unusually long time, but she had a pleasant look on her face and didn't seem concerned. She clicked buttons and shifted her wand, pressing and pausing, pressing and pausing. Finally, she said, "Alrighty, abdominal anatomy done. Let's check on this baby, shall we?" Val let out a forceful breath full of relief. Julia hadn't even realized that she, too, had been holding her breath until she heard herself let it go. The tech went back to work, totally oblivious to the tension in the room. "There we go! Wow, a wiggler!" Julia and Val stared at the screen, in awe, as baby McKnight squirmed and rolled before their eyes. The tech continued pausing and clicking, moving and pressing, "Well, mommy, would you like to find out your baby's sex today?"

"Really?" Julia pushed up onto her elbows. "I didn't think you could tell yet! My next ultrasound isn't for another month or so!"

"Well, it's not always possible. But your baby definitely wants us to know," she laughed at her own words.

Julia looked to Val, "Do I want to know?"

"Well, I know I do, but it's up to you," Val responded.

"Oh my gosh! I want to know, too!" She turned her face to the tech, "Yes! Tell us!" The tech turned the monitor toward Julia a little more, and then she carefully explained the image on the screen, bit by bit.

"This is a little foot, and a little leg, and here's the other little leg, and this right here is, well…"

"It's a boy!" Val shouted. She leaned over to hug Julia, who began crying immediately. "It's a baby boy!"

~

Julia made it very clear that she wasn't happy with her ER doctor's order that she remain on bedrest until she could see her OB. Though she was emotionally fragile, Julia was also determined and the exact opposite of lazy — characteristics Val loved about her, but also characteristics that could cause her to become stubborn. It was this budding stubbornness that prompted Val to call Joe's mom and ask her to come and stay at the house with Julia while she and Joe traveled to Germany. Julia needed someone to keep her in bed, to keep her fed and to make sure that she didn't overexert. As far as Val was concerned, the best person for the job was her mother-in-law. Joe's mom was a caretaker to her core, and as strong willed as they came. She was sweet, but firm, and she didn't take anything off anybody. Val had never seen someone shut down drama as politely or as effectively as she did.

"I don't need a babysitter Ms. Valerie," Julia said.

"Julia, honey, she's just going to be here to take care of meals and cleaning, and to make sure you stay in bed. Besides, Beau wanted you here so we could take care of you. This is exactly what he would want." Val watched as Julia's eyes glassed over with tears.

"You have the ultrasound picture, right?" Julia questioned as she wiped her cheeks with her fingers.

"Of course," Val answered.

"I want him to have it after I tell him. Promise me I'll get to tell him as soon as he can talk to me."

"I promise. And as soon as you do, I'll give him the ultrasound picture. I'll even put it in a frame before we leave."

Val reached out to squeeze Julia's hand as they waited for Joe to pick them up. Her thoughts were all over the place. She thought about Eli, about Beau, about traveling to Germany, about becoming a grandmother and about how everything seemed to be happening so fast. She tried to focus on her gratitude, about the good parts, because being grateful for the good, despite the bad, had seen her through the previous two years, she saw no reason to stop now. She closed her eyes and silently gave thanks. She told herself that Eli was awake, talking and laughing, that Beau was alive and would soon know about Eli's miracle, and that baby boy McKnight was currently thriving, growing and safe. She tried to calm her stress by counting her blessings.

By the time Joe arrived to get them, both Julia and Val had dozed off. He walked through the sliding glass doors of the ER and found Julia and Val leaning on each other in the vinyl seats of the waiting area, asleep. He walked over to his wife and gently touched her shoulder. When she stirred, he whispered, "Val, it's me."

"Oh, hi," she murmured. She stretched in her seat and Julia began to awaken beside her. "Guess what?"

Joe gave her a peculiar look, "What?"

Val reached into her bag, which she'd been holding on her lap, and pulled out one of the two ultrasound photos the tech had given them, "It's a boy, Gramps!" Val giggled to herself and scrunched her nose. She handed Joe the photo and then gave him a playful jab on the arm.

"What? It's a boy?" Joe took the photo from Val's hand as a broad smile spread across his face. Julia was awake and watching the scene unfold. She smiled as Joe wrapped his arms around Valerie. When he pulled away and looked at them both, he said, "But let's get one thing straight here. I am not a Gramps. I'm going to have to veto the Gramps business." Both Val and Julia laughed and continued laughing as they slowly made their way to the car.

~

The drive home was light, but also informative. Valerie told Joe all about the bedrest and his mother's agreement to stay with Julia, and Joe told Valerie all about his conversation with Cpl. Ballantine and their current travel arrangements. He also shared that Ballantine should be calling with an update on Beau's condition from the hospital liaison before their trip.

"Maybe we can get home, finish packing and get back to Houston to see Eli again before we leave?" Val formed the question as if it were already a given.

"We'll fly out of Houston tomorrow, so, yeah we can. Maybe we can stay in the hotel room Pete got and have him drive us to the airport tomorrow," Joe said.

"Your mom should be at the house soon. When we get there, Julia, you need to get right in bed." Val turned to look at Julia, who seemed to be taking it all in.

"I'd like to shower first. Do you think that will be alright?" Val could hear the slight sarcasm in Julia's voice, but she pretended not to notice.

"I think so, but if you feel the least bit weak or have the slightest pain, you tell me and get right in bed. Okay?"

"Agreed," Julia returned. "I still wish I was going with you."

"I know sweetheart," Joe said. "But, after talking to Cpl. Ballantine, I don't know if you could have gone anyway. And you need to take care of yourself and the baby. That's the most important thing."

"I've heard that a lot tonight," Julia responded.

"We'll keep you updated every step of the way," Val reached for Julia's hand.

"I know. I'm just, well, I cry all the time and I'm tired and I just... " Julia took a deep breath.

"You're pregnant," Val stopped her short and tried to reassure her. "Cut yourself some slack. Everything will be alright."

"Yeah, kiddo," Joe said. "If I remember, when Val was pregnant, she cried watching fabric softener commercials."

Val laughed, "That little bear just killed me! It was so cute, I couldn't take it!" She squeezed Joe's hand and then turned around to look at Julia again, "And I wasn't dealing with half of what you are. So, if you need to cry, you just cry. It's okay. And remember, prayer really does work. We love you, and Jesus does too."

Julia paused. She still wasn't sure about the whole faith thing, but she had to admit, the McKnights definitely had something she didn't have. Something she knew she wanted, but couldn't figure out why. So, if faith was something they recommended, it couldn't hurt to at least consider it. "Thank you Ms. Valerie. Thank you both." She leaned her head back against the seat and let her mind wander.

CHAPTER EIGHT

Joe put the last of the bags into the back of their SUV and yelled for Val, "Move it or lose it, Val. We gotta go if we're going to get to spend any time with Eli." He then called back toward the door, "Bye, Mom, love you!"

Joe's mom was waving in his direction as Valerie gave her some specifics about Julia. "You have the list of numbers and you know where my mom and Pete are staying. Some of my other family is coming in, too, but they know we're headed out. They'll get hotels. Don't worry about anything," Val chattered on.

"Me? Don't *you* worry about anything Valerie. I've got this," Mimi, as the boys had called her since they were little because having two "Nanas" was too confusing, shut down Val's babbling by telling her exactly what she needed to hear.

Val hugged her and turned to trot down the sidewalk toward Joe. "Be safe and keep us posted. We'll be fine here," Mimi assured her.

"I've already been in to see her, but will you remind Julia one more time that everything is going to be okay?" Val knew Julia was still upset about being left behind.

"I will," Mimi answered.

As Joe and Valerie drove away, Mimi waved until they were out of sight. She turned back toward the stoop and decided it needed a good sweeping. Mimi believed that keeping oneself busy was an art form, an art form that seemed most enjoyable during times of stress and crisis. The magazines called this a coping mechanism, but Mimi called it good, old fashioned horse sense. She walked into the house, grabbed the broom, and went straight to work.

~

By the time Joe and Valerie had reached the hospital, they had discussed the events of the day, the plan for their flight and even potential names for their soon-coming grandson. Val had jotted down a list for Eli and Pete and had created a second list of every phone number and email address they might need, from the insurance company to the church office. She tucked it into her bag as Joe searched for a parking spot. Evening had come, working hours were over, and that meant parking spots were few and far between. After what felt like an eternity in the parking garage, Joe and Valerie finally made it back to Eli's room.

Val didn't even wait for a greeting when she breezed through the door, holding it open for Joe to come in behind her. "Well," Val began, "we've had quite the day." She began to tell the story of how she broke the news of Beau's injuries to Julia and how the stress of it all brought on contractions. She told them about their mad dash to the hospital, her ride in the ambulance, and that Julia had been put on bedrest until she could see her doctor. She also told them about their early morning flight.

"What? Contractions? Is she going to be okay? Is the baby okay?" Pete asked urgently, as he jumped to his feet. You could tell by his body language that he wanted to do something, as though through action he could somehow help the situation. Eli sat motionless. It was almost too hard to keep up. He felt strangely distanced from his own family, having been out of the loop for so long. He had missed out on a lifetime of experiences and was now trying desperately to fill the gaps in his mind.

Valerie assured Pete that the ER doctor believed everything would be fine and that, for now, the baby appeared to be healthy and showed no signs of distress. Finally, after talking herself blue in the face, and explaining that she and Joe had driven back to Houston so they could see Eli and catch an early flight the next morning, Valerie added, "And, we got some other news today too!" Her demeanor changed and she became almost giddy. Joe watched as her face lit up. He couldn't help but smile. To him, nothing was more beautiful than Valerie's face, especially when she was bubbling over with love. He knew what she was up to immediately, and before she even had to ask, he walked over and grabbed her bag, handing it to her with a wink. She reached in and pulled out the ultrasound photo, looked at it for a moment, and then practically skipped over to Eli's bedside.

He cocked his head to the side and took the small image from her hand before he read the words aloud, "It's a boy," he paused. "Wait! It's a boy! I'm going to have a nephew?"

"Yes! It's a boy!" Valerie jumped up and down a few times and Pete let out a whoo-whee, slapping his ball cap against his knee.

"I knew it! A baby boy!" Pete announced, "James and I were taking bets." Val's brothers had been betting on everything from football to who could eat the most pizza for as long as anyone could remember. He looked at Val with a big grin on his face, but she was staring at him in a way that made it clear she didn't approve. "What?" Pete asked. "Don't look at me like that."

"Well, I'm not sure how I feel about you betting on the baby," Val answered. She glanced at Joe. He knew she still felt awkward about the pregnancy. She never expected to plan her grandson's baby shower before she even became a mother-in-law, and she secretly worried about what people might think, but he also knew that she already loved the baby fiercely.

So, to ease the tension, Joe spoke up, "I feel like we have something to celebrate! When's dinner in this place? Maybe they'll let us get something from the cafeteria for Uncle Eli! Besides, we're staring down the barrel at airline food and I hate airline food.

"I like the sound of that! Maybe me having a nephew will soften them up to a meatball sub!" Eli announced laughingly.

~

Ivy made her way down the long white hallway, taking in the smells and sounds of the hospital and feeling an eerie sense of déjà vu as she passed the nurse's station. She didn't need to ask directions. She didn't need assistance with finding the right room. Though it had been well over a year since she'd walked the halls, the familiarity hadn't completely left her and she moved effortlessly through the labyrinth of corridors as though she'd never left.

She had received a flurry of texts while she was somewhere over the South Atlantic Ocean. When she landed and turned her phone on again, she also had a dozen missed calls, voicemails and notifications providing her with Eli's room number and the shocking news that Beau had been wounded in action. As she walked the halls, she replayed Val's messages in her head. It didn't seem real. She just couldn't seem to think clearly. The past thirty hours had been some of the most hectic she'd ever experienced, and now, hearing the news about Beau and learning that Joe and Val had made an immediate trip to Germany caused her head to spin.

In an attempt to relieve some of the pressure in her head, she put her thumb and index finger on either side of her nose and pressed hard as she made her way down the hall. All the while, coping with the reality of jet lag and the memory of her mother's voice in her head telling her she needed to rest. As she walked, she also battled feelings of overstimulation, brought about by her sudden submersion back into American culture. She'd never realized how much noise she'd lived with all her life until she spent time in a truly quiet place. Sure, there were cities in Zimbabwe, but the hustle and bustle there was nothing compared to home. And having spent most of her time there in the rural villages, she knew the people there lived a markedly slower pace of life. There, people did life in a completely different way — a simpler way.

She felt her phone buzzing. It was Mark — again. She sighed and slid the device back into the rear pocket of her jeans. He'd called four times already, once before she'd even left the ground in Zimbabwe, and twice more while she was in the air, even though he knew she wouldn't have service — and now this. She wanted to answer, but she was too close to Eli's room and, somehow, it didn't feel right. She secretly hoped she'd take one look at Eli and forget all about Mark, well, at least forget all about how she felt about him. The closer she got to Eli's room, the easier it became to convince herself that nothing had changed. She didn't plan to say anything about Mark, no matter what — it was too soon and Eli had a long road to a full recovery ahead of him. The last thing she wanted to do was hurt him, so secrecy felt like the best option.

She shook Mark from her thoughts as best she could and allowed her mind to follow Beau to Afghanistan. She didn't know all the details, but trying to imagine Beau McKnight on a battlefield was next to impossible. Then again, he definitely hadn't been the same Beau she knew from high school by the time he left for boot camp. Despite her initial anger, she had forgiven him, and she feared for his life. Come what may, he was still like family to her.

When she reached Eli's room, she paused outside the door and took a deep breath. She smoothed her soft brown hair and adjusted her handbag on her arm. She pushed the door open slowly and eased her way inside. Pete was asleep in the recliner and the TV was on, but there was no one else in the room. She looked around. The bathroom door was open and the light was off, nobody there either. Should she wake Pete? Should she sneak in and wait? After a few moments of indecision, she decided she would walk to the waiting room down the hall, get something from a vending machine and give it some time. She felt awkward as it was. It would be even weirder to just sit in silence while Pete slept.

When she arrived in the waiting room, she pulled some cash from her purse and bought a bag of trail mix and a bottle of water. She sat down to eat her snack and began playing with her phone to fight her own anxiety. Her missed call from Mark was a glaring reminder of his existence and she thought about calling him to touch base, but she immediately vetoed that idea. She hated herself for even considering it. "What kind of person calls another guy while she sits in a hospital and waits to see her boyfriend of four years after he's woken up from a coma?" she asked herself. She lightly hit her own forehead with her palm, as if to snap herself out of it. The confusion in her troubled heart was almost more than she could bear.

~

Ivy's inner turmoil was interrupted and she sat straight up in her waiting room chair when she heard Eli's voice. The orderly rolled him right by the open doors of the waiting area and kept on rolling. Eli was talking about food. "Well, some things don't change, I guess," Ivy said to herself with a grin. But, she didn't get up right away — she couldn't. Instead, she sat, frozen in place, almost afraid to stand. Finally, she gathered her bag and her phone, willed herself up onto her feet and made her way to the door. She dropped her trash in the receptacle as she turned down the hall toward Eli's room and took a deep breath. As she walked, she wiped the palm of her hand on her jeans, not because she'd had a snack, but because she was full of nervous energy.

When she reached Eli's room, she found herself once again frozen, standing outside the door — but her fear was interrupted when the orderly pulled the door open and began to back out with the rolling bed he'd just used to deliver Eli. She jumped, somewhat startled. "Here we go," she thought.

She wasn't quite prepared when she heard Pete shout, "Well, well, look what the cat dragged in!"

"Hi!" she said as she walked slowly through the door, holding her bag close to her chest.

"Ivy!" Eli was pressed up on his hands as far as his strength would allow. "You… you… you're beautiful!"

Ivy smiled as the tears filled her eyes. She dropped her bag onto the floor, ran to Eli and threw her arms around his neck. Pete sniffled behind her and Eli lifted his gaze to look at his uncle. "I'm not crying! You're crying," Pete exclaimed with a laugh. Eli smiled and Ivy wiped her eyes, as she let out a laugh.

"Wow," Ivy said, "I can't, I mean, I can… I don't even know what to say! I can hardly believe this is happening." She hugged Eli again, squeezing him tightly. He was living proof that miracles are real, and just seeing his smile somehow brought Ivy into God's presence, right then and there.

Eli scooted over in his bed, taking advantage of his now-thin frame to make room for Ivy next to him. She instinctively climbed up onto his bed and he grabbed her hand, interlocking his fingers with hers. She stared at their hands and guilt washed over her body like a wave. "I'm so glad to see you," Eli was smiling broadly.

"You look…" Ivy started.

Eli cut her off. "Skinny? Emaciated? Hungry?" he chuckled.

"I was going to say 'vibrant,'" Ivy scoffed. "But yeah, hungry works too." She laughed, as the tears once again began to flow. "This is just so, so, miraculous!"

"That's what they tell me," Eli joked.

"So, what did they say? What's happening? Are you going home?" Ivy peppered Eli with questions. All the while taking in his frail frame and the vicelike way he held her fingers in his own.

"We don't know all that yet," Pete said as he stood up from the recliner and stretched.

"But, I do get to start eating some solid food," Eli said, as he patted his belly.

"Yep," Pete said, "and he's been trying to get me to sneak him a meatball sub ever since they told him he could start eating some regular food."

"Apparently, I have to ease into it and wean off the tube. All I want is a meatball sub, but the nurse said I should eat some simple stuff first. They seem to think it's weird that I'm so hungry. One of the nurses said most feeding tube people don't get a normal appetite back right away. So, I just told her my appetite was never normal to begin with!" Eli let out a succinct laugh.

Ivy smiled and nodded her head. "Well, that's certainly true," she said.

Eli went on to tell Ivy and Pete about the brain scan he'd just had — the first one he'd ever had while awake, and mentioned that Dr. Davies would probably come in again before nightfall to give him the results. He also confirmed that he had trouble moving, he reckoned because his muscles had atrophied so much. After giving Ivy all the updates he could think of, he began to ask her about Zimbabwe. Her guilt made it difficult for her to answer questions. Nearly every memory she had of Zimbabwe for the last year included Mark.

"You know what, let's skip me for now and talk about Beau. Any word from your parents yet?" Ivy made the transition seamlessly, though her stomach was tied in knots.

"Not yet. The last we heard, they had talked to the hospital liaison and he was stable, but that's all we know. I reckon they'll call us once they know more. I think they should be landing pretty soon." Pete took it upon himself to answer. "How long was their flight again?"

"They said twelve hours or so," Eli answered.

"Well, I guess that gives them twelve hours to figure out how they're going to tell him everything that's going on. I mean, how do you walk into a hospital room to see your war torn son and go, 'Hey, your twin brother is awake after two years in a coma, and oh, by the way, you're having a son'?"

"Wait, what?" Ivy sat straight up, lifting both her hands as if she were signaling 'stop.' "What do you mean, 'having a son'?" Her forehead crinkled with disbelief, "Are you for real right now?" Her mouth hung open. "Is Julia pregnant? And how did I not know this?" Ivy sat in a state of shock as Pete and Eli filled her in on the newest addition to the McKnight clan. She knew Julia had come back into the picture for good, and that she'd been staying with the family, because Val had filled her in during one of their phone calls, but this — this was so, so, huge.

She and Julia knew each other in middle school, but they'd never been close. They ran in different circles. But why hadn't Val mentioned it? A baby seemed like an incredibly noteworthy topic of conversation. As she began to feel hurt and somewhat offended, she stopped her own thoughts short when it dawned on her that having another boyfriend in Zimbabwe seemed like a noteworthy topic, too. And yet, she'd kept her mouth closed on that point for months. Her stomach became knotted with guilt once again, and her hurt melted into acceptance.

CHAPTER NINE

Beau could hardly move as the pain of his injuries began to settle into a place of permanence. He was stiff and sore, and despite the ample amounts of pain medication he had been given, he still felt uncomfortable. Nearly the entire right side of his torso was covered in bandages, from his right jaw line all the way down to his right hip. The majority of his wounds were concentrated in the area of his right shoulder, clavicle and neck. His surgeons had bandaged them in such a way that moving his neck was nearly impossible. He could shift his shoulders a little bit, but doing so was excruciatingly painful. Antonne continued to ramble on, and Beau began to wonder if talking back to him was the only thing that would shut him up for a while. But, at least for now, Beau didn't have anything to say.

This time, when the nurse came through the door, she was followed closely by a doctor. The doctor wore green scrubs, a lab coat and running shoes. He didn't appear to be very old, at least so far as Beau thought, but he carried himself as though he were both authoritative and exhausted at the same time. "Hello there Marine," the doctor said, as he tucked his clipboard under his left arm. "I am Maj. Elston and I am your attending physician. I was part of the on-site surgical team responsible for patching you up." Beau didn't know it yet, but Maj. Elston was a blunt, well-educated, to-the-point physician. His bedside manner was specifically suited to working with members of the military, because he'd never been described as warm and fuzzy and he preferred to keep unnecessary words to a minimum. He was also brutally honest — and never, ever minced words.

Beau did his best to clear the fogginess from his mind, a task that proved much more difficult than he thought it would, given the effects of the pain medication coursing through his veins. "Thank you, sir." Beau hesitated, "I would salute, but…"

Maj. Elston interrupted Beau's words with a chuckle, "No need for that." He moved to Beau's bedside and placed his clipboard onto the bedside table next to the lingering dinner tray. "Let me start by letting you know that you are a very lucky man. You took quite a bit of shrapnel, and one of the pieces in your neck missed your carotid artery by mere millimeters."

Elston moved around to the other side of the bed, leaning in to inspect Beau's bandages. "The quick treatment you received in Afghanistan likely saved your life." He began to lightly touch Beau's right shoulder and bicep. Reflexively, Beau tensed up, but the doctor didn't touch him with enough force to inflict pain. "You need to know that we had to put a significant number of stitches in your right deltoid after we removed the shrapnel, your right bicep tendon was completely detached and your triceps was nearly severed at the medial head. Essentially, we had to put your muscles back where they belong. The blast nearly tore your right arm completely off. That means the rehabilitation for your shoulder and right arm, as well as your neck, will be hard work. I'm not going to sugarcoat it, I'm still very concerned about nerve damage and it will be your desire to heal and your willingness to work through it that will be the determining factor in whether or not you regain full function in that arm."

Beau painfully nodded his understanding, at least so far as his immobilized neck would allow him to nod — which was barely more than a dip of his chin. He wasn't completely clear on the details, his head was still too fuzzy, but he clearly understood that he could have died. And though some days he actually *wanted* to die, in this moment, he was grateful to be alive. "Thank you," Beau said.

"'Ol Hangdog here is a man of few words, Doc," Antonne spoke up, "a grumpy, crotchety man of few words." He laughed at his own joke, and Beau caught the doctor holding back a chuckle.

"I would also like to report that, upon initial inspection, your prognosis was far grimmer than your current level of progress would indicate. The proximity of the shrapnel to your carotid artery was critical. The trauma itself had caused a pseudoaneurysm to form at the right bifurcation." Beau struggled to hang onto the doctor's words. Even on a good day, this kind of talk would have been over his head, but adding IV pain medication made it nearly impossible to follow. The doctor paused when he noticed Beau's expression and checked himself. "Basically, that means that the point where your main carotid artery splits to supply your head and neck," he touched his own neck with his fingers, "blunt force trauma from the blast and the physical embedding of the shrapnel into your neck resulted in injury to the blood vessel wall, causing blood to pool in the surrounding tissue." He paused again, "Let's just put it this way, you were millimeters from death, and you survived."

He grabbed his clipboard and began to jot a few things down. He then looked back at Beau and explained the process of communicating with the liaison officers, the eyes and ears of a military hospital, as he called them, and informed Beau that he'd arranged for travel orders for his parents to be by his bedside — and confirmed, that because of his original prognosis, the Marine Corps had immediately agreed to arrange both travel and lodging.

Beau's forehead furrowed with concern. "My parents are coming here? To Germany?" he asked. There was both surprise and reluctance in his voice when he responded. He wasn't sure how he should feel.

"They are very likely already in the air." Maj. Elston pulled a pair of reading glasses from his lab coat pocket and propped them on his nose. He reached for his clipboard and read over some of his notes. "As your attending physician, I believe their presence to be both warranted and of benefit to your recovery." He continued reading as he spoke in an unmistakably matter-of-fact tone. "And according to my information, your liaison officer has also supplied your unit with all your information. I expect you will begin getting correspondence at any time." Maj. Elston stood up and removed his glasses, tucking them back into his pocket. "I'll be back to follow-up with you again in the morning. In the meantime, you're in good hands with your nurses. It's important that you eat to keep your strength up. Susan here tells me that you've been a little bit stubborn in that department."

Beau's nurse made a face. She hadn't expected Elston to call her out. Then she walked over to the bedside table next to where Elston stood and lifted the cover off the tray, revealing a meal that had barely been touched. "I'm going to heat this up again. It's all soft foods and should be easy to swallow. It's important that you try to eat." She looked at Maj. Elston and made her way to the door.

Elston started to follow suit, then he looked back at Beau and asked, "Do you have any questions for me?"

Even though he had a million questions running through his foggy brain, Beau answered, "No, sir. Thank you."

"Like I said, a man of few words." Antonne shook his head and then continued, "Thanks for coming by, Doc." He threw up a hand and waved goodbye. Beau wondered how it was possible for someone to be that jovial while stuck in a hospital bed. He knew he was far too medicated to form a rational string of thoughts, but something in him still managed to ache for his work. He *wanted* to be with this unit. He didn't want to be incapacitated. And today, he didn't want to die either.

~

Joe and Valerie were dragging when they deboarded their plane at Ramstein Air Base. They'd hardly slept at all the night before their trip and the twelve plus hours of flight time had been anything but relaxing. Cpl. Ballantine had provided them with so much information that Valerie felt she was suffering from some kind of sensory overload. But, despite their fatigue, they both acknowledged that the Marine Corps had gone above and beyond to ensure they were well taken care of. The liaison had arranged for lodging and transportation, and had even assigned a Marine Corps escort to meet them upon landing, to ensure they didn't have trouble with the security protocol. Their names had been placed on a specific list of base-allowed travelers and, truth be told, they were both grateful to avoid the stress of handling it themselves. Early on in Beau's time as a Marine, they'd learned the hard way that being civilian resulted in significant road blocks when it came to getting on base.

"Mr. and Mrs. McKnight?" Their escort approached them instinctively. Val reasoned that they must have stuck out like sore thumbs. They were the only people on their flight who were obviously civilian.

"Yes," Joe said, as he stuck out his hand.

"Pfc. Carroll. Nice to meet you, sir." The young Marine was dressed in his service C uniform, which consisted of dark green pants, a khaki short sleeve shirt with his rank emblazoned on the sleeves and a garrison cap. He appeared neat and poised, and somehow that alone made Joe feel more at ease. Pfc. Carroll introduced the McKnights to two other Marines and assured them that their luggage and belongings would be taken care of. Valerie welcomed the offer to take her carry-on bag and Joe reluctantly followed suit once he accepted that the attending pair of Marines had been given the task as part of their jobs. Something in him made it difficult to hand over his bag, because he was perfectly capable of carrying it himself. The group moved together toward the baggage claim area and Joe and Valerie were in awe as the two assisting Marines stood by, waiting for them to point out their bags.

"I've been instructed to take you to the Landstuhl Fisher Houses. It's within walking distance to the medical center. You can get settled in and then go from there. The management is expecting you," said Pfc. Carroll.

"Do you know what we should do, or where we're supposed to go after that?" Joe asked.

"Not entirely, sir. Headquarters should have provided you with the contact information for your liaison, who should also be expecting you. I imagine you'll head straight to the hospital as soon as your lodging is secure." Pfc. Carroll was polite and knowledgeable, though it quickly dawned on both Joe and Valerie that he likely wasn't privy to all the details and may or may not be pulling some of his information from past experience. Joe reckoned his specific job was to get the family from point A to point B and decided to hold his other questions.

"The liaison, of course," Joe said, with a tone that revealed his realization that calling the liaison should have been his first option. "Sorry."

"Not a problem, sir. Let's get you to your home away from home."

Valerie was deeply moved by the Marine Corps' care and consideration, so much so that the sight of the two Marines loading their luggage into a government vehicle caused her to tear up. She leaned in to Joe and whispered, "It's really amazing, isn't it?" She gestured toward the Marines with her hand.

"What do you mean?" Joe whispered in return.

"This!" This time she was whisper-yelling, "All of this." She waved her hand in a more dramatic gesture toward the two Marines, now closing the trunk of the vehicle, and to their young escort.

"Oh," Joe whispered in response, "I know. It's almost overwhelming."

"That whole band of brothers concept is a real thing, I think," Val continued.

"I think you're right," Joe responded, as he put his arm around her waist. He pulled her to him, squeezing her close. They could both sense the awe and pride the other felt and they let themselves bask in the warm glow of what it meant to be a small part of the extended Marine Corps family.

CHAPTER TEN

When Eli's dinner tray arrived, Pete decided it was time for him, too, to fill his belly. Since it was his turn to stay the night at the hospital, he opted for the hospital cafeteria.

"I'm going to head down for some food. Ivy, do you want to come, or maybe I can bring you something?"

"Um, I'm okay for now, thanks Pete." The truth of the matter was that Ivy's stomach was a tangled web. She had so hoped to take one look at Eli and experience a flood of old feelings and a definite certainty that he was the one. But she hadn't. She was overcome with emotion, yes. She felt love and gratitude for Eli's miraculous recovery, yes. She experienced a familiarity that she'd missed and longed for since the night of the accident, yes. But did she immediately forget about her feelings for Mark? Was she flooded by visions of a future with Eli? No!

"Okay. Shoot me a text if you change your mind. You two have fun," Pete said and winked at Eli as he left the room. Sweet Pete never let the opportunity to cause his nephews embarrassment pass him by.

"Will do," she said. Ivy smiled at Pete as he left and then stood up and moved out of the way so the hospital attendant could roll Eli's bedside table closer to the bed. She reached out and took the lid off his tray as the attendant left the room.

Ivy glanced at his plate, "Hmm. Appetizing," she joked. She smiled when Eli glanced at the bland collection of food items on his tray and made a dissatisfied face.

"This is *not* a meatball sub," he said as he reached for his spoon and placed it into the bowl of hot broth, but when he moved to bring the spoon to his lips, his arm was shaky. "Seriously?" he murmured, taking a deep, slightly frustrated breath. His fine motor skills were sorely lacking and he was surprised by his own inability to perform such a simple movement.

"Here, let me," Ivy said as she took the spoon and lifted a spoonful of broth to Eli's lips. He blew it for a second and watched the steam dissipate. After he swallowed the broth, Ivy gave him another spoonful. He took a few more bites and then shook his head, not wanting any more soup.

"I'm going to try for some bread. Surely I can do that," he said. He reached for the soft roll on his plate and tore a small piece off. He lifted it to his mouth and had no trouble feeding it to himself. "Success," he exclaimed, holding out a fist for Ivy. After she met his fist with hers, he stopped and stared into her eyes for a long beat, "I love you. I'm so glad you're here."

Ivy smiled, but she couldn't return his words. She did love him, but she knew what he meant, and she couldn't bring herself to say the words the way he meant them. She wanted to, so badly, but when she tried to make them come, all she could think about was Mark. "Keep eating," she said, still smiling. Though she didn't mean to, her energy, her very presence, created a tension in the room that was nearly palpable. It was as though her inner turmoil was changing the environment around her. There was awkwardness where none had existed before and a lack of comfort in a place that had once felt like home.

The strangeness wasn't lost on Eli. He felt her hesitation. The tension she had created was as physical as she was, but he chose to ignore it. He forced himself to overlook it, rationalizing that she was probably just exhausted. He reasoned that living in another country for as long as she had probably meant being back in America would be an adjustment. He watched her, seeing for the first time what two years had done to her physically. She looked the same, but different. She looked mature, womanly and gorgeous. So much so that Eli began to feel self-consciousness, because he knew he didn't look like the person she remembered and he certainly couldn't do the things he used to do, at least not yet. He equated self-sufficiency with manhood, and he couldn't even feed himself soup. Vulnerability hit him like a ton of bricks. It was the first time since waking up that the sensation of total peace had left him. He didn't like it. But before he let it take hold, he silently gave thanks to God for his life and for the moment he was living right that second, and the worry began to disappear immediately — but the awkwardness between him and Ivy didn't.

To beat back the feelings of uncertainty, Ivy began to ask questions again. Eli revealed his fear about sleep, and confessed that he'd only slept a few hours since arriving at the hospital — not because he wasn't tired, but because he was scared. He told her about what Dr. Davies had said, and confided in her that Dr. Davies' assurance had done little to still his nerves when it came to a good night's sleep. Soon she and Eli were having an animated discussion about rest and, for a while, things felt normal again. They'd always had good conversations and this moment was all the assurance Eli needed to forget the tension in the room. Ivy told Eli that rest was important for healing and that he should try to sleep, while he asserted that he'd been resting for two years and that he didn't really need sleep in order to rest. As they chatted on, Ivy began to register a comfortable familiarity between her and Eli — a sensation that reminded her of why she fell for him in the first place. But, try as she might, thoughts of Mark never left her and she found herself engaged in a game of emotional ping-pong. Her exhaustion, coupled with her emotional fragility, made the whole world feel surreal. She told herself as long as she could keep talking, she would be okay — so that's what she did.

~

Dr. Davies came through the door, trailed by Eli's nurse. Pete was passed out in the vinyl recliner by the window, allowing his full stomach to lull him into a satisfying sleep. Eli was lying back against his bed watching TV, as Ivy sat quietly next to him, pretending to watch as her mind wandered and her stomach churned.

"It's almost time for me to call it a night, but I wanted to come by and let you know that I've got the results of today's brain scan." Dr. Davies seemed energized — almost childlike.

Pete stirred when he heard the doctor's voice and wiped his face with his hands.

"I'm sorry, what?" Pete asked. He moved from groggy to alert in a blink.

"He's got my scan results, Uncle Pete," Eli repeated what Dr. Davies said.

"Right, well, it's remarkable," Dr. Davies said. "The results are truly remarkable. Eli, your brain scan shows no visible evidence that you were ever in a coma at all. Literally everything about everything is one hundred percent spatially normal." Dr. Davies was smiling as he spoke. His face was a testament to the awe he felt inside. He'd been carrying that awe like a torch since he first got the call that Eli was awake and it showed no signs of dimming. Eli McKnight had renewed his love for his work and his appreciation for the majesty that is the human body.

Pete clapped his hands sharply and let out a single deep laugh, "Yes, sir! God is good, I tell ya'! God is good!"

Eli couldn't help but feel excited. His smile was broad, and despite her internal struggles, Ivy was excited too. She felt an instant sense of relief, as though two years of invisible weight lifted off her shoulders. Her feelings of elation in hearing the news only made her more confused about her feelings for Eli and Mark. She was beginning to distrust her own emotions.

"Wow! Thank you," Eli reached a hand toward Dr. Davies, who had moved to the right side of his bed. Eli shifted his body weight toward Ivy. He noticed she didn't lean into him, as she would have done before all this, but she didn't pull away either, so he let the moment pass.

"Dr. Davies, will you help us settle something?" Ivy asked.

"If I can, absolutely," Dr. Davies ran his hand through his hair and then stuck his hand into his pocket.

"So, I say he should be sleeping more, letting his body heal, and he says he doesn't need sleep to rest."

"Oh boy," Eli said, "here we go." He laughed.

"So, should he try to sleep at bedtime, to get into a rhythm? Or is an hour here and there okay?" Ivy legitimately wondered which approach would be better for Eli. Matters of the heart aside, she still cared for him deeply and wanted to help him heal, but she also just really wanted to be right.

"Well, that's really up to him. If he thinks he could sleep, he should. If not, we'll have to trust his body will catch up to a rhythm on its own, based on his activity," Dr. Davies spoke directly to Ivy. She was a far cry from the weepy young girl he remembered from two years ago. Ivy nodded her understanding.

"So, sleep if he's sleepy and don't fight it, right?" Ivy asked.

"Right. Natural sleep is healthy and it's very different from a coma." Dr. Davies began to pick up on Ivy's line of questioning. "Are you still struggling with anxiety about sleeping, Eli?" He turned to Eli with a medical-professional expression on his face.

"Great," Eli sighed, but with a smile on his face. "She's let the cat out of the bag." His smile faded after a moment and he answered, "Some."

"Well, you do need sleep, so if you aren't sleeping, we'll get you something to help you." Dr. Davies nodded at Eli, "Okay?"

"I'd prefer to go without if I can," Eli answered. He didn't want a pill to force him to sleep, because he didn't want to sleep at all if he could avoid it, much less have no control over it. Once again, he found himself fighting to feel God's peace.

"I'm going to order it for you. If you don't sleep again tonight, your nurse will have it. How about that?" Davies stepped back, tucking Eli's file under his arm, back to where it had been when he came in, "Tomorrow, we're going to do an

EEG to check electrical conductivity in your brain, but based on your earlier exam and your scan, and your general cognitive reasoning skills, I don't anticipate any issues.

"EEG?" Eli questioned. He'd heard of it, but didn't know exactly what it was. "What is that exactly?"

"Electroencephalogram... " Dr. Davies began.

Pete cut him off, "What a mouthful!"

"Exactly," Dr. Davies confirmed. He made a funny face, raising one eyebrow, which caused Pete to chuckle. "It's EEG for short. Anyway, it's a simple test to measure electrical patterns in the brain. It doesn't hurt, no anesthesia or anything, but you will end up with some goop in your hair. But it'll wash out."

Eli paused for a moment, but Dr. Davies could tell he wanted to ask something else. Finally, Eli got the words out, "Speaking of that, when can I take a shower? And, well," he leaned toward Dr. Davies and spoke more quietly, "I'm working on a couple days here already. How long am I going to have to do this whole catheter thing? I am not a fan."

Dr. Davies couldn't help himself and grinned widely, he stifled a laugh before responding. "I think we could probably start moving in that direction tomorrow. But you do need to know that your muscles have atrophied pretty severely. You absolutely cannot get up out of that bed without a nurse in the room to assist you. Understood?"

"Yes, sir," Eli responded. "But, for real, the sooner we can move on that the better."

"Are you in pain at all?" Dr. Davies slipped into care mode.

"Oh, no, no. I'm okay. I just know it's there, and that alone is enough to make the hair on the back of my neck stand up. I've always kind of considered that *area* an exit, not an entry — I feel like we're going the wrong way down a one-way street, if you get my meaning." Eli tilted his head down and raised his eyebrows in Dr. Davies direction. His face spoke a thousand words and Davies thought every single one of them was funny. He threw his head back and laughed out loud.

"I hear you loud and clear," Davies returned. He continued laughing as he finished up. "We'll try to get that matter taken care of. Now, how about food? Did you tolerate your dinner okay?"

"I think so. I feel fine," Eli answered.

"Um, 'tolerated' isn't the word — demolished is more like it." Ivy reached for the tray that was still on the rolling table and lifted the lid. "Not a crumb left, except for a little broth."

"Alright then," Davies said, crossing his arms across his chest, Eli's file still held firmly in place. "I'll order formula as we wean you off the tube, but maybe for lunch we can up the ante a little."

"I'm not going to be satisfied until I get a meatball sub," Eli responded, jokingly. "I'm kidding," he paused, "but seriously, I can't think of anything but a meatball sub."

This time Pete couldn't contain himself and began to crack up, "I've missed you, boy!"

Dr. Davies chuckled. He was beginning to see for himself what so many people had told him in the past — Eli McKnight was special.

CHAPTER ELEVEN

The drive from Ramstein Air Base to the Landstuhl Fisher House was just over ten minutes, and both Joe and Valerie took in as much of the surrounding landscape as they could during the ride. The architecture made Valerie feel like she was living in a movie or in the chapters of a book. Despite the fact that they were in Germany under terrifying circumstances, they both felt a certain sense of gratitude for the experience in and of itself. They drove past fields and farmland for several miles before arriving on the outskirts of Landstuhl. As they made their way through the small city, Joe and Valerie were growing increasingly eager to see Beau. They were nervous but somehow relieved at the same time. Val held tightly to Joe's hand, and he held her delicate fingers firmly in return, thankful to have her there by his side.

Pfc. Carroll was quiet for much of the ride, only speaking to point out locations he considered to be key points of interest for an American family, places like the McDonald's and the supermarket. When they finally pulled up outside the Fisher House, Valerie made a mental note of its unique beauty — a two-story building with a terracotta tile roof and deep reddish brown shutters flanking the windows. It was homey, a little different from American style, but homey nonetheless. As Pfc. Carroll made quick work of driving under the veranda in front of the building, Joe and Valerie noted the neat margins of the landscape and the richness of the wood trusses supporting the roof above them.

Once they'd carried all their bags in through the doors, they were greeted by volunteer staff and said their goodbyes to Pfc. Carroll. They were given a quick tour of the facility and the common areas, and then they settled into their room. When they were finally alone, Joe called their hospital liaison. They were both exhausted and in dire need of sleep, but neither of them had any intent of taking a nap before they saw Beau. Joe left a message for the liaison and sat on one of the two twin beds in the room. He patted the bed next to him, signaling Val to sit. "Twin beds," he announced, as though she hadn't noticed, "interesting."

"Beggars can't be choosers, Joe. We are staying here free of charge, remember?" Val pointed out the obvious.

"True," Joe answered. "Do you want to go ahead and walk over to the hospital? Who knows when the liaison will call back? Maybe we can get a jump on the whole thing if we head over there now."

"I thought you'd never ask," Valerie returned. "What time is it at home? We should call everyone." She was in a bit of a fog and Joe could see the fatigue in her face.

"I think it's early morning at home, like seven o'clock," Joe answered.

"I'm going to call Mom and Mimi, and I might try Eli's room to let them know we made it. Then we can head over, okay?"

"Okay. I'll try that hospital lady ag... " Joe hadn't finished his sentence when the phone began to ring. "Speak of the devil," he said as he looked at the number. Valerie signaled to Joe that she was going to make her calls while he worked through the day with their liaison. After getting all the information he needed to navigate the medical center and find Beau's room, and after receiving the latest update on Beau's condition, he hung up the phone feeling a true sense of calm and a depth of faithfulness he'd largely been faking up until now. He fought to keep his eyes open in the quiet room and had just begun to doze off when he heard Valerie speak.

"Well, everything is good at home. Are you ready?" She asked.

"Oh, I was almost asleep there for a second." He stretched as he stood up, "Well, my dear, I have very good news for you." He paused.

"Well?" Val asked impatiently.

"The liaison spoke to his case manager today and the case manager, uh, Captain, or uh Ms., something… " He paused trying to recall the name he'd been given just minutes before, but a lack of sleep and an overload of information resulted in an evaporation of his recollection. "I can't remember." He shook his head.

"It doesn't matter! What else?" Elation filled Val's voice. The good news was all the news she cared about at the moment.

"Beau is awake and he's talking, and his prognosis is very good, much better than they thought at first. With therapy, he's expected to make a full recovery!"

"Really? Really, really? Thank God! That's fantastic news!" Valerie jumped up and down where she stood, her body reenergized by hope. "Let's go see him right now!"

Joe was smiling a broad McKnight smile and, as he stood up, he said a silent prayer of thanks. Life still felt like a whirlwind of chaos, but somehow he also felt confident and safe, and at ease knowing that his trust in God had not been misplaced — everything really would be okay. "Sounds good," he laughed as he reached out to grab the hand she'd extended in his direction. "Today is a good day."

~

Beau was leaning back against his pillow with his eyes closed as Antonne shared all the details of his life, from his childhood memories to his position on toothpaste. Beau began to wonder why he always managed to wind up in close proximity to people who never seemed to shut up. His thoughts turned to Andy, the original chatterbox. Andy had managed to somehow claw his way into Beau's life and went from being nothing more than his motor-mouthed bunkmate to one of his closest friends. Was he still a motor mouth? Yes. But Beau had come to love him like a brother. Thus far, Antonne had not clawed anything except Beau's nerves.

In the hopes he would stop talking, Beau was doing his best to convince Antonne that he had fallen asleep, after all, he *was* heavily medicated, but Antonne paid no attention to Beau's efforts and seemed to be completely engrossed in his own words until the door to the room opened and Capt. Pickett, Beau's nurse case manager at the hospital, walked in. She turned and looked over her shoulder. "Right this way," she said quietly, "it appears he's asleep now." When Beau heard the words, his eyes shot open immediately. He watched as his father and mother tentatively followed Capt. Pickett through the door into the room, and he recognized that, for the first time since he'd woken from surgery, Antonne was quiet. "Oh, maybe not!" Capt. Pickett made her way to the head of the bed on Beau's left side.

Valerie was beaming when she saw Beau's eyes open. She saw his bandages, she saw the bruises and cuts that were left to heal, she saw the IV and the machines, but his eyes were open and after two years of looking at Eli's sleeping face, seeing Beau's open eyes was a huge relief. "Beau!" She moved quickly to his bedside. She wanted to squeeze him, but his bandages and bruises made that seem like a bad idea. Capt. Pickett stepped backward to give Valerie more room, and Valerie laid a gentle hand on Beau's head, rubbing his short hair with her fingers, before leaning in to kiss his left cheek. After she did, she lingered for a moment and laid her forehead against the crown of his head. When she stepped back, Beau saw the tears in her eyes, but he also saw a loving smile on her face, a smile that made him secretly happy she'd come. Joe was standing behind her, his right hand covering his mouth. He didn't speak, but Beau could see that his eyes, too, glistened with tears. Valerie was wiping her cheeks as she moved out of the way to make room for Joe.

"How are you feeling, son?" Joe moved close to his boy and reached out to take his left hand. He held it in an underhand fashion, almost as if they might arm wrestle — but with a tenderness that Capt. Pickett rarely saw. Working in this environment, she had grown largely desensitized to trauma, but joy and love had never been lost on her, and she had never become desensitized to the emotions of a reunion between a service member and his family.

"I will let you visit for a while," she said, "and then I'll come back so we can talk about what happens next." She quietly left the room, letting the door shut gently behind her.

"It looks worse than it is, I think," Beau said, still holding his father's hand. Joe was still holding his laptop in his right hand, and he turned his body to hand it to Valerie. She put her bag and Joe's laptop on a small table under the window. Then, as she pulled a chair up next to the bed, motioning for Joe to sit, Beau noticed the exhaustion in their faces. "When did you get here?" he asked.

"It's probably been two hours since we landed," Valerie answered. "They put us at the Fisher House. We can walk there from here."

"Well, the Fisher Houses — I thought those were for the families of people who were, you know, really bad off," Antonne heavily emphasized the word *really*, so as to make his point unmistakable. He couldn't resist joining the conversation. Interjection just happened to be one of his finest skills. Valerie was startled by his words. Having been completely focused on Beau, she hadn't even been aware of his presence in the room. "I'm Antonne, by the way. Nice to meet you." He was holding out his hand. Valerie took a few steps toward him, reaching her hand out to take his. Beau made an audible groan, but Joe couldn't tell if it was a groan of frustration or of pain.

"I'm Valerie McKnight, and that's my husband Joe. We are Beau's mom and dad." She smiled as she shook his hand.

Antonne started to speak again, but Beau cut him off short, "I've wanted to pull that curtain all day!" He pulled his hand from Joe's grasp and pointed toward the room dividing curtain with his left hand, "Could you pull it for me, Mom? It won't drown him out, but at least I won't have to look at his mouth moving every second of the day like I have so far."

"Beau!" Valerie couldn't believe her ears.

Antonne started to laugh immediately, seemingly unscathed by Beau's snarky comment. "Fine!" he said, as he reached out and grabbed the curtain, yanking it closed with urgency. "You're no fun to talk to anyway," he said laughingly. "It's time for my beauty nap anyhow!" Joe and Valerie could hear movement on the other side of the curtain for a short period of time, along with the squeaky sound of Antonne's traction device and his bed rails. After that, the room fell quiet.

Valerie gave Beau a look that expressed her confusion, coupled with a mild maternal frustration over his behavior. Joe shook his head in Valerie's direction, in an attempt to brush off the experience. He turned to Beau and said, "We'll let you fill us in on that later."

Beau looked in Antonne's direction out of the corner of his eye, as though he could somehow see through the curtain. He used his left hand to gently tug his father closer to himself, then he whispered, "His name is Antonne Young, he's Army, and he has literally been talking every second since I woke up in this bed — I am about to snap." Joe couldn't help but laugh. He chuckled to himself under his breath and covered his mouth with his hand. The fact that Beau was well enough to be irritated by a talkative roommate was funny. Mere hours earlier they were worried for his life, and now his chief complaint was an annoying roommate. Joe sat back in the chair Valerie had pulled over for him and took a deep breath. How quickly the tables had turned.

"Has the doctor been in? What are they saying?" Valerie moved close to Beau's bedside. She stood in front of Joe, who patted his knee, signaling for her to sit.

"He says I'm going to be fine," Beau's answer was short. Joe and Valerie glanced at each other, making note of the fact that his ill temperament hadn't seemed to change since he left.

"And?" Valerie added, but Beau simply shrugged his one working shoulder.

"If you don't answer, she's just going to get a nurse, you know that right, son?" Joe joked. From behind the curtain, they heard Antonne laugh, too. Immediately, Valerie covered her mouth, trying to hold back a laugh of her own. Joe didn't hold back, and though he didn't think his own statement was that funny, knowing that Antonne was eavesdropping on their conversation changed the dynamic entirely.

"Shut up!" Beau yelled, as he used his left hand to throw one of his pillows against the curtain. It hit the curtain with a small puff-like sound and slid to the floor with a soft plop.

"Hangdog, boy, you answer your mama or I'll do it for you," Antonne shouted back.

Beau growled under his breath, Joe watched as he made a fist with his left hand, squeezing it until the tension was visible in his knuckles. "I can't take this guy!" Beau yelled. "Fine! God knows if I don't do it, you'll find a way to make the conversation last all night long!" He inhaled sharply and then winced in pain. After a short pause, he cleared his throat and began to speak. Joe and Valerie weren't quite sure how to take the dynamic between their son and his roommate, so they wordlessly, collectively chose to accept it as part of the surreal experience they were living. "The doctor said that I'm lucky to be alive, that some of the shrapnel in my neck was within millimeters of my carotid artery and that I could've bled to death if the people who took care of me in Afghanistan hadn't done such a good job. He also said that I've had a lot of muscle and tendon damage and a lot of stitches. My rehab will be hard, and he said I'll get out of it what I put into it. If I want full range of motion and feeling back, I'll have to work for it." He paused again and then yelled, "Are you and your big fat mouth happy now?"

"Very," Antonne answered calmly.

"Well, we know hard work won't be a problem for you, son." Joe laid a hand on Beau's left shoulder and squeezed it lightly. "Right?" Instead of an answer, Beau again dismissively shrugged the one shoulder he could move. Laying there in his bed, he had plenty of time to think about getting what he deserved. He *needed* to live for the sake of his unborn child, but nothing said he had to live free of pain. Part of him felt that having lingering effects from his injuries would be part of a punishment he deserved.

"How's everybody at home? How's Julia and the baby? How's Eli?" No matter how hard he tried to build a wall of indifference around his feelings, Beau genuinely cared about the people he loved. No amount of self-loathing or guilt could totally harden his heart. He watched as Valerie's smile spread across her face. He glanced at his dad, and his smile was broader still. Joe could see the suspicion in his son's eyes before he asked, "What's going on, Dad?"

"Let me! Let me!" Valerie bounced to her feet and moved toward her bag, she pulled out her phone and held it tightly in her hand. "First, we have some news." She looked at Joe, smiling, and she couldn't stop tears from forming in her eyes — something that had become part of her norm over the last couple days. "Then, I'll let you call Julia. Dad brought his laptop so you can get her on Skype!"

"Okay," Beau responded tentatively. He could tell there was something strange in his parents' demeanor, but he couldn't imagine what it might be. What could possibly be worth all this? "What's going on, guys?"

"Valerie, Beau wants to know what's going on." Joe's smile almost swallowed his entire face. Valerie fiddled with her phone and then quickly thrust it in front of Beau's eyes. What Beau saw rendered him speechless. He snatched the phone with his good hand and watched as a video of his brother, in his hospital bed, talking and laughing, played out before him. He was staring at the screen in disbelief. He dropped the phone into his lap and squeezed his eyes shut, breathing heavily, as if he'd been running, but then he heard Eli's voice emanating from the phone and his eyes shot open. He lifted the phone to his face and watched as Eli delivered a message.

"Hey there big brother, surprise!" Eli laughed and then continued, "I hear you're a Marine now. I can't believe that! You're way too big of a wuss to be a Marine, and besides, you always looked stupid with a buzz cut." He laughed again and then finished, "I can't wait to see you! Keep your head down. I love you! You're still my best friend, even with that haircut!" The video ended with Eli lifting his thin fingers toward the screen and smiling as if it were any other day.

Beau was silent. He didn't move. He held the phone in front of his eyes until the screen went black. When he finally set the phone back in his lap, his stunned silence gave way to tears. He lifted his left hand and covered his eyes with his fingers. His shoulder rose and fell in short succession as low sobs broke the silence of his voice. Valerie had been weeping since the moment the video had started, and now Joe was crying too. Beau's sobs were perforated only by his attempts to quiet himself. Antonne pulled the curtain back just long enough to take in the scene, but immediately closed it back — he clearly didn't belong in this moment, and for once, he was speechless.

Valerie started to speak, but before the words came, Beau had the phone in his hand again. He revived the screen and replayed the video without a word, as tears continued to pour down his cheeks. The bandage on his right jaw was dripping onto his bedding. He replayed the message from Eli over and over again, staring at the screen, as Joe and Valerie looked on, each trying to compose themselves, as they waited for the questions they knew would come.

"When?" Beau finally asked. "When did he wake up?"

"Just over two days ago." Valerie took the phone from Beau's lap and opened the gallery so Beau could see the pictures she'd taken. She continued to wipe her eyes. Joe couldn't stop crying long enough to speak. He had prayed for the heaviness in Beau's spirit to lift for so long, watching it unfold unleashed a torrent of emotion he was powerless to stop.

"He seems... good, like nothing is wrong," Beau said, but he looked at his mom with questioning eyes.

"He's perfect. One hundred percent perfect," Joe finally spoke up.

"Except for muscle atrophy. He will have rehab too," Val added.

"I can't believe it," Beau said, clearly stunned. "I just can't. I mean, I can, but I can't." He reached for his mom's phone again. "Can I watch it again?" He was like a little boy. Innocence and sweetness bubbled up from somewhere inside him, a part of him the entire world had forgotten existed. Val found the video again quickly and Beau held the phone close to his face as he watched it again and then again a second time. Beau's mind snagged on the possible timing of Eli waking up, "Two days ago?" He dared not mention it, at least not now, but he could hear Andy's voice in his head, crying out to God on Eli's behalf. He replayed the moments in his mind. He recalled the searing pain as shrapnel tore through his flesh and he could smell the heat and smoke in the air, but over and above the memory of the pain, he could hear Andy. He remembered the stillness, the peace in Andy's face and the strange presence he felt all around him before he lost consciousness. Could it be possible? Did Eli wake up at the very moment Andy called out to God? Impossible! "Mom, can we call him? Can we call him now?"

"Of course, baby." Val was overcome with her motherly feelings. The love she felt for her boys had taken control of her senses. At that moment, all she could see was the child in him. She shook herself free from the web of maternal emotions so she could step back into the present. "But, maybe you should call Julia first. What do you think Joe, should he call Julia first?" Val wasn't sure how to move from Eli's miracle on to a completely different kind of miracle, but she knew Beau would want to know, and she knew Julia *needed* to hear from him.

"I think so," Joe said, wiping yet another tear from his cheek with the back of his index finger. He stood up from his chair and reached for his laptop bag. "I think a video chat will be just what the doctor ordered for Julia. She's been worried out of her mind."

Beau sniffed, "Oh, wow, I guess she probably is." He wiped his eyes again, "I just can't believe all this is real." Joe laid the open laptop on Beau's lap as the Skype logo appeared on the screen. Beau used his good hand to enter his user name and password. He scrolled down his contacts list and found Julia's name. Opening their previous chat, he read her urgent message from the night Eli woke up. He used his index finger to find the call icon and pressed it.

As the call connected, Joe and Valerie moved closer together. He put his arm over her shoulder and she wrapped her arm around his waist. They stood, holding tightly to each other, watching the breadth of emotions Beau experienced as Julie cried over his wounds and shared her fears with him. They held tightly to one another as Julia put her own experiences aside to offer Beau a first-hand account of Eli's first few minutes awake, and watched Beau fight tears of both joy and relief as he listened to the mother of his unborn child recount Eli's miracle from her perspective. They listened as, over and over, Julia said, "I wish you could have been there." They held tightly to each other as they watched their son's demeanor soften and heard the tenderness in his voice when he spoke to her. Valerie laid her head on Joe's shoulder as the reality of Beau and Julia's love for one another became all the more apparent. They looked at each other knowingly as Julia told Beau about the hospital and the ultrasound, noting that she downplayed her own emergency room experience in order to spare Beau the added worry and stress. And finally, they held tightly to one another as their baby boy learned that he would soon have a baby boy of his own. They watched as Julia stood to show Beau her growing tummy, and they cried as they watched Beau kiss his fingers and then gently touch them to the screen, resting them on Julia's stomach. And as Valerie pulled the framed ultrasound photo from her bag, they knew, in that moment, the overwhelming love shared between a father and his son would soon change Beau forever.

CHAPTER TWELVE

Less than two weeks from the day he arrived at Landstuhl, Beau was set for transfer to Bethesda Naval Hospital in Maryland. From there, thanks to the ample efforts of his case worker and his hospital liaison, he would fly home to Texas and begin rehab in Houston, alongside his brother, at TIRR Memorial Hermann rehabilitation hospital. Joe and Valerie had been approved to travel with him and, as a result, had developed an undeniable pride and appreciation for the Marine Corps and the military as a whole. They developed a short-lived, but significant, bond with Beau's doctors and nurses, and even with Antonne, who was scheduled for yet another surgery on the very day Beau would fly out. He hadn't totally won Beau over, but Beau had learned to accept him, and to respect him as well.

Joe had sat and nodded for hour after hour as Antonne rambled on about his parents and family, or lack thereof, and it became clear that Antonne just needed someone to care. He'd had no visitors, no family by his bedside, and no real expectations to even get a phone call from home. Some of his Army buddies had sent cards and called, and when Joe saw how Antonne lit up at such a small gesture, he made the decision to invest in his life. Come what may, Antonne would have an *adoptive* family for as long as he needed!

The anticipation of laying eyes on Eli made Beau's constant pain feel like less of a burden. After some of his swelling had subsided, his doctors had agreed he'd need at least one more shoulder surgery before he could begin rehab, a surgery that would take place in Maryland. Thus far, he had regained only some of the feeling in his right hand, and his doctor had grown increasingly concerned about nerve damage.

He was eager to see Julia, eager to see his family, and eager to leave the confines of the hospital. But, he also harbored a nagging desire to return to his unit. He felt as though he had abandoned his team and that he was somehow laying down on the job and neglecting his duty as a Marine. And only Antonne knew that Beau had struggled with nightmares for the last two weeks, waking abruptly in the night.

Beau used Skype and his dad's computer to communicate with Andy and the other members of his squad, all of whom assured him he'd be back by their sides in no time, joking about how much better they were eating than he was and assuring him they would save him some powdered eggs and MREs.

He spent much of his time in a fog — swimming in a thick soup of pain medication and immobility. Physically, his wounds had begun to heal. Despite that, his pain was near constant. On one hand, he was elated that Eli was awake, that he would soon be a father, and that his name might be cleared from wrongdoing now that Eli was recovering. He had expected to find relief and solace from his guilt, but, for some reason, the feelings of guilt had only multiplied. Not only did he still carry guilt about what had happened to Eli, but now, he also carried guilt over leaving his squad to fight alone. He knew some of his fellow Marines had died on the day he was wounded, and he carried guilt that he hadn't been there to mourn them. He carried guilt that he hadn't done more to help them, somehow. And, he carried guilt that he had lived while others had died — in his mind, others who didn't deserve it, while he did.

When they first spoke via Skype, Beau had forced Eli's address onto Andy, insisting that he write. Andy hadn't asked for it, but Beau persisted. He *needed* Eli to know the man who might be responsible for his recovery. Andy took Eli's address down and, in his typical vernacular, agreed to write him by saying, "Well, it ain't like I got other stuff going on." Beau had managed to keep Andy's battlefield prayer a secret from his family, but word had traveled quickly throughout their unit — everyone had heard about Big Mack's battle-ending convoy prayer and Eli McKnight's miraculous recovery. Prior to Beau's injury, nobody in his unit knew Eli existed, except for Andy. But during that initial Skype call with his squad, Beau's first words had been, "Eli is awake!" While everyone else sat listening in confusion, Andy had simply smiled, shrugged, and said, "Well, yeah. That's how God works." After that, there was no stopping the talk and Andy had been given the unofficial task of praying over every mission. Even the men who, before the war, had considered themselves atheists would stand around Andy as he prayed, rationalizing their actions with questions like, "What can it hurt?"

Internally, Eli's recovery plagued Beau's thoughts. He needed to know the truth. He needed definitive answers. Could it really be possible? Was Andy's faith responsible for Eli's wakefulness? His mind had become a jumbled knot of thoughts and emotions that wouldn't untangle. Where he should feel peace, instead he felt uncertainty. There was a void in his spirit and he didn't know how to fill it. Laying in his hospital bed, he had nothing but time to think. He felt so useless.

~

After visiting her obstetrician, Julia was given an order of modified bedrest. She was still at risk for preterm labor, and though the doctor didn't think she was in imminent danger, the risk was still high enough to warrant some medical precautions. Modified bedrest meant Julia had been forced to quit her job, but Mimi had been taking care of her every step of the way. She'd definitely taken her job seriously and gave daily updates to Valerie when she called. When the order of complete bedrest was lifted a bit, she finally allowed Julia to come down and eat her meals in the kitchen instead of in her bed. She also began letting her take real showers, without setting a timer or sitting outside the bathroom door asking, "How are you doing?" repeatedly.

Julia had Skyped with Beau every day and she knew something wasn't quite right. He seemed *off*. Though she could tell his excitement about coming home to her again, and seeing Eli, was definitely genuine, there seemed to be something else between them — a wedge that she couldn't see. She knew he was in a great deal of physical pain and had been medicated during every conversation they'd had since he'd been wounded, but she didn't believe his distance was pain induced. It felt like something else. She found herself hoping that seeing Eli face-to-face would somehow jolt him back into the person he used to be. She loved him just as he was, but she really wanted to be with the Beau she knew before the accident — fun loving, full of life and full of promise. She had expected and anticipated that the transformation would come when Beau first found out about his brother, building it up in her mind, but it hadn't happened, not with the impact she had expected anyway, and she was disappointed.

She knew she couldn't fly to Maryland. For one, she wasn't medically allowed to, and for two, she couldn't afford it. Relying on the McKnights for her survival had taken a toll on her sense of self-worth. She felt like a burden, no matter how many times Joe and Valerie told her she wasn't. She knew, in her heart, that things between her and Beau were far from the fairytale romance Joe and Valerie had wanted for their son, and she wondered what it was about them that still made them so willing to accept her into their world. Not many people would be so loving, and she knew it. Because she knew there would be no flying to Maryland, she asked again and again when Beau's next shoulder surgery would be and when he'd be transferred to the rehab hospital in Houston. Nobody had answers for her, but it didn't stop her from asking each and every day. She wanted to be waiting when he arrived in Houston, ready to hold his hand and help him through whatever pain he would endure. And, she had to admit, the idea that Beau would be present for the birth of their son felt like a dream come true. She had braced herself to go it alone, but now, she wouldn't have to. She felt guilty that she had even an ounce of gladness that Beau had been wounded, but she did — as hard as it was to admit to herself — she did! She wanted him there with her, and his suffering guaranteed she'd get her wish. It was a horrible thing to know about herself, but it was true and she was willing to accept it.

~

When the orderly came to get Antonne for surgery, on the day of Beau's transport to Bethesda, the McKnight family, Beau grudgingly included, made sure Antonne knew he was an honorary member of the family. Joe surprised him with his very own laptop and made sure he had all their information, that he could reach them day or night and vice versa. They invited him to visit Texas on leave and even to stay with them during the holidays, if he wanted to. Somehow, Beau already knew Antonne would take them up on the offer and felt just a little bit annoyed. But, he had to admit, he'd rather be annoyed by Antonne's non-stop talking on Christmas morning than to stomach the idea that Antonne might be somewhere alone, with no one to miss him or care. When they wheeled him out for yet another operation, Beau called behind him, "Take care of yourself, brother. Skype me when you get out of surgery."

Antonne's voice could be heard echoing down the hallway, "See, I knew it! He loves me! I knew it — 'ol Hangdog has a heart after all!"

Joe and Valerie were smiling as Beau shook his head and said sarcastically, "We're making a huge mistake with him. You know that, right?"

Beau's case worker stopped by his room for a final meeting before the transport flight. She briefed the McKnights on his recovery for the long term, what his USMC health assessment might entail and informed them that Beau should expect a mental health assessment at some point in the near future. She gave Val a packet of information that included her card, as well as the contact information for their next hospital liaison. As she continued discussing logistics, expectations and immediate plans, all Beau could focus on was the prospect of a medical review. What did that mean? When would that be? What would it mean for his future with the Marine Corps? Then, his mind jumped to his own mental health. He was having nightmares and, despite his efforts to try and hide it, he was secretly paranoid that everyone he saw already knew it. He felt like the world could see right through him. Between the nightmares and just the overall disruptive nature of the hospital, he hadn't been sleeping well and the lack of sleep only seemed to make the cycle worse. Less sleep meant more nightmares and the nightmares meant less sleep. He took a deep breath and forced himself to think about what was happening now.

His parents would accompany him on the flight, as would several other service members requiring transfer. He would be admitted to the hospital upon landing and would probably be scheduled for surgery within a day or two. He felt a marked indifference about the prospect of another surgery. In fact, he felt a marked indifference about his entire situation. If not for his deep desire to remain a Marine, he wouldn't have given his wounds a second thought. He still believed he deserved them. Maybe it was the influence of painkillers, maybe it was something else, but he was not very concerned about his own physical wellbeing — something that the *old* Beau had been acutely focused on.

~

Joe and Valerie had managed to see a little of Germany during their stay, and the fact that they'd been so very blessed, during what they originally expected to be a life and death journey, hadn't been lost on them. Every post and picture Valerie put up on social media received hundreds of reactions, and Eli and Pete had confirmed that he'd had an endless stream of visitors since the day they left town. They knew the hand of God had ordained their situation. Not only had Beau's prognosis improved dramatically, while they were still in mid-air, affording them some freedom to explore the local area during their stay, but his doctors and nursing staff had graciously arranged for them to travel back to the states with their son, free of charge. What could have been a tragedy had, strangely, turned out to be a blessing. And now, they'd go home and tag team their trips between Texas and Maryland, until the happy, and much anticipated, day their entire family would be reunited.

As they waited for the team to prep Beau for travel, Joe turned to Valerie and marveled at what a surreal ten days they'd just experienced. And then, as they recognized they were about to embark on yet another adventure, Valerie was the one to speak up, "This is going to be a very good day."

Joe put his arm around her and gave her a caring squeeze as he laughed and adjusted the bag on his shoulder, "Hey woman, you just stole my line!"

CHAPTER THIRTEEN

Beau had not allowed himself to feel excitement in over two years. He had not allowed himself to look forward to anything, to anticipate his future in a way that made him happy he was alive. But, as he and Valerie waited for him to be released from the hospital in Bethesda, he allowed himself the luxury of excitement — he was going to see his brother! Eli was still inpatient at the rehab hospital, at least for a couple more weeks, because he still hadn't put on enough muscle to fully support his own body weight. His doctors felt it would be best for him to undergo daily therapy for a while longer, before being released for outpatient care. Beau knew that he would be inpatient too, at least for a little while. His surgeons had confirmed he'd likely have some permanent nerve damage and that his rehab would be significant if he wanted to regain meaningful use of his arm. He had decided he wanted to return to duty as soon as possible — he needed to. He needed to be with his unit and he needed to be able to support a family. He was determined to do the work to get there. In his mind, he would soon be back to one hundred percent, but in is body, at least at the moment, he needed more Vicodin.

This time around, they'd be flying on a commercial flight. The Marine Corps covered Beau's travel, but Joe and Valerie were on their own once again. They'd spent so much money traveling back and forth from Texas to Maryland that Joe had decided to pick up extra work as soon as the family was together in one state. His company had been very understanding and supportive, but he was a salaried employee and he knew more money meant a second job. He didn't know what he was going to do, but he refused to dip into their investments any further than he already had, and he knew there would likely be more big expenses on the horizon, so he wanted to prepare. Besides that, he *needed* to be back at work. He needed the injection of normalcy into his life. He needed to feel like a provider and, if that meant two jobs, so be it.

Val and Beau would be landing in Houston, where Joe would pick them up and drive them to the rehab hospital for immediate admission. Beau had already been given special handicap privileges and was splinted, strapped and tightly bandaged on the right side of his body, from the waist up. He wore a neck brace to prevent over-rotation and tearing, as his doctors believed further nerve damage was likely if things didn't heal and rehabilitate in a specific sequence. Valerie had been writing down notes for two days, things to watch for, things to do, things to ask. Between Eli's coma and Beau's wounds, she felt certain she'd do pretty well on a nurse's exam if push came to shove. It had been a full week since Beau's last surgery, and even though his doctors assured him it was time to move on, he felt like his body was worse off than it had been before he left Germany. It didn't matter though, he was ready to go. He was ready to see Eli, and the hospital had already confirmed Beau and Eli could share a room. He'd almost forgotten what excitement was.

Their story was so unique that the entire community was buzzing about it. The family had tried to keep everything quiet, but Eli had entertained an endless parade of visitors from schools, churches, local charities, even some of the local government officials had been by — everyone in town wanted to see a real life miracle, so it was impossible to know who had done the most talking. Local reporters had been calling the hospital for days hoping to get a tip on Beau's arrival. Joe and Valerie had been screening calls since the news of Eli's miracle first became public, Mimi had simply turned the phone off at the house, and since the world learned that Beau McKnight was now a wounded warrior, members of the media had been coming out of the woodwork. Valerie knew that Rev. Hinkley had probably contacted Kevin, who had grown into a successful Senior Airman in the United States Air Force, to tell him Beau was coming home, and Kevin probably told everyone he knew, because, well, he wouldn't be Kevin Hinkley if he didn't.

Their story was media gold, and the reporters weren't going to let the family forget it. The McKnight brothers' saga had gone viral on social media and the frenzy showed no signs of slowing down. Everyone in the family had been bombarded with messages and calls — some welcomed, some not. Pete had taken to flinging insults like they were confetti and had grown quite proficient at slamming the phone down in Eli's hospital room. The nursing staff was on alert and had become diligent about visiting hours and poking their heads in regularly to determine whether or not each visitor was a welcomed guest or a stranger seeking a sneaky interview.

Eli couldn't believe how much attention he was getting. The hospital had even started discussions about beefing up security once Beau arrived. He'd been getting messages online from people he'd never met, asking all kinds of strange questions and making all kinds of unusual requests. People wanted locks of his hair, his prayers, information about what he saw and how he felt. One lady had even asked if she could have his bedding from home, hoping she could use it for her own son, who'd spent two months in a coma due to a drug overdose. Eli read the request out loud to Pete, who dismissed her immediately, "She's a nut. Don't message her back."

"I don't think she's a nut. I think she's desperate," Eli said. "I should say something to her."

Pete instantly felt bad. She probably was desperate, a desperate mother. "How did these people even find you?"

"I have no idea, but they did. I was just going to shut all my stuff down, but then I thought I might be able to help someone." Eli looked up at his uncle.

"You're a good man, Eli McKnight." Pete shook his head. He was humbled by his nephew's way of seeing the world. "Just be careful. There are a lot of crazies out there."

"I know. I will," Eli promised.

Beau, on the other hand, had ignored his social media. Julia had been keeping tabs on everything for him, but she dared not say a word about the seven hundred and twelve friend requests he'd received from random strangers. She was happy that he had become content to use Skype alone and she certainly didn't relay comments she read or the shared news stories and other posts about their situation. Some people were downright cruel and the last thing Beau needed was to have his guilt corroborated. Though, admittedly, she knew he'd eventually read some of the negative comments, she hoped that, by then, he'd be beyond the guilt.

Instead of filling his head with the drama, she kept things vague, telling him the story had gone wild, but nothing more. She talked to him about Eli's progress, her growing tummy, feeling their son move for the first time and about how excited she was to see him. She wasn't technically allowed to travel to Houston, but she'd bribed Joe into letting her join him. Mimi had put up a little bit of a fuss, just for show, knowing that it was her job to keep Julia on doctor's orders, but she hadn't forgotten what it felt like to be young and in love either, and she wasn't about to stop the reunion for a second.

~

Travel day had been a blur, security had been a nightmare, and Valerie's energy was gone. Taking care of Beau and the bags all by herself had proven a ginormous task. She gave Beau his pain medication as they waited at the gate, wondering what the altitude might mean for his pain, if anything. She honestly prayed he'd sleep — because she wanted to sleep too. Three solid hours would do her body good. When boarding finally began, she and Beau were allowed to board first. A member of the airline staff was kind enough to help Valerie with the bags, and when she handed the attendant the tickets and their identification, the young woman inspected their credentials and turned to click a few things on her computer screen. She turned back to Valerie and said, "We're going to bump you up to first class today. Thank you for your service, sir."

Valerie was taken aback. She had tears in her eyes when she looked back over her shoulder to thank the attendant again. She leaned over and kissed the top of Beau's head as she pushed his wheelchair down the jetway. Beau, his eyes only half open as the effects of his pain medication set in, finally spoke, "First class. Maybe I should get blown up more often?"

"Shut up, you! Don't even joke about that," Valerie snapped back before beginning to chuckle. She pretended to smack him. She and Joe never flew first class. They could have, but they chose not to. Joe believed coach seats were overpriced, let alone first class seats. No, he believed no "extra wide butt cushion" in the world would ever be worth the cost of a first class plane ticket. Val couldn't help but smile at the thought of telling Joe she got to fly first class.

~

Three hours and thirty eight minutes later, the flight attendants helped Valerie transfer Beau back into his wheelchair. He was woozy from the medication, but had enough strength in his legs to help himself a little. If not for the sharp shooting pains, he might have been able to walk. A male attendant helped Valerie back Beau through the narrow passage into the jetway and voluntarily carried their carry-on bags all the way to the gate. Valerie thanked the man at least seven times as they walked. When he bid them farewell, Val threw her carry-on over her shoulder and used all the strength left in her legs to hang Beau's Marine issue rucksack onto the back of his wheelchair. He had traveled from Afghanistan to Germany with nothing. His nurse case manager had procured some slippers and the hospital had provided other essentials. He wore either a half-open hospital gown or just his skivvies every day until Joe and Valerie went out and purchased some ball shorts and a few oversized button-down shirts that could be easily slid over his broken body. While at Bethesda, Beau received a package from his unit. The orderly had delivered it on a rolling cart. In it, his squad had put a few letters, pictures, get well cards and his rucksack. The rucksack contained as many of Beau's personal effects as they could shove into one bag, and now Valerie was trying to haul it around while managing her own belongings and Beau's chair. Beau felt the front of his chair come off the ground a little as the weight of the bag came crashing down onto the back of the chair. It startled him, which resulted in a wince of pain.

"I'm sorry sweetheart. It's the heaviest backpack I've ever tried to lift!" She was breathing heavily and sweating a little as she pushed off and began rolling Beau toward the elevator and the baggage claim area where she'd planned to meet Joe. They didn't have checked baggage, but the pickup outside baggage claim made the most sense.

"That's okay. Just wasn't expecting it," Beau said as he started to become more alert.

The elevator moved like molasses, or at least it seemed that way to Valerie. She was beyond ready to pass the baton. She needed a break and she needed to see Joe's face. They'd been apart too long, passing like ships in the night as they tag teamed from one child to the other. When they finally reached the bottom floor, the elevator doors slid open and Valerie pushed Beau's chair into the open space near the first baggage carousel. As soon as they crossed the threshold, they heard the sound of applause — booming applause.

Valerie looked up quickly and was surprised to see a large crowd congregated behind her sweet husband and Julia. People were holding signs, waving flags and cheering. Everyone was there — classmates and teammates from high school, Valerie's brother James, Pete, Nana and Pop, Mimi and Gramps, Mr. and Mrs. Zellway, Ivy, the Hinkleys, along with about thirty others from their church, even Beau's recruiter was in the crowd. Julia had tears streaming down her face as she dropped her sign and ran toward them. She fell to her knees beside Beau and began kissing his face, gently and repeatedly. He couldn't hold her in return, but the entire crowd could see the love in his eyes when he teared up as she held him.

Joe followed closely behind Julia, taking Val into his arms and hugging her tightly. He kissed her forehead as she wiped tears from her cheeks. "How?" Valerie motioned to the crowd and looked back at Joe again, "How did you pull this off. We had no idea!"

"It was Julia. She arranged the whole thing." Joe looked down at Julia who was smiling up at Val as she knelt at Beau's feet.

"You'd be amazed what you have time to do when you're stuck in bed all day!" she laughed. "I admit, I didn't expect this turnout though. I really didn't." She stood up and stayed next to Beau. As he sat staring into the crowd, a broad, shocked McKnight grin on his still-tattered face, she bent down and whispered into his ear, "They're all here for you, because you're a hero." Beau closed his eyes, blinking back the tears he didn't want to shed.

The crowd began to slowly shift from applause to laughing, crying and hugging. Valerie noticed cellphones out all across the room. There wasn't a dry eye to be seen. Ivy moved to the front of the crowd and knelt down beside Beau. She didn't say a word, but she kissed his cheek. Beau couldn't really move, but he could smile — and so he did. He smiled a lot. He was in shock to see so many people. He'd spent a long time feeling ashamed and believing that he was hated, so long, in fact, that a room full of people thanking him and cheering for him was almost too much to handle.

After everyone in the crowd had offered Beau a personal greeting, chatted with him, hugged him or thanked him, Joe began to slowly push him toward the sliding glass doors. Airport security had allowed Joe to keep the SUV parked in the loading zone without issue, an unusual phenomenon to be sure. As the crowd moved toward the doors to see them off, they noticed a long line of men lining the sidewalk on both sides, holding American flags. Instinctively, everyone began straining to get a glimpse of the flag bearers. As Joe rolled Beau out onto the sidewalk, the crowd began to fill in behind them to behold a sea of motorcycles lined up behind Joe's vehicle. In front of the SUV were two police officers, also on motorcycles, lights flashing. As it became clear the riders were there to honor Beau, several people in the crowd began to clap and soon everyone was cheering. Julia bent down and spoke into Beau's ear, "They're here for you!"

"Are you serious?" Beau called back as the rumble of engines began to emanate around them. His mouth hung open in shock as he maneuvered his mangled body to see as much of the crowd as he could. He raised his left hand and wiped his eyes with his fingers.

"Yep, they're called the Rolling Thunder. They're going to escort you to the hospital!" Julia was beaming with pride.

Valerie pressed her cheek against Joe's shoulder, her hand over her mouth and tears in her eyes. As she looked around, there were cellphones out all over. People were cheering and clapping. Even the passersby who had nothing to do with the homecoming surprise had stopped to join the moment. Beau couldn't believe his eyes. "But why?" he shouted, looking at Julia, and then up at his parents.

"Because you're a hero, son." Joe reached out with his hand and roughed his son's short hair. Beau shook his head. Joe began pushing him toward the passenger door of their SUV and one of the flag bearers, dressed in jeans and a leather vest, handed his flag to the man on his right and ran over to hold the door open. Joe, Val and Julia slowly helped Beau into the passenger seat, as he stood, the weight of his pack on the back of the chair caused it to tip over. Ivy ran up to lift it and Pete opened the hatch as James hoisted the heavy pack onto his shoulder to load it. Pete struggled with the wheelchair for just a moment, before it folded for loading. Valerie hugged as many people as she could, knowing she'd see most of her family at the hospital in a very short while. She was overwhelmed by the outpouring of love and support, and she suddenly felt an affection for Julia she hadn't experienced before. Knowing that Julia had planned this hero's welcome, to honor Beau's service and sacrifice, allowed Val to see her with new eyes.

Once Beau was safely inside the SUV, Joe rolled his window down. Julia ran up to kiss him goodbye. "I'm going to meet you there. I have to attend to all your adoring fans!" she laughed and kissed his cheek again.

Valerie climbed into the backseat. As Julia backed away from the window, the deep rumble of motorcycle engines began to grow louder as the entourage of riders prepared for their exit. Two of the flag bearers saluted as Joe pulled forward. Once Joe had passed them, they broke ranks and carried their flags toward their own bikes. Valerie turned to look out the back window, watching as the men mounted the flags to their motorcycles and waited their turn to join the procession. "This is seriously amazing!" She turned to look at Beau and Joe in the front seats, "Am I the only one who thinks this is totally amazing?"

"Definitely not," Joe answered. "None of us even knew about the motorcycle thing! Julia kept that a total secret! I'm trying to keep it manly here, but I kind of want to cry." Joe laughed at himself, glancing in the rearview mirror at his wife.

Valerie laughed along with him, and then smirked and said, "Well, I'm not gonna lie, I am strongly considering purchasing you a leather vest." She raised both her eyebrows simultaneously and whistled. Joe burst into laughter.

Beau, on the other hand, groaned, "Ew. Gross! Cut it out you two," causing Joe and Valerie to cackle. After that, they rode along in silence for a while. Each of them watching as cars stopped and people stared, kids waved, people clapped, and all along the route, not a single person turned away from the rumbling procession. Beau found himself speechless, overwhelmed by the idea that every single person in attendance was there just because of him. After a while, he turned and looked at his father. "I'm not a hero."

"What?" Joe asked.

"I'm not really a hero. I'm not. All these people, all this because I got hurt. The real heroes are the ones who are still there. My unit, my squad — the people who kept me alive, and mostly, the guys in my convoy who didn't get to come home, those are the heroes. I just don't feel like a hero. I'm kind of embarrassed by all of this, I didn't really earn it." Beau leaned back against his seat, shifting slightly so he could see out the window, his splinted arm awkwardly touching the door.

"You are a hero! And what you just said makes you all the more heroic." Valerie leaned forward and touched his shoulder. "Don't undervalue your service or what you've been through."

Joe reached over with his right hand and placed it on his son's left forearm, "I am so proud of you, son. And this is a very good day."

~

The procession couldn't follow into the hospital lot, so as Joe turned under the blue awning to obtain a parking ticket, the riders proceeded slowly behind them, moving down Moursund Street slowly and deliberately. The riders waved flags and saluted, some of their passengers held up posters and signs that said *thank you* and *you're a hero*. Valerie read them aloud as they passed. She was on her knees, hanging out the window, waving as the riders passed by. Joe pulled forward when the gate arm lifted. The long line of riders continued past them as spectators stopped and stared, and once again, Val was crying. Joe drove slowly toward the main entry of the hospital. "Drop off is up here. I'll take the car to the garage once we've unloaded." As they approached the main entrance, Joe fell silent. Valerie's breath caught in her chest. There, in his wheelchair, waiting with a nurse, sat Eli. He held a small flag in his right hand. He was dressed in sweatpants and a Texas State sweatshirt, his thin frame swallowed by his clothing. He was smiling broadly, his chin lifted slightly, waving the little flag every so often.

Eli's demeanor reflected his almost childlike joy. He had the same look as that of a little boy, excited to receive a gift. Beau's breathing deepened as he attempted to stifle his tears. Joe's eyes were brimming at the sight of Eli's smiling face. Valerie didn't hold back, and no one expected her to. Eli made a goofy face and waved his little flag again, and Beau began to laugh. He was laughing through his tears as Joe brought the vehicle to a stop, directly across from where Eli and his nurse were waiting. The nurse was beaming, clearly happy to be part of the reunion. By the time Joe got around to Beau's door, orderlies were already waiting. Eli watched as they moved Beau into a wheelchair and placed his bags onto a rolling cart.

One of the orderlies helped Valerie from the back seat and the other began to push Beau toward the sidewalk. He wheeled the chair over to the place where Eli was waiting and everyone watched in exuberant silence as they embraced, truly embraced, for the first time in years. Eli leaned his thin frame forward, carefully placing both his arms around his brother. Beau used his left arm to pull his twin close. He gripped Eli's sweatshirt in his hand and buried his battered face into his shoulder. He began to sob as the weight of his guilt and pain gave way to a new future. "I'm sorry," Beau choked out the words, as though he were dropping an unbearable burden at Eli's feet.

"It's okay," Eli's words were soft and reassuring. "It's okay," he repeated, slowly and carefully, as if to emphasize that Beau had been forgiven long before.

They separated, smiling. Even the orderlies were holding back tears as they began to wheel the brothers toward the sliding glass doors. Joe and Valerie walked behind them, wrapped up in each other's arms as the tears of joy flowed freely. They watched from behind as Eli turned to Beau and said, "I assumed you'd think you were a big deal now, what with the motorcycle army and all, so I brought you a little gift to remind you of your roots." He reached into his seat and pulled out a tube sock. As they wheeled along, side by side, Eli reached over and laid the tube sock across Beau's good shoulder. "I think you forgot this." Beau began to laugh as he used his good arm to give Eli a little shove. He left his hand on his brother's shoulder for a long beat as they rode along. They were together again, and despite the tough road ahead, they seemed new, refreshed. Their futures had been reborn.

HANGDOG II
Rebirth

PART TWO

CHAPTER FOURTEEN

Mark's shoulders slumped under the weight of his overstuffed backpack. When he left Zimbabwe, he shoved everything he could into one bag. Money was tight and the last thing he needed was an extra expense. The cheapest flight he could book meant multiple layovers, sleeping in airports, and five whole days of travel. Now that he was about to set foot on the ground in Texas, he prayed the time, expense and the literal weight on his shoulders would be worth his effort. It had been more than three months since he'd laid eyes on Ivy and their daily phone conversations had become a poor substitute. For the last week, he'd lied to her, telling her it was business as usual in Africa, when in reality, he had been hurtling toward her, one changeover at a time, hoping to surprise her.

He knew Ivy had been spending her days with Eli, as he worked to strengthen his body again, to help his mind catch up on two years' worth of missed information. He knew the medical community considered Eli a miracle and that, other than muscular atrophy, he suffered from no residual effects of his accident or his coma. But, he also knew Ivy, and she would never dream of hurting anyone — especially someone like Eli, who had been through so much already. So, in a way, he understood why she'd never breathed a word about his existence to anyone. He had to admit to himself that his surprise visit came not just from his love for Ivy and his desire to see her, but also from his longing to claim her for himself alone, from his unspoken jealousy and from some admittedly misguided, masculine desire to *win*. When confronted with his presence, Ivy would have to choose. In his heart, he already knew what her choice would be. So, when he stepped off the plane and onto the jetway in Texas, he shook off his feelings of anxiety about how she might react and what she might say, took a deep breath and began putting his plan into motion.

First, he would rent a car and drive to Longview. After that, he would find a hotel, take a much needed shower and, hopefully, if he could turn off his mind long enough to rest, sleep. The following morning, he would call Ivy and casually try to find out where she was, and then he would wait for the most opportune and least disruptive time to simply show up. He didn't want to surprise her while she was with Eli, and because she had confirmed the day before that she was going to spend a few days with her parents, the timing was right. He was ready, or at least that's what he kept telling himself.

~

Ivy sat across from her mother at the kitchen table, sipping some hot tea. As much as she missed her work in Africa, and her mission team, she really was happy to be home. Somehow, both places felt right. Mrs. Zellway could sense a change in her daughter, something that wasn't related to her growing maturity or her travels. Eileen Zellway had always been perceptive. She was insightful, and she could tell Ivy was preoccupied, but she couldn't put a finger on why. She'd always been good at reading people. She'd always been the family's chief advice giver and Ivy's sounding board for all things related to life. In her mind, there were no secrets between them, so the fact that Ivy seemed distant, and not her typical, joyful self, was dominating her thoughts. She had to know what was going on and since she knew Ivy would be home for a few days, home with no place to hide, she decided to ask straight up, "What's going on with you, little girl?"

"What do you mean?" Ivy asked.

"I mean, something's up. I can tell. And I want you to tell me what it is." Ivy's mother took a nonchalant sip of her tea, staring over the edge of her cup straight into her daughter's eyes. "Something is different about you, off. You're wrestling with something. I can see it. So, spill it."

Ivy could feel her heart pounding in her chest. Her cheeks grew flushed with heat. She thought she'd been doing so well hiding her secrets, but Mark had been written all over her face the entire time. She took a deep breath and opened her mouth. Her first intention was to deny, deny, deny, but somehow, she found herself powerless to utter another lie. Words from her heart began spilling out of her mouth. She'd wrestled with feelings of guilt and shame, and she'd lived under the weight of secrecy for months now, so when the dam finally broke, there was no holding it back.

When her mother saw her eyes filling with tears, she immediately put her cup down and slid her chair closer to Ivy's, placing her hand on her little girl's forearm, "Oh honey, honey, what is it?" Ivy instinctively reached out and took her mother's hand, like a toddler who needed to feel the comfort of her mommy's love.

"Oh Mom, I'm a horrible, awful person. I don't know what to do." Her tears flowed freely.

"What?" Eileen was shocked. "No, you absolutely are not a terrible person. You're the best person I know! Don't you dare think otherwise!" She released Ivy's hand and put both arms around her gently. She didn't squeeze her but, instead, chose to hold her like a baby. Ivy began to sob and didn't speak for a long time. Her dad walked to the threshold of the kitchen when he heard her tears and questioned his wife silently with his eyes. Ivy's mother, holding her close, shook her head and shrugged, telling her husband that she had no idea why their little girl seemed so broken. If Eli's coma hadn't broken her and Africa hadn't broken her, whatever this was had to be big — a thought that could quickly bring fear to a mother's heart.

Finally, Ivy began to speak, "I met someone. I met someone in Zimbabwe and I can't stop thinking about him, but I still care for Eli, so much, and I can't bring myself to tell him the truth. I love him, too. I think I love them both, in different ways. I thought I was meant to be with Eli forever, but then I met Mark — that's his name, Mark — and now I don't know what to do. I thought I would forget all about him when I got home, I even hoped I would, but I haven't." She wiped her cheeks as she pulled back from her mother's embrace. "I developed feelings for another guy, in another country, while my boyfriend was in a coma. Some Christian I am, huh?" she sniffed and let out a deep sigh.

Though she knew Ivy's hurt was genuine, her mother couldn't help feeling relieved. She breathed a silent prayer of thanks that her jolt of fear was caused by nothing more than what she considered to be boy drama. She could deal with boy drama, but she didn't want to inadvertently minimize Ivy's struggle or push her away by accident, so she tried her best to put herself into her daughter's shoes, "Oh honey, no. You can't think of it that way." Eileen brushed Ivy's hair off her forehead.

"How can I not? Eli seems so certain about me, about us. He's constantly telling me how excited he is to start our life together and how he wants to pick up where we left off, how he can see us together. It makes me feel like the worst person in the world, because I don't know if I want that future anymore. I mean, maybe I do, but I might want to be a missionary for a while longer, and what if he doesn't want that? But I can't bring myself to talk to him about it. He's got a white picket fence vision of the future and I just, I do love him, but I just... " Ivy looked down at the table in front of her.

"But you told me yourself that, to him, graduation just happened. In his mind, no time has passed at all. You're in a different place now, a different season. You grew without him and that is not your fault. You didn't choose the circumstances, but you chose to thrive in them, and that is a great thing. It's an amazing thing. Your father and I are so proud of you. I know you don't want to hurt Eli, but by keeping these feelings a secret, you're hurting yourself in the process." She took hold of her teacup again. "If you think there's even a chance he's not the one, then you need to come clean, for your own sake and for his. It's not fair to him to believe things are just fine when they aren't."

"But, he's still in rehab. He's not back on his feet. He's still struggling. How could I do that to him?" Ivy was practically holding her breath, thinking about what it might mean to tell Eli she had feelings for someone else, that she'd kissed someone else.

"If Eli is the one for you, he'll be willing to work through it. If he's not, then out of respect for him, for yourself, and yes, even for this… this Mark, you can't carry around this burden. You haven't done anything wrong, really. But if your heart is heavy because of this, well then young lady, you've made your bed." Ivy's mom raised her eyebrows at her daughter, "You will feel better after you've come clean. I think you know that, don't you?"

"I'm scared," Ivy said, flatly. She looked up at her mom and continued, "What if Eli is hurt enough to just walk away? What then? I don't know what I want, but I do know I don't want to lose him for good. I do love him. But do I *love* him?"

"Well, honey, he might, but I doubt it. I don't think he's the type. I don't think he has it in him to dismiss anyone, especially someone he cares about — especially you." Ivy's mom took another sip of her tea and pushed Ivy's cup closer to her. "Drink your tea."

"Mom, what you're saying is he could never hurt me, but here I am, thinking about breaking his heart, telling him I met another guy while he was in a coma — a coma, Mom! Tell me again, *how* am I not a horrible person?"

"Ivy, a horrible person would go on living in secret and continuing the lie. That's not you." She took a deep breath and gave her daughter a knowing look.

"It's eating me alive," Ivy responded.

"Exactly. I could tell the minute you walked through the front door that something was wrong. If I can tell and Dad can tell, you know Eli can probably tell, too."

"Well," Ivy took a breath, "he does a really good job of hiding it. He tells me how great I am almost every day, and it's like a punch to the gut every time."

"You have to talk to him. I promise, you'll feel better." Ivy's mother continued sipping her tea, sharing bits of wisdom like it was the easiest thing in the world. "It will be hard, too. I can promise you that. But in the end, it's the right thing. The truth will set you free, remember?"

"Ugh, Mom," Ivy threw her head back and looked up at the ceiling. "Do we have to bring the Bible into this?" She laughed at her own words, knowing her mother was right, but resisting all the same.

Eileen smiled and reached out to touch her daughter's cheek, "Everything will be okay, baby girl. I promise you, it's all going to turn out fine. You may get some bumps on the way, but you'll come through this better than you ever were before."

"Do you promise?"

"I promise," she smiled. "And look at it this way, you would never have been in Zimbabwe if Eli hadn't gotten hurt. And you would never have met Mark. What if God used something bad to bring you something good?"

"But if my something good means something bad for Eli, how could that be God?" Ivy's mind reeled.

"You don't know it will be something bad for Eli. If you aren't the one for him, then someone else is his *good*, right?"

"Why does that make me feel jealous? I don't like the idea of him with someone else, either." Ivy whiningly complained.

"Well, you can't have it both ways. What's good for the goose is good for the gander." Ivy's mom raised her eyebrows. Ivy knew she was right, but she didn't want to admit it. Her mind, her heart and her emotions were tangled in knots. Who would she choose? Who *should* she choose? Should she choose at all? She didn't know. But she did know her mother was right. She had to come clean with Eli, but how?

CHAPTER FIFTEEN

Beau rifled through his duffle bag, searching for his stashed bottle of pain pills. He hadn't even started his rehab session for the morning and he was already in pain. Eli watched him dig, noting the look of panic on Beau's face when the bottle proved harder to find than he expected.

"Didn't you just take the one the nurse gave you an hour ago?" Eli asked, as he reached down in an attempt to pull on his tennis shoes. "For the record, I'm pretty sure I have been sore every single day for months."

"Don't worry about it." Beau finally located the pill bottle stashed in the bottom of his duffel bag. "You seem to be making progress though. You're not quite the skinny little runt you were when I got here." He popped the pill into his mouth and reached for the bottle of water resting on his bedside table.

"Besides, we'll both be out of here soon, back at home. I've only got five more weeks until my medical eval and my range of motion is still garbage. Can you believe they scheduled it on Julia's due date? Literally, on the exact day. Everybody keeps telling me that the chances of her actually going into labor on that day are slim to none, but still." Beau took another sip of his water as Eli stood up on his own two feet.

Though Eli found himself fatigued more quickly than he'd like to admit, he was now walking unassisted and had gained enough muscle mass to forgo a nurse escort when he made trips to the bathroom, and he was even allowed to take himself all the way downstairs for his rehab appointments, by himself. For him, the luxury of a trip to the toilet without company felt as rewarding as a trip to the beach. "That scheduling glitch is easier for me to believe than the fact that you're actually going to be a father." Eli reached both arms into the air, allowing himself a short stretch. His arms were still thin, but he had begun to regain some muscle tone, along with some of his confidence. "The bigger Julia gets, the harder I pray for that kid," Eli laughed at his own words and reached out to give his brother's good shoulder a quick punch.

"Shut it, Eliza." Beau grabbed his water bottle and opened the door to their shared room. "After you, Princess," he said to Eli, gesturing toward the door. Together, the two of them headed to the elevator to make their way downstairs for one of their final inpatient rehabilitation appointments. As luck would have it, they were both scheduled for release to outpatient therapy within days of one another. They were both beyond ready. They wanted to go home. They wanted to get their lives back. They wanted to find that comfortable place called *normal*.

~

True to form, Beau and Eli sat at lunch, talking about dinner. Everyone in the family had returned to their own respective routines. Pete had gone back to work, James was back to running his company, their grandparents had gone back home, and for now, the only strangeness to the family routine was the three hour drive Joe and Valerie made every night for dinner. With the exception of one or two nights, Mr. and Mrs. McKnight had left home around four o'clock and battled the traffic to enjoy dinner with both their sons in Houston. After dinner, they would make the three hour drive back home. A few times a week, Julia joined them, even though travel was against her doctor's wishes. Ivy spent most of her days in Houston, milling about and visiting with Eli between therapy sessions. A few times, Beau had mentioned that Ivy seemed different. But, he was content to blame the changes in her disposition on the passage of time and the fact that she had spent a lot of time in a foreign country. He wasn't the same person he used to be either, so he kept his criticisms to himself.

"Do you think Ivy is going to go back to Africa?" Beau asked Eli as he popped a French fry into his mouth.

"I really don't know," Eli shrugged and took a sip of his drink. "For some reason, she won't talk about Africa with me. Every time I bring it up, she changes the subject. I've heard from everybody I know how much she loved it there, but when I ask her about it, she gets all weird. I honestly think she might be trying to convince herself that she would rather be here, even though she wants to go back, but I just don't know. She's definitely different than she used to be. She doesn't seem as, I dunno, joyful maybe? She doesn't laugh at my jokes as much. She doesn't smile as much. It's almost like she's worried about something, but she refuses to say what it is." He wiped his mouth with a napkin and pushed back in his chair. "To be honest, it makes me feel like I'm walking on eggshells all the time, like I know her, but I don't know her at the same time. It's eating me up, but I haven't said anything because, well, because, I'm almost afraid to find out what it is. And, really, what right do I have to complain about anything? I was in a coma for two years and she still showed up. Plus, I'm alive.

Apparently, I'm a walking, talking medical miracle, so complaining about anything makes me feel like trash, like I'm ungrateful for my life. It feels like a disservice to God somehow. Does that make sense? Anyway, she's going to be home with her parents all week this week. I don't think they want to pay for her short-term lease anymore," he laughed. "When they agreed to it, I think they expected a few weeks, not a few months."

"She really only goes there to sleep, anyway," Beau's mouth was full as he spoke.

"I guess it's a good thing we are out of here soon. Because if they don't pay for it, she can't afford to be here. She's basically tapped out."

"Dude, you still have a savings account. I'm just saying."

"Mom and Dad would kill me if I had tried to take money out of my savings to pay for my girlfriend's studio apartment that she doesn't even actually need." Eli put his elbows on the table.

"They probably would, but I mean, if you're absolutely sure she's the one, like, *the* one, and she's being weird, you might need to let her know somehow, maybe. You know, let her know that you're still serious. You are sure, right? I mean, there's lots of fish in the sea, as they say, and it ain't like you've done much fishin', if you catch my drift." Beau took a sip of his drink and winked at his brother.

"C'mon, man. You know that's not me. When I said I loved her, I meant it. I do love her, but, it's just that, well, sometimes, I don't know if she's still the her I fell in love with. I mean, it feels like I fell in love with one girl, took a nap, and she became somebody else while I slept. It's weird. She's still just so amazing and she's still the same person, but, somehow she's not. But, at the same time, I couldn't imagine my life without her." Eli responded to Beau's question with real, heartfelt truth. He was showing a vulnerability he hadn't allowed himself to reveal since waking up. Beau was taken aback.

"Look, given my track record, you're probably better off doing the opposite of what I say, but I say, if you love her and you want it to work, you need to tell *her* all this stuff." Beau pressed his lips together. "Maybe she's feeling the same way about you. Maybe she's scared something else will happen. Maybe she's worried you'll be upset about Africa. Wait, *would* you be upset if she went back to Africa?"

Eli became thoughtful. "I don't think so. I'd pine for her until she came home, but the truth is, I think I might like to go for a while myself. I've missed out on a lot. African missions might be just what I need to kick start my life again."

"Okay, I've had enough of this ooey gooey *feelings* talk." Beau changed the subject abruptly, taking Eli off guard. "Why don't you go get us some dessert, Eliza," Beau threw a wadded up napkin across the table with his left hand, striking his brother in the chin.

"Oh, I saw that. You should be doing that with your right hand. I know you're a delicate flower and all, but stop favoring it."

"Shut up and go get that dessert." Beau took another sip of his drink and watched his brother stand. Eli walked away from the small table they shared in the cafeteria and made his way back to the buffet line. As soon as he was out of view, Beau reached into his pocket and pulled out another pain pill. He popped it into his mouth and swallowed it down with a sip of his water. He knew it wasn't time, but as he reached up to his right shoulder with his left hand and felt his scars, he didn't care — he needed it. He leaned his head far left stretching his neck, feeling the rigidity of the scar tissue that had taken up permanent residence in his shoulder. He reached his right arm up into the air and tried in vain to make a full circle. It was stiff and uncooperative. His therapist had been manually manipulating his shoulder for weeks to try and loosen the scar tissue, but he still felt weak. His grip strength was, in his mind, pathetic. For now, he knew he wasn't fit for duty. But, he didn't want anyone else to know that.

As Eli made his way around the corner, balancing what appeared to be four tiny dessert plates in his hands, Beau found himself battling a strange and sudden fear. What if? What if he was discharged from the Marines? The Marine Corps was the one thing he'd been good at since he graduated high school. He lost football. He dang near lost his mind. The Marine Corps had given him an identity. Now, the Marine Corps would be his way to provide for a family. If they took that away, what would he do? He had nothing else. The Marine Corps had helped him to reestablish himself as a person who had something to offer. His squad and his unit valued him. In a world where his failures, his mistakes, had been splattered about on local news and social media, the Marine Corps had given him a renewed sense of purpose. The Marine Corps had given him a chance to redeem himself. He'd only been a Marine for about a year, but it was in his blood. He wanted to finish his enlistment, at least. He needed to, for himself and for his son.

When Eli reached the table, he awkwardly placed all four dessert plates on the table. "I didn't know what to get, so I got everything," he smiled broadly as he handed his brother a fork.

Beau forced himself back into the present, "I like the way you think." He grabbed the plate holding what appeared to be coconut cream pie and peeled the cellophane back. He cut the piece in half and looked up at Eli, "We'll split each one down the middle, fifty-fifty." He scarfed down a bite of the pie, leaving some of the whipped cream on the corners of his mouth. "I go to the pool next, what do you do?"

"Resistance training. They're making me use those rubber bands. It makes me feel like Mom." Eli didn't look up from his plate.

Beau smiled, whipped cream still intact. "Mom's in pretty good shape, too. You're well on your way to a girlish figure," he laughed, and then laughed some more.

"Wipe your mouth, you Neanderthal." Eli stared at him from across the table, maintaining a straight face as his words echoed his dry sense of humor. Beau smiled a wide grin and lifted his eyebrows repeatedly in his brother's direction. Eli just shook his head, returning to his pie.

~

Joe and Valerie walked into the boys' room to find Eli's physical therapist, Dr. Brendell, preparing to leave. Eli was grinning from ear to ear as the doctor greeted his parents. And as soon as the door closed behind him, Eli burst open with excitement, "I get to go home! He said I've progressed enough to go home and continue treatment with outpatient physical therapy. I'm going home! I get to go home! It's great news, right?"

"Eli! That's fantastic news!" Valerie exclaimed. She ran over to hug him.

"Wow! That's awesome, son! When did they say you'd be released?" Joe questioned.

"At the end of the week!" Eli answered.

Beau grumbled, "Guess who gets to stay!" He feigned an excited tone. "Apparently, neurotherapy is," he cleared his throat and mimicked his doctor's tone, "a bit more complicated."

Eli stood and walked over to his brother, placed his hand on his left shoulder and said, "I win." He burst into laughter. Since they were old enough to understand competition, they'd been able to make a contest out of anything, from who could eat the most pizza to hotel elevator racing. Apparently, even their treatment had evolved into a competition.

"Give me a break," Beau replied.

"This is so exciting! We've already moved the hospital bed out of your room. Joe, I think it's time for a trip back to the attic!" Valerie began chattering on about the possibility of some new decor and updating Eli's room for his debut back into normal life. She loved all things home, and any excuse to upgrade their home decor gave her a charge.

"You know, he did say I would probably get to be home before the baby comes," Beau interrupted as the thought popped into his mind. He stood and made his way across the room toward the bathroom door as he spoke.

"That's excellent!" Joe returned. "We're definitely getting pretty close to baby time."

Beau opened the door to the bathroom and stepped inside, he turned on the water for the sink and reached into his pocket. He pulled out a bottle of pain pills and popped one into his mouth before putting the lid back on the bottle and returning it to his pocket. He rinsed his hands, turned off the water, shook the water from his hands into the sink and then patted them against his jeans to finish the drying process. He walked back out into the room and asked, "We gonna eat?"

"Let's!" Valerie said. "We are going to celebrate!"

"Where's Julia tonight?" Eli asked.

"The doc said she needed to take it easy," Beau returned. "The farther along she gets, the more bedrest they have her taking. I guess to avoid any chance of premature labor."

"Anything to take care of my nephew," Eli smiled as he spoke.

"She was planning on a frozen waffle and instant grits for dinner. Pregnant ladies eat the weirdest stuff," Beau added. Joe and Valerie laughed, but Eli didn't.

"I don't think that's weird. Waffles with grits sounds amazing!" Eli looked around the room, as if everyone else was crazy. His parents laughed at him. His brother simply shook his head.

"I caught her drinking pickle juice the other day, straight from the jar!" Valerie chuckled.

Beau shook his head, "That is so weird."

"I hope the pickles were hers," Eli said. "Otherwise, remind me not to eat any pickles when I get home." He made a heh-heh sound, feigning a taunt, and pushed his father's shoulder slightly.

"Oh yeah," Joe said. "She's been going through a jar every couple weeks."

"Dang!" Eli said. "That's a lot of pickles. No wonder her blood pressure was up a little bit." Beau laughed, but Valerie appeared thoughtful.

"Oh, wow. That's actually a good point," she paused for a moment with a thoughtful look on her fact, but then, she suddenly stood and grabbed her purse, signaling to the entire family that it was time for dinner. "Okay that's it, I'm starving."

"Alright then, let's eat." Joe stood up and took a step toward Eli. He'd been helping Eli up for months, the act had become a habit.

This time, when he reached out a hand to Eli, Eli responded, "Nope, I've got this, Dad!" Eli held both hands straight up into the air, positioned his feet squarely on the floor in front of him and stood to his own two feet. "See? No hands!"

"Nicely done, son! This is a very good day!" Joe said, turning to his wife with a smile.

"A good day indeed," Valerie responded, as she took Eli's face in her hands, planting a big kiss on his cheek.

CHAPTER SIXTEEN

Ivy walked out onto her parents' front porch, wearing her favorite comfy sweats and an oversized T-shirt. She had her hair pulled up on top of her head in a messy bun and wore only chapstick on her otherwise freshly washed face. It was the first time she'd been alone in over a week. With her mom out running errands and her dad spending the day at the office, she decided it was the perfect time for a little self-indulgent relaxation. She settled down on the porch swing, slid her feet out of her slippers and pulled them up under her body. As she sat staring out at the sky, she rolled a bottle of clear nail polish dismissively between the palms of her hands. She bent one knee and pulled her foot up close to her body. Just as she was about to open the bottle of polish, she saw movement out of the corner of her eye. As she raised her head, she saw a strange car turning into the driveway.

She set the bottle down on the arm of the swing and watched silently as the unfamiliar car slowly approached the house, moving down the driveway between the trees tentatively but also seemingly with a purpose. If the turn had been a mistake, the driver would have figured it out by now and turned back, but, instead, the car kept coming. Ivy squinted, trying to see the driver behind the wheel. But the car was still too far away and the reflection of the sunlight on the windshield made visibility impossible. She stood up and made her way to the edge of the porch. As the car got closer, she noticed that it had an out-of-state tag. "New Jersey?" She asked herself who they knew from New Jersey. Nobody.

She stepped down onto the first step of the porch as the car pulled closer to the house. She still couldn't tell who was driving. She placed her right hand on the banister and watched. She didn't feel alarmed, though she probably should have. After all, she was alone and now there was a stranger in the driveway, all the while she stood there barefoot, with no phone and no way to contact help if she needed it. The driver put the car into park and she watched as the door opened. Ivy gasped as she watched Mark step into the sunlight. She blinked hard. Was he a mirage? He had to be. Mark slowly took off his sunglasses and just looked at her for a moment, and then he smiled. Ivy covered her mouth with both hands. She was unable to move and unable to speak. She felt her eyes brimming over with tears, but she didn't know why. Mark walked around the front of the car and Ivy felt herself running down the remaining stairs. It was as if she moved automatically, for reasons beyond her own control. Still, no words would come. Before she could even think, she was in his arms. He wrapped her in a tight hug as he pulled her off the ground. "Surprise," he said, as he held her close. He absorbed the fact that she seemed happy to see him, and he felt an immense sense of relief.

Ivy finally found the ability to form words. "What are you doing here?" she squealed with excitement. Mark lowered her back to the ground and she squeezed him again.

"I'm here for you. I couldn't take it anymore. I had to see you." Mark's smile was near perfection and Ivy couldn't help but smile back at him.

"I… I don't know what to say." She stood in surprised silence for a second before she gathered herself enough to speak. "Come on." She made her way back toward the porch, holding Mark's hand as he trailed behind her. "Can I get you anything? Oh, goodness, I'm such a mess right now."

"Well, a trip to the bathroom would be phenomenal," he laughed, "and you look beautiful! You're the prettiest thing I've ever seen. I mean it." Ivy smiled. She opened the front door, and Mark grabbed it and held it for her to walk through first.

"The bathroom is the second door on your right down that hall. If you get to the kitchen, you've gone too far." Ivy pointed down the front hallway. She still couldn't believe Mark was here, in America, let alone in her house.

The light poured in through the window above the kitchen sink, filling the hallway and dancing off the hardwood floor. "Your house is amazing," Mark said, as he made his way down the hall.

"Thanks! I had literally nothing to do with it. My mom has really good taste." She chuckled at her own words as she darted into the living room to check her face in the mirror over the fireplace. She pulled her hair out of the bun she wore and tossed her head around to loosen it. As she fluffed it with her fingers, she leaned into the mirror, scoffing at her own face. "Ugh," she thought. She pinched her cheeks lightly with her fingers and wiped beneath her eyes for good measure. As she inspected her reflection, the realization of what was happening settled in her spirit. She closed her eyes tightly and prayed silently, "God, help me. What am I doing?"

Thoughts of Eli filled her mind and the burden of guilt weighed heavily on her heart. She stared at her own reflection. It was time to admit the truth, but how? She heard Mark's footsteps approaching and she stepped away from the fireplace, turning toward the doorway. "Come sit," she said.

Mark made his way toward the sofa, but he stopped where Ivy stood. He put his arms around her and leaned in to kiss her. For a brief moment, she thought about stopping him, but she didn't. Before she knew what was happening, she was kissing him back. After, the two walked hand in hand to the nearby sofa and sat down. "I've missed you, so much. More than I thought I would," Mark said softly.

"I've missed you, too," Ivy said, being truthful. "How is everyone? How is the irrigation system working? How are the kids?"

"Everyone is doing great. The system had some kinks, but mostly, it's been phenomenal. Everyone is really excited for harvest season. The kids miss you. Everyone misses you. It's not the same without you." Mark leaned his back against the cushion and tried to look relaxed, but his heart was pounding inside his chest. "I'm going back in two weeks. I'll stay a week here, then I'm going to see my family and, Ivy, I... I want you to come with me." He leaned forward and squeezed her hand. "I want you to come meet my family. I want you to come back to Zimbabwe with me. You said yourself you were called to missions and that you fell in love with it. And... and, I want my chance. I want a chance. I want you to pick me. Choose me. We can finish out the year in Africa and then, who knows? All I know is I believe God put us together and that I *had* to come here. And if you say 'no,' I'll spend the rest of my life wondering why, but I won't ever regret trying. I can't share you anymore, though. I won't!"

Ivy stared at him. She took in his words like a sponge. She was silent for a long time, or at least it felt like a long time. "Okay," she said finally.

"What? Really?" Mark looked confused. He couldn't believe what he was hearing. He'd expected a more wordy response. He'd expected, he really didn't know what he expected, but he definitely didn't expect that it would be this easy.

"Okay," Ivy smiled. Not even she had expected the decision to be so fluid, so right, so fast, but she could no longer deny how she felt about Mark. She *did* care for him. She *did* want to be with him. She *did* miss Africa. She *did* love missions. But, she *didn't* want to hurt Eli. How would she explain it? How would she find the strength to break his heart?

Mark pulled her close and hugged her tightly. She hugged him back. Though she couldn't bear the idea of hurting Eli, she couldn't deny that being with Mark felt right. If she didn't follow her heart, she'd always wonder if she'd missed out on what God wanted her to do. The idea that she might spend the rest of her life with Eli out of obligation, out of fear, made her stomach hurt. He deserved better.

"So, this is it then? We're a thing? A couple? You're my girlfriend as of this moment, right?" Mark looked at her intently.

Ivy laughed, "Yes!"

"Okay, I just wanted to clarify. Months of being 'the other guy' takes a toll on a man." He smiled broadly and kissed her forehead.

Ivy took a deep breath. "I still have to tell Eli." Tears puddled in her eyes. "It won't be easy."

Mark did his best to repress the burning sensation of jealousy in his gut. He had no reason to feel animosity toward Eli. By all accounts, Eli sounded like a great guy — someone he'd probably like under different circumstances. His only fault was that he'd found Ivy first. Mark didn't want to dislike him. He genuinely felt bad for Eli, but not bad enough to let Ivy go. "He still has no idea I exist, huh?"

Ivy shook her head, ashamed. "I couldn't. He's been through so much, and he really is an amazing guy, a wonderful guy. He'd never hurt me in a million years, so I feel bad enough for letting myself fall for you, much less for breaking up with him and causing him more pain."

"I'll go with you, if you want."

"No. I need to go alone. This needs to be between me and him."

"When?" Mark asked.

"I guess tomorrow. The longer I wait, the harder it will get." Ivy was bluntly honest. There was no sense in mincing words now. Mark knew exactly where she stood.

"Well, then go now," Mark smiled and raised an eyebrow. "I don't want you to have time to change your mind."

Ivy laughed and touched his face. "I'll go tomorrow. Tonight, I'll introduce you to my parents. My mom already knows about you. Maybe we can even go on a real date?"

Mark threw his head back and gestured toward the ceiling, letting out a sigh as he spoke, "From your lips to God's ears."

Ivy chuckled, "I need to go change. We really shouldn't be here alone. My parents would flip out."

"I understand," Mark replied. "How about I head to my hotel and get some lunch. Then I'll come back here. You just say when."

"That sounds perfect." Ivy had butterflies in her stomach. She'd almost forgotten how cute Mark was.

Mark stood up and Ivy followed suit. "You have no idea how happy I am right now. I'm going to sweep you off your feet, you'll see." Mark brushed the hair back from Ivy's face and leaned in to kiss her. She put her hand on his chest and stopped him.

"I realize this is a step back, but, technically, we haven't even been on that first date yet. So, I'm going to make you earn that kiss." Mark had kissed her twice already — really, truly, fairytale-style kisses — and they hadn't even been a couple. She now felt the need to slow things down. She *wanted* to kiss him, so much. But, she needed to feel "in control" even more. Instead of trying to explain, she narrowed her eyes and then winked at him playfully.

Mark raised both eyebrows, "Oh, so that's how it's going to be then?"

Ivy nodded, "Mmm-hmm." She smiled at him with closed lips.

"And I thought it wasn't possible to like you more than I already do, but here I am." Mark shook his head slightly.

Ivy hugged him tightly. "Now, go. I'll see you in a few hours, okay?"

"Can I at least get a kiss on the cheek? I mean, I did fly all the way from Africa for this moment. Please!" Mark leaned in toward her, exposing his right cheek. He drew out the word "please" like a small child begging for candy.

Ivy grabbed his face and pressed her lips against his cheek. As she pulled away, they were both smiling. "I'll see you in a little while. Now, get out of here."

"I don't want to go!" Mark exclaimed.

"You have to go," Ivy responded, as she playfully pushed him toward the door.

"Fine, fine," Mark said. "But let the record show that you're kicking me out against my will. I would just as soon wait on the porch."

"Duly noted. Now scoot."

Ivy ushered Mark onto the porch, and he headed down the stairs toward his rental car. Ivy watched as he unlocked the door. Before he got in, he called up to her, "You've made me very, very happy, Ivy Zellway."

Ivy smiled. As she watched Mark turn around in the driveway to head out, she bit her bottom lip and her smile faded. Tomorrow would be the hardest day of her life to date.

CHAPTER SEVENTEEN

Beau sat quietly, once again rereading the letter he'd received from Andy three days ago. In it, Andy had described some of the lighter details of life in Afghanistan. Beau knew their tour would be over soon and he'd missed most of it. He couldn't forgive himself for not being there. He felt as though he'd abandoned them when they needed him most. Of course, none of *them* blamed him, but he blamed himself. His squad had been without internet access and had resorted to letters to keep in contact with friends and family. At best, the letters would take two weeks to arrive, and probably wouldn't arrive until after internet access had been restored, but none of them cared. Andy Mack had a knack for writing letters. He wrote exactly as he spoke. Beau could almost hear his voice as he read the words Andy had written.

After neatly folding Andy's letter and sliding it back into the envelope, Beau reached for the card Andy had included with his letter. He'd read the card at least ten times in the last three days. The words were simple, but Beau couldn't get them out of his head:

I am praying for your complete healing and peace so that you may continue to move bravely through this life for many years to come, fulfilling God's purpose for you each step of the way. Semper Fi, Marine.

~ HN. Juan Gabriel

Combat medics often see dozens of wounded men and women every day, depending on where they serve. And Beau knew that Juan Gabriel had seen lots of wounded men that day. Did he write cards to every unit, for every person he helped? That seemed not only unlikely, but almost impossible. Something about the card stuck with Beau. Somehow the corpsman had managed to speak volumes through a single sentence. Beau rolled the words over and over in his mind. Continue to move bravely, fulfilling God's purpose, Semper Fi.

Beau didn't feel brave, especially not now. Instead, he felt useless. He tossed and turned at night, fighting battles in his mind. What peace? He certainly didn't think he was fulfilling anyone's purpose, let alone God's. He read the card again before closing it and sliding it back into the envelope with Andy's letter. He sat for a few minutes wallowing in self-pity at his lack of accomplishment, looking around the room and taking in the image of Eli's book lying open on the bed. Eli would be gone in a few days, having beat severe muscular atrophy and a two-year coma, meanwhile, Beau couldn't even make a full circle with his arm. He felt like a failure. He felt sorry for himself. Everyone had been calling him a hero since he'd arrived back in the States, but he didn't *feel* like a hero. He reached into his pocket and pulled out his bottle of pain pills, popped one into his mouth and swallowed.

~

Julia was more excited for her baby shower than she had been for any event she could remember. Her mom was coming — Valerie had made sure of it. Her friends were coming and even some of Val's friends. Valerie had decorated the great room and kitchen beautifully. Everything was blue with soft gray accents, and incredibly elegant. The cake was a three-tier masterpiece, donated for the event by one of Valerie's friends from church. Julia marveled at how beautiful everything looked and how sophisticated she felt. She'd grown to love Joe and Valerie like a second set of parents. Valerie knew that Julia's father had been distant since learning about the baby, so she made certain Joe was present in Julia's life — even when he didn't feel like it. "Where do you want this ice, Val?" Joe called into the kitchen as he came through the front door carrying two heavy bags.

"Oh, thank you! One goes in the freezer and one will go into that big ice bucket." She gestured to the gleaming silver ice bucket on the kitchen island.

"Are there any other men coming to this thing?" Joe gave Val a pained look.

Valerie laughed, "Both the Hinkleys are coming!"

"Thank the Lord," Joe said.

"You will love the baby bottle chugging contest!" Valerie practically sung the words.

"What?" Joe asked, shocked. Valerie cackled with laughter as Joe added, "That's just lovely. It's a good thing you're cute, woman."

"It's going to be so fun, and Julia is so excited. Let's make this special for her, okay? Especially since Beau can't be here with her."

Joe took a deep breath and let it out slowly. "You're right. Give me her corsage. I'll go pin it on for her."

"That's my Joe." Valerie reached into the refrigerator and handed Joe a lovely corsage of three white rosebuds and gray and blue ribbon, and there was a small, sterling silver baby elephant pendant in the middle. Julia had decided on baby elephants to decorate the nursery and Val couldn't resist the simple pendant — Julia's first token of motherhood.

~

Ivy led Mark into the den and cleared her throat before she announced his presence to her parents. "Mom, Dad, this is Mark Sandoval." Eileen stood up immediately. Don followed, having taken his wife's cue.

"Hello Mark, I'm Eileen, and this is my husband, Don." She reached out her hand and took Mark's. She'd been anticipating this moment all afternoon. She was almost as nervous as Ivy.

Don shook Mark's hand firmly. "Nice to meet you, son." He wasn't sure how to feel. He'd grown to care for Eli, so this experience wasn't exactly welcomed. But, he wanted nothing but the best for his daughter, and this was her choice.

"Thank you, sir. It's very nice to meet you both." Mark's heart was pounding in his chest. "You have a really nice home." He didn't know what to say, and that line seemed safe.

"Thank you! We love it here." Eileen was beaming. Ivy almost giggled at her mother's reaction.

"We're going to go for dinner and then we'll see a movie," Ivy said, as she turned to make her way toward the door.

"Okay, sounds good," Eileen answered.

"Do you have your key?" Don asked.

"Yes, sir. I do. Love you!" Ivy sang.

"I want a hug," Eileen said. As Ivy leaned in to embrace her, she whispered in her ear, "He's so cute!"

Ivy tried to stifle her smile. "Mom," she said flatly, drawing out the word like an embarrassed teenager.

"Well, he is." She smiled and squeezed her little girl's body like only a mother can. Ivy shook her head.

"I won't be too late."

"Okay, be safe. Keep your phone on you," Eileen added.

"Yes, ma'am."

When Ivy joined Mark on the front porch, she couldn't help but laugh. He looked at her through nervous eyes. "I'm glad that's over."

"Oh, come on. It wasn't so bad. It was like, sixty seconds of your life." Ivy bumped his shoulder with her own.

"I know, but, you know, I'm 'the other guy,' and what if they don't like me?" Mark looked at her with an expression of genuine concern.

An involuntary smile curled Ivy's lips, "Trust me. They like you just fine."

"Even your dad?" Mark questioned, raising one eyebrow in Ivy's direction.

"Well, yeah. He might take longer to warm up, but trust me, if he hadn't liked you, I'd already know." She took his hand and squeezed it. "And my mom, well, she's totally transparent, and she thinks you're cute."

"Really? Does she now? And how do you know this?"

"She literally just told me!" Ivy laughed with abandon and grabbed his bicep with her left hand, leaning into him.

"So, do they know about tomorrow?" Mark asked. His entire life seemed to hang in the balance. Would Ivy go through with it? Could she sit with Eli face-to-face and end their relationship? At this point, he knew she wanted to be with him, but he also had doubts about her ability to follow through with the breakup. He knew she didn't want to hurt Eli.

"Yes, they know. I told them all about it this afternoon."

"And?" Mark asked.

"Well, my mom had already told me to come clean, so she's happy. Dad didn't have much to say, except that he loves me and supports my choice. He's always liked Eli."

"See? I told you. Your dad is going to hate me," Mark retorted, as he opened the door for Ivy to get into his rental car.

"No, he won't!" she responded. "He needs to get to know you, that's all."

"Well, how does he feel about you coming to meet my family in a week?" He closed the door and ran around the front of the car to the driver's side. As he got in, he looked at her intently.

"Well, I haven't mentioned that yet. Baby steps, right?" Ivy batted her eyes in his direction, her body language pleading for his understanding.

Mark smiled, "So, to be safe, let's make sure I'm nowhere around for that conversation."

"Deal." Ivy reached for his hand.

"And maybe we should just double that for the day you tell them you're going back to Africa for a few more months, too." He wasn't kidding, but he laughed to mask his concern.

"I'm more worried about asking for their financial help to get there." Ivy rubbed her temple with her right hand.

"You know what, let's just forget about all this stuff for tonight. It'll work out. God's got this. Tonight, let's just worry about having fun, okay?"

"Yes! I'm totally on board with that idea. And, I'm starving," Ivy said. She allowed herself to put all her worries on hold, trusting that everything would, in fact, work out just as it should.

"I'm hungry, too. I was too nervous to eat anything all afternoon, and now that I've met your father and lived to tell the tale, I could really go for some steak," Mark joked, glancing at Ivy as they left her driveway and pulled out onto the main road.

The entire day had been surreal. Everything had happened so quickly. He'd practiced his speech all the way from Zimbabwe, even planning how he would answer her objections, but she didn't have objections. In fact, she seemed just as ready as he was. It had all gone exactly as he'd prayed for, so far. He'd been asking God to bring him the right girl for three years, and when he met Ivy, they'd shared an instant connection. But then she told him about Eli, and his certainty was met with an equal amount of resistance. Still, he believed he was exactly where God wanted him to be. If Ivy was still his tomorrow, he'd be happier than he'd ever been. But, he had to admit, it still felt like a very big *if*.

CHAPTER EIGHTEEN

Eli stared at his phone, silently willing Ivy to call him back, to text him back, something. He'd been trying to reach her since yesterday morning and it was unlike her to go so long without responding. He had begun to worry about her. He had an uneasy feeling in the pit of his stomach, but he didn't know why. He sat in the chair by his bed, holding his phone with both hands. He closed and opened his text window several times, and though it accomplished nothing, it gave him the feeling he was doing something and that seemed better than doing nothing at all.

Beau was stretched out on his bed, asleep. He seemed to sleep a lot lately. Eli couldn't put a finger on it, but he definitely seemed off, weird almost. He knew his brother was sick of the rehab hospital, sick of doctors, sick of his injury and, truth be told, at this point, they were both stir crazy. Despite being overwhelmed with gratitude that his brother was awake, well and happy, Beau was bitter that Eli would go home in a few days, and Eli knew it. Beau had barely left Eli's side for the first four weeks at the hospital. Eli knew he'd felt immense guilt, and being Beau, he'd chosen to make it up to him through the art of pestering. Eli hated to leave him behind at the hospital, but he was also beyond excited to go home. He couldn't wait to ease back into his life, to enroll in some college classes, to jump start life with Ivy, to begin living the future they'd been planning. Despite his reluctance to leave his brother, he knew it would only be a few more weeks and Beau would be home too, and then, life would really be back on track. So, he rationalized his feeling of excitement at going home by including Beau and chose to keep his eye on the prize — an amazing future.

Eli closed his eyes and imagined what it would be like to see Ivy every day again. If he hadn't suffered the coma, he'd probably have proposed by now. He knew she wanted a long engagement. He imagined what it would be like to marry her, then to one day have kids of his own. He couldn't help but smile as he thought about becoming Uncle Eli, but it was still hard to imagine Beau as a father. He silently decided that Ivy's strange demeanor since returning from Africa was a product of her own desire to start the life they'd been planning. He reckoned she'd grown impatient. After all, she'd been waiting far longer than he had. That had to be it.

~

Ivy sat in the hospital parking lot, motionless behind the wheel of her car. Her stomach ached. Her heart pounded in her chest. She heard her phone buzz again on the passenger seat. Eli had called her four times since yesterday morning and texted her five times. She'd imagined the buzzing was him again, but this time it wasn't. She opened the message from Mark. It consisted of only four words <IT WILL BE OKAY>. She swallowed hard and put the phone in the console. She placed her purse behind the back seat and turned off the ignition. She pulled down the visor and stared at her own face. She'd cried off and on for the last three hours and the sight of her reflection in the mirror spoke a thousand words. She took a deep breath and grabbed her keys. Once she was outside the car, her legs stopped working. She focused on breathing in and out, willing her body to cooperate with her mind.

When she finally managed to take a few strides toward the hospital doors, her mind began to reel. "What are you doing? This is Eli! The Eli you planned to be with forever.

You're a terrible, awful person." She stopped in her tracks and almost turned back. Fear gripped her, but not the fear of ending things with Eli — instead, it was the fear of *not* going through with it. What would it mean for her life if she committed to Eli because she felt guilty? What would it mean for their relationship if every day she thought about another man? "Lord, if You want me to stay with Eli, I'm really going to need You to let me know. I don't want to mess this up." She stood in place for a moment, waiting. Waiting for what, she didn't quite know. A sign? A voice from the Heavens? As she stood there, thoughts of Mark swirled in her brain. She'd never planned to fall for him, but it had happened. In her spirit, she knew what she had to do. Eli deserved to be with someone who was fully devoted to him. He deserved something she couldn't give. Yes, she loved him still, but now her love for him was different. It had changed. She began walking toward the doors again, determined to break the news to him, face-to-face. Not just for her sake alone, but for his too. Because even if she didn't go through with it, she'd still never be able to give him her full heart. He may not notice right away, but, eventually, he'd figure it out — and then where would they be? She wanted to be with Mark. She didn't want to hurt Eli, but she reasoned that her desire to be with Mark was greater than her desire to avoid breaking Eli's heart. She knew in her heart that God had placed

Mark in her path for a reason and she let that be the guiding force driving her to go through with it. "If God put Mark in my path, that must mean He has a better plan for Eli, too," she murmured to herself as she went through the door.

~

Mark paced back and forth in his hotel room. He looked at his phone — nothing. He looked at the clock. "She's there, right now. It's happening right now," he thought. He turned on the TV and tried to focus his attention on something other than Ivy and Eli. What if she couldn't go through with it? What if she'd changed her mind? He found himself staring blankly at the TV screen as a talk show droned on, but he had no idea what was said or why, because his mind was fully preoccupied with thoughts of Ivy. "Oh, God, please let this work out. Please give her the desire and the courage to go through with it. And give her the right words to say." In the same breath, Mark thought about what Eli must be feeling. He felt his stomach churn. He was jealous of Eli, but why? He couldn't seem to keep himself from feeling just a little bit of disdain for Eli, despite having never met him. Eli had never done him wrong and, by all accounts, he sounded like a good guy, but something in him caused him to carry a mild sense of dislike. Perhaps it was territorial? Ivy was his, and now, Eli was the other guy. He glanced at his phone again. "Two minutes? That's all it's been?" He tossed it onto the bed. The last two minutes had felt like two hours and the suspense of the situation was literally driving him mad. He grabbed his room key and wallet and decided to head down to the hotel restaurant, purposely leaving his phone on the bed in the hopes he could stop obsessing. He knew it wouldn't work, but he decided to try it anyway.

~

Eli checked all his social media accounts. Had Ivy posted recently? No. Where could she be? Was she okay? He decided to call again. He knew it hadn't been long since he'd last tried, but he didn't care. He dialed her number and lifted the phone to his ear, as it began to ring, he heard the door open. He looked up quickly. His nurse noticed that he was on the phone so she whispered, "Everything okay in here?" Eli nodded a yes, listening to ring after unanswered ring on the other end of the line. When Ivy's voicemail picked up, he opted out of leaving a message and chose to hang up. What good would another message do? He could sense his nurse waiting in the doorway, so he placed his phone on the chair arm beside him and looked up again — but it wasn't the nurse.

"Ivy!" Eli stood up quickly. "I didn't think you were coming back until the weekend!" Beau grumbled and sat up in his bed. He reached for the water on his bedside table and dismissively threw a hand up in Ivy's direction as he reached for the remote control. "Thank God!" Eli put his arms around Ivy. "I was beginning to worry about you."

Ivy felt sick. "I'm sorry," she said. She hugged him back, but just to appease him. Eli stepped back, smiling.

When he looked at Ivy's face, his smile faded. There was no mistaking her expression. Something was wrong. "Oh, no. What's happened?"

Ivy looked down at her shoes and then back at Eli, she cleared her throat and glanced over at Beau, who was holding the remote and flipping channels. "I need to talk to you," she said, "in private." She glanced at Beau again. This time, he was looking back at her. There was palpable tension in the air.

"Um, sure," Eli responded. "Just let me get some shoes on." He sat on the chair and reached for his sneakers. The room was deathly silent. Beau watched Ivy watching Eli. This was bad. This was very bad.

As they walked out the door into the hallway, Eli held out his hand for Ivy to take. She hesitated. He noticed. But she took his hand anyway and he interlaced his fingers with hers, allowing the feeling of her hand in his to ease his nerves. "Want to go to the courtyard?"

Ivy nodded. She tried to focus on her breathing. She watched Eli's profile as they walked. He was so handsome, so tall, and she could tell he was getting stronger by the day. She blinked back tears. They rode the elevator in silence. Eli put his arm around her, and she had to admit, it felt easy, comfortable. She breathed in the scent of his cologne and absorbed the warmth of his body next to hers. She leaned into him. He would never feel the same way about her after this. He would never see her the same way. She was about to shatter his image of her, and she knew it. She wanted to savor these last moments. He had been *her* Eli for so long, and knowing that in just a few short moments, he would no longer be hers felt somehow heartbreaking. They walked out into the courtyard through sliding double doors and Ivy made a bee-line for the nearest bench. She needed to sit down. Her legs felt heavy. Eli followed and sat next to her, scooting close and turning his body to see her clearly.

He took a deep breath, "Okay, what's going on? Is everything okay? Are you okay?" He reached for her hand and held it gently in his.

"I… Well… First, you need to know that I care about you, so much. This is going to be really, really hard for me."

The tears that she'd been fighting now flowed freely down her cheeks. "I want you to hear my heart — I missed you so much, and the last thing I ever want to do is to hurt you."

Eli's heart began pounding inside his chest. "What is it, Ivy?" He breathed in and out through his nose. His usually jovial expression was flat and stoic.

Ivy closed her eyes. She had come this far, there was no turning back now. "I... I met someone. There's someone else." She looked down as Eli pulled his hand away. It was a crushing moment. She felt it to her core.

"What?" Eli blinked hard and shook his head in disbelief. "Who? When? Who?" He felt like he was suffocating. They were outside, but it felt like there was no air to breathe. His mind couldn't process her words and he sat staring at her, in shock. As Ivy started to speak again, she watched his face change, as his shock made room for his heartache. She had to look away when his eyes filled with tears. She couldn't bear to look at him. Once again, she stared at her feet.

"He's a missionary. His name is Mark Sandoval. We met in Africa."

Eli cut her off. "Since Africa?" he asked, shock filling his voice. "All this time, Ivy?" He pressed his tear filled eyes with the fingers of his right hand and soaked in her words. "How could you?" His expression was one of not only pain, but anger. Ivy had never seen it before. "How could you let me believe... " he paused. "Does this guy even know about me?" His nostrils flared slightly and his face was red. His eyes were wet, but his jaw was set in stone. He felt betrayed. He felt like a fool.

"It wasn't like that!" She was sobbing now, too. "He knows about you, but..." The pain in his voice tore her to shreds. "We weren't... we didn't..." she took a deep breath. She felt the need to justify herself, but she knew there was no justification to be found. She had no justification. She had feelings for another guy and she'd kept them a secret for months. "He showed up yesterday morning and asked me to be his. It isn't what I planned."

"I trusted you. I believed you, every word. I... who are you?" He pushed away from her. Ivy tried to grab his hand, but he made a fist and pulled it back.

"It wouldn't be fair to either of us to build a life together now, not like this. Not if my heart isn't in it. You deserve better. You deserve so much better." Eli could hear the truthfulness of her words as they poured out of her in broken sobs.

"There is no one better," Eli spoke softly, blinking against his tears. He stared at her intently and felt awash with indescribable grief. His stomach knotted as he took in the curves of her face. He'd thought he knew her. He'd thought she was his future. "I thought you were going to tell me you wanted to go back to Africa to finish out your mission or something. I… I didn't see this coming." His voice grew louder, "I didn't see you with another guy! I can't…" He checked himself, bringing his voice back to his usual tone. "I can't believe you've been lying to me all this time. I feel like an idiot."

"Eli… I'm sorry. I'm so sorry. You have to believe that I didn't want this. I didn't. It wasn't supposed to be this way." She couldn't help herself. She leaned forward and wrapped her arms around him, tears flowing like glass over her skin. She wanted desperately to comfort him, to take the pain away. And yet, she *had* to follow through. She was watching his heart break before her eyes and it was even harder and more painful than she could have imagined. "I'm sorry."

Eli stiffened for a moment. He debated pushing her away, and then he slowly lifted his arms and wrapped her up in them. He pressed his lips against the top of her head, taking in the smell of her hair. He could almost physically feel the shards of his heart piercing his insides. He put his lips close to her ear as he held her close, "But I love you." Ivy could hear the breath catching in his chest. "Please don't leave me." His voice was quiet and calm. But there was no desperation in his tone, instead, his words were filled with anguish — he spoke as though she had died, like he was mourning a death.

The finality of the moment took Ivy's breath away. She pulled back and slowly rose to her feet. She had to. The reality of his pain was enough to make her stay, but she knew she couldn't. She shouldn't. Except for his tears, Eli's face was as perfect as it had ever been. "I'm so sorry," she whispered.

Eli stood to face her. "So, this is it, then?" he paused. Ivy wiped her tears again, staring at him. He could see it in her eyes — she was already gone. He hugged her again, allowing himself to accept the inevitable. "How will I not call you in the morning? How will I not text you goodnight every night?" He tried to smile again, for her benefit, but it was forced and pained. He hated to see her cry — no matter the reason. "What will I do without you?"

Ivy sniffed hard in the midst of her tears. She had no answer. She knew Eli would find someone else, too, eventually, but she couldn't bring herself to say so. Despite the fact that it was her choice to end their relationship, she also found it difficult to imagine him with someone else. The very idea made her strangely jealous, but she wanted it and expected it for him at the same time. She put her hand on his chest. "I should go."

"Can… Could I kiss you goodbye? Would that be okay, maybe?" He didn't know why, but he needed to feel her lips against his one last time. Ivy nodded. Eli stepped back. Ivy watched as he tried to blink away tears. He reached up with his hand and took her chin in his fingers gently. He bent towards her and kissed her softly. His touch was tender and the kiss was sweet. He lingered there for a few moments, his eyes closed, his lips against hers. He didn't want to pull away, because pulling away would make it real. When he pulled away, she would leave, and he'd be left to face the night, alone.

When they finally parted, Ivy looked up at him and wiped away the single tear on his cheek with her fingers. "I have to go." Eli nodded reluctantly. She reached out and squeezed his hand and turned toward the sliding doors. He held her fingers, allowing them to slide one by one from his grasp.

He watched her as she walked away, her long hair blowing slightly in the breeze. "Hey, Ivy," he called to her before she reached the doors, "if you ever change your mind…" He couldn't finish his sentence, the words were caught in his throat. But she knew what he was trying to say. She looked down to mask her own pain and nodded.

As she disappeared from sight, Eli turned back to the empty courtyard. He stood breathing in and out, unsure of what to do next. He walked slowly back to the bench and sank onto it. He leaned forward and buried his face in his hands. He wanted to pray, but he couldn't, so instead, he gave in to his emotions, he gave in to his despair. As the dusk gave way to darkness, Eli cried — mourning his broken heart, mourning the loss of his first love and mourning the loss of a future that could never be.

CHAPTER NINETEEN

Joe was relaxing on the couch with his feet propped up on Valerie's favorite tufted ottoman, flipping through channels, when his phone rang. Valerie and Julia were decorating Julia's bedroom to include a nursery. Joe could hear the girls giggling and talking about colors and discussing the placement of a crib and changing table. No one was sure how long she and Beau would be in the McKnight home, but they didn't care. Both Joe and Val had allowed themselves to become attached to Julia and they were already so in love with their grandson that the thought of him living under their roof felt like the biggest blessing in the world.

Julia knew that they had not approved of her choice to engage in a physical relationship with Beau outside of wedlock. She knew that her presence and an unplanned pregnancy was outside the scope of what Joe and Val wanted for their son, so she was amazed at their ability to welcome her into their home and into their hearts. She was grateful for their understanding, and though they had made it very clear that they had expectations and house rules and that they did not approve of the choices she and Beau had made, they had also made it clear that she was safe, loved, and welcome.

Joe jumped when his phone rang. The sound of his own ring tone startled him. Nobody called his cell phone when he was at home. "Hello?"

There was a pause on the other end of the line before Joe heard a familiar voice, "Mr. McKnight? Um. This is Antonne."

"Antonne! It's good to hear your voice, son!" Joe had kept in touch with Antonne via email since arriving home from Germany. At least once a week, sometimes more, he would send the young man a short message from his work email, reminding him to call if he needed anything and expressing care and concern for his well-being. "What's new?"

"Well," Antonne began, "remember in my last email when I told you that the medical board was deciding on my fitness to serve?"

"I remember," Joe answered.

"Well, sir, they decided. I'm out. Well, I'm not out yet but I'm going to be, and it won't be long."

"Oh, no — I'm sorry to hear that, son." Joe had been praying for Antonne's well-being, but he had to admit he hadn't given much thought to the medical board process. In fact, he hadn't been concerned about it at all. It hadn't even dawned on him that things might not go Antonne's way.

"It's okay. I kind of expected it, really. The only problem is, I don't know what to do now... I was... I was kind of hoping maybe you could give me some ideas." Antonne didn't come out and ask, but Joe could sense he needed their help.

"Do you have a place to stay when you get out? Someplace to go?"

"I have a little money saved, and I'll get some kind of disability severance thing. I think I can apply for VA disability too, but my Aunt Sylvia is willing to let me sleep on their couch. She ain't really my aunt, she's a lady who used to work in the cafeteria at my school. She'd sneak me food to take home at night. Anyway, I called her to see if she had a room I could maybe rent. But, her daughter has moved back in with her baby so she said I could have a couch. At least until I decide what to do." Antonne did not want to sleep on Sylvia's sofa. Joe could hear it in his voice.

"Well, how about a visit to Texas? We've got the room, and you could stay here as long as you needed to. I know some people, I'm sure you could find work here." Joe thought about it for a second and realized he'd invited Antonne to move into their home without so much as mentioning it to Valerie. "I'll have to clear it with Ms. Valerie, but I don't think it'll be a problem."

Antonne was elated. He hadn't wanted to ask, and he was glad he didn't have to. The McKnight family was the kind of family he'd always wanted. "Really?" Joe could hear the excitement in his voice. "Would it really be okay?"

"Let me talk it over with Val, and I'll call you back, okay?"

"Yeah. I mean, yes, sir. Thank you," Antonne answered.

"Okay, bye. I'll call you back." Joe hung up his phone and immediately stood up to head into the spare bedroom. He needed to break the news to Val — he'd just donated their basement to Antonne. What they had expected to be an empty nest was rapidly becoming a flock.

~

Beau was sitting up in his bed, texting with Julia when Eli finally came through the door. He knew immediately something was going on with him and Ivy. "Trouble in paradise?" he asked with a laugh. Eli moved quickly toward his bed, snatching his framed picture of Ivy from off his bedside table. He turned and hurled it, with all the force he could muster, against the wall above Beau's head. Beau ducked instinctively. "What the... What was that for?" he shouted.

"Just shut up, okay?" Eli shouted back.

"For real, what's going on?" Beau asked, with genuine concern this time.

"I don't want to talk about it." Eli collapsed face first onto his bed.

Beau texted Julia, <ELI AND IVY MUST BE FIGHTING. HE JUST THREW HER PICTURE AT ME AND SMASHED IT AGAINST THE WALL.>

<UH OH, WHAT HAPPENED?> Julia responded.

<HE WON'T TELL ME.>

<THAT DOESN'T SOUND GOOD.>

<I'LL FIND OUT.>

<TEXT ME WHEN YOU KNOW – XOXO> Julia put down her phone and walked into the kitchen. Joe and Val were still sitting at the kitchen island, discussing Antonne. "Beau just told me Ivy and Eli are fighting. Apparently, it was bad enough that Eli threw her picture and smashed it."

Val's mouth fell open, "What?"

"That doesn't sound like Eli," Joe added, a look of concern on his face.

"Should I call him?" Val looked back at Joe.

"I don't think that's a good idea, Val," Joe answered. "It will probably blow over."

"I doubt he knows that I know anyway." Julia made a pained face. "I probably shouldn't have told you. I was just surprised is all."

"I wonder what happened. I don't think those two have ever had a fight." Val began to speculate. "I wonder if she told him she wanted to go back to finish her mission?"

"Who knows? But it doesn't help us to sit here taking shots in the dark." Joe raised his eyebrows at Val, in a way that reined her in, preventing her from creating her own imaginary scenario.

"Beau said he'd text me when he finds out." Julia walked over to the fridge and opened the door, she stood there for a moment, staring at its contents. She reached inside and pulled out a stick of string cheese and her jar of pickles. Joe and Valerie glanced at each other. Val giggled under her breath, pulling her shoulders up toward her ears. When Julia turned around again, she saw them both watching her. "What?"

Both Val and Joe burst into laughter. "Nothing," Val answered. "Nothing at all." Julia smiled and then laughed out loud. She knew she was huge, pregnancy overwhelmed her thin frame, and she couldn't seem to stop snacking. "Shut up," she said teasingly, as she laughed with them. They continued to talk, laughing and joking about Julia's appetite, oblivious to Eli's pain and Ivy's betrayal.

~

Beau slid off the edge of his bed and walked across the room. He sat down on his brother's bed, not sure what to do. When he realized that Eli seemed to be crying, he reached out and laid his hand on his brother's shoulder. "What?" Eli asked gruffly, his voice muffled by his pillow.

"What happened?" Beau asked gently.

"I said I don't want to talk about it." Eli lifted his face and spoke flatly.

"I don't care that you don't want to talk about it, I'm asking anyway. Tell me," Beau responded, vehemently.

"She broke up with me, okay? Are you happy now? There's another guy. Now leave me alone." Eli was short. His emotions were raw.

"What?" Beau's voice went shrill, unbelieving. "Who? When?" Beau sounded legitimately angry. Eli resigned himself to the conversation and rolled over onto his back. He let his head fall backward forcefully onto his pillow.

"Some guy named Mark. He's a missionary. He apparently showed up here the other day and it forced her to come clean." He put his hand over his eyes, trying to hide his hurt from Beau.

"Ivy was cheating on you this whole time?" Beau's voice emanated disbelief.

"Apparently," Eli said and took a deep breath. "Well, I guess."

"What a b…" Beau started to shout, but Eli cut him off.

"Don't."

"Well, it's true! Who does that? I mean, it's really messed up." Beau could feel his face getting hot. "Who is this jackwagon anyway? He's here, right now? Let's bolt and go find him. They'll never know we're gone. We should go kick his a…"

"Stop it. It wouldn't help anyway." Eli cut him off again.

"Maybe not, but we'd both feel better." Beau stood up. "I can't believe her. I can't believe she would do that — of all people, Ivy Zellway. That little two-timing tramp!"

"You are not helping," Eli raised his voice. "Don't talk about her like that."

"Dude, I can't believe you're *not* talking about her like that!" Beau paced the floor. "I want to see this guy. Did he know about you two? Oh, if he did... that makes him the biggest jerk ever. I want to drive my fist through his weasely little face."

"He knew. But she tried to tell me it wasn't like that. She tried to say they weren't *them* until he got here the other day. Now I know why she was acting so weird lately." He rolled to his side and pushed himself up onto his elbow. "I thought she wanted to go back to Africa and was afraid to tell me. I'm such an idiot." He looked at Beau. "I really believed she was, you know, the one."

"You're not an idiot. She played you for a fool." Beau's forehead was creased with concern.

"I don't think so. I mean, she did, but I don't think that was her plan. She said she didn't want it to happen, and I saw her face. I believe her. Then she said it wouldn't be fair to either of us to stay together if she had feelings for someone else..."

Beau cut him off, "Blah, blah, blah. That's just something cheaters say to make it seem like they're doing you a favor while they're stabbing you in your back. Trust me. I know."

Eli didn't know how to respond. He knew Ivy. He couldn't believe she would hurt him on purpose. But then again, he didn't think she'd fall for another guy behind his back either. He didn't know what to think, or how to feel. His mind was jumbled up and messy, for maybe the first time in his life. "Do you think…" he paused. He didn't want to sound foolish. "Do you think Ivy and I might wind up like you and Julia? You know, later?"

Beau stopped and sat down in the chair by Eli's bed. He pressed his lips together and shook his head. "I dunno." He blew his breath out through an o-shaped mouth. "I mean, I was what, thirteen when that happened? That's a lot different. You're about to be an actual grownup. It's not the same thing, I don't think." Eli just nodded silently. He seemed so broken, Beau's heart hurt for his brother — the look on his face was more than Beau could bear. "But, who knows. Anything is possible, right? Maybe you *will* get back together." He stood up again and ruffled Eli's hair, trying to look hopeful, before walking back to his bed.

He knew he should say something else. Something in him pushed the words out of his body. "I have a buddy. His name is Andy. We all call him Mack, or Big Mack, on account of the fact that his last name is Mack. He's this country, slow talkin' guy in my squad. He was my bunk mate and basically harassed me into being his friend. Drove me insane for the first few weeks I knew him…" Beau could tell Eli was eager for him to get to the point, but he was afraid. He was afraid to admit that Andy had something he didn't. He was afraid to admit it to Eli, but moreover, he was afraid to admit it to himself. Andy had a peace, a power, a... a something different. He was afraid to let Eli know that he'd been thinking about his faith at all, let alone that he'd begun to consider it as a possible truth. But knowing that Andy's prayer probably took place at the exact time of Eli's recovery, he had no choice — it couldn't possibly be coincidence. He almost stopped himself from saying another word, but Eli needed something to hang on to. "Anyway, he's literally the best Christian I've ever seen. Different from everyone I know. I mean, he defies the B.S. and calls it what it is. He knows the Bible like he knows his own face. It's almost weird. No, it *is* weird. In fact, on the day I got hurt, he prayed..." he stopped himself. Not now. Did he want Eli to know about Andy's prayer? He wasn't sure, but either way, it seemed like the wrong time. "Well, anyway, he once said that what Satan means for your harm, God can use for your good. He said God doesn't do things to hurt us, but when bad things happen, He can use 'em." He moved toward his bed and sat down.

Eli thought about Beau's words for a few moments, but he wasn't ready to be hopeful. He was angry. For the first time in his life, he felt like God had abandoned him. "I'm going to go walk around for a while."

"Do you want me to come?" Beau asked.

"No, I want to be alone," Eli answered. Beau nodded his understanding. Eli slowly opened the door to their room and walked out into the hallway as Beau grabbed his phone. He'd missed a text from Julia.

<WELL?>

<IT'S BAD. SHE DUMPED HIM. SHE'S BEEN SNEAKING AROUND WITH SOME A-HOLE SHE MET IN AFRICA.>

<WHAT? NO!!!! HOW IS HE?> Beau could read the heartfelt concern in Julia's words.

<NOT GOOD.>

<POOR ELI. OH MY GOSH. WHAT SHOULD WE DO?>

<WHAT CAN WE DO?> Beau set his phone down on the bed beside him. He didn't know what to do for his brother. He was angry. He hurt. He rolled toward his bedside table and opened his pills, swallowing two in a single, dry gulp. He closed his eyes and waited for his pain to melt away. Hard things all seemed easier when he was numb.

CHAPTER TWENTY

Valerie was so excited she couldn't sit still. She had been anticipating the day Eli would come home since the day he started rehab. He hadn't said a word to them about his breakup with Ivy, but it had only been two days. She assumed he would open up about it in his own time. But, she had made it a point to remove reminders of Ivy from the house. She had also mandated a "circle of silence" where Ivy was concerned. Both Joe and Julia had been sworn to silence concerning all things Ivy, until Eli was ready to open up on his own. Despite her concern for his emotional state, it did little to dampen her excitement about his homecoming. She'd spent the morning preparing his room, cleaning house and cooking as many of his favorite foods as she could feasibly pass off as *reasonable*. As afternoon approached, she grew increasingly impatient for Joe's return so they could make their dinner trip to Houston — only this day, when they drove home, they would have Eli with them.

Despite her eager anticipation, Valerie knew that leaving the hospital would be bittersweet. She found it difficult to imagine leaving Beau behind. She tried to tell herself that it would only be a few more weeks and he'd be coming home too, but the idea of leaving him alone in Houston still brought tears to her eyes. She was torn between pure joy and sadness.

As she sat thinking about Beau, she remembered that Joe planned to tell him about their plan for Antonne to move into the basement. Beau had an affection for the basement. In fact, both boys did. With its own kitchenette, lounge area, TV, game area, bedroom and bathroom, it had been the perfect place for both Beau and Eli to host their friends, hang out and have fun. Joe and Valerie loved the basement too, Joe in particular. He readily admitted that finishing the basement was one of the best household projects they'd ever completed — despite the expense. Why? Because no matter how many boys their sons had entertained, no matter how loud the music or the TV, Joe never had to yell at them to keep it down. Valerie loved the basement because, as the boys grew, the mess stayed downstairs. She could close the door to the stairs and feel as though the house was in relative order. She had "ventured into the abyss," as she called it, once a month since Joe deemed it ready for use. And up until the accident, it had been a total mess every single time.

Valerie giggled to herself at the thought of telling Beau that he would have to share his living space with Antonne Young again, at least until he returned to duty. She knew Antonne got on Beau's nerves, but she also knew that Beau had a big heart — despite every effort he made to convince people otherwise. She knew he would secretly be happy that his family was able to help Antonne, especially after having learned about Antonne's absentee family during their time together in Germany. Valerie walked to the island in the kitchen, grabbed an orange from the fruit bowl and then sat down to begin peeling.

Her mind began to move from Antonne to Beau's impending medical review. In a few short weeks, his case would go before a medical evaluation board and they would decide whether or not he was well enough to return to service. Beau was so anxious to get back to work that he hadn't allowed himself to consider the possibility he might not be ready. Valerie knew he wasn't ready. Despite the great strides he'd already made, he still had a dramatically limited range of motion in his right arm and shoulder. He still had pain with certain movements and the doctors had already told him he had developed quite a lot of scar tissue and had some thickening and inflammation in his shoulder capsule. Beau had found it difficult to accept that, despite his surgeries, rehab and painful manual therapy, he may need yet another surgery to improve the scar tissue. Though this surgery would be arthroscopic and much less invasive, it was still another surgery and Beau wanted no part of it. Instead, he was trying to convince his doctors that he was ready to go back to work.

About the time her mind turned to the subject of her grandson, she heard the front door open. She heard the telltale sounds of Joe's keys hitting the console table in the front entry and then she heard her husband's voice, "Val?" She could hear him moving through the great room.

"I'm in the kitchen!" Valerie called back.

"I'm going to change real quick, then grab a snack and we can go. Julia is going with us tonight, right?" Joe had already begun to unbutton his shirt and remove his belt.

"Yes, that's the plan. She's upstairs getting ready." Valerie stood up from her chair, wrapping her arms around her husband. She kissed his cheek. "Welcome home! I don't think I've ever been more excited to get to the hospital!"

Joe smiled. "I don't know about that. I'm thinking you were probably more excited to get to the hospital when you were in labor." He laughed to himself and then added, "Eli is coming home today!"

"You're awful!" Valerie said, chuckling. "You're right, but you're awful." She jumped up and down a few times and then looked at Joe and said, "Eeeek!"

"The house looks great by the way," Joe said as he headed toward the stairs. "And it smells like you've been cooking all day."

"I have been! And cleaning and rearranging furniture and hanging pictures and trying to make Eli's bedroom perfect..." Joe cut her off.

"Okay, okay. Stop trying to one up me! I had a busy day too you know." He laughed as he called out over his shoulder "I'll be ready in ten minutes."

Valerie began to buzz around the house, preparing to leave. Julia moved slowly down the stairs toward the front room, toting a small handbag and a very large belly. Valerie ran into the kitchen to grab her own purse and noticed a string hanging from the bottom of her sweater. She grabbed the string between her thumb and index finger and walked to the junk drawer to retrieve a pair of scissors. When she opened the drawer, her eyes were drawn to a newspaper article that had been clipped from the paper over two years ago. She had several copies of the article, given to her by a number of

different people. Because she had several, when her friend from
church handed her yet another copy, she slid it into the drawer
and didn't think any more about it. The article depicted a
picture of Beau and Eli and a police photo of Eli's mangled
truck. As her eyes rested on the image of the truck, she began to
cry. Looking at it, somehow seeing it through fresh eyes, it
became all the more apparent how blessed they were that Eli
was alive at all, let alone well enough to live a completely
normal life.

At the same time, it dawned on her that Beau, too, had
been involved in the same crash. The fact that he had managed
to walk away with minor cuts and bruises was miraculous in
and of itself. For over two years now, she had failed to see the
magnitude of the miracle of Beau's life because she was so
focused on Eli. It was as though the Holy Spirit was speaking
directly to her heart, as she recognized that Beau's life had been
spared not just once, but twice. He'd experienced a miracle at
the time of the crash and another miracle during the battle in
Afghanistan. Something in her spirit felt reassured. Beau had a
purpose beyond himself, and he didn't even know it yet.

By the time Valerie had said a silent prayer of thanks,
wiped her eyes and composed herself, Joe was downstairs. As
she turned the corner and walked back into the living room, she
saw her sweet husband helping the very pregnant Julia up off

the deep sofa. Julia was laughing at her struggle to get up and Joe began to laugh along with her. Valerie smiled. "Do you need me to push from behind?" she called out before laughing herself. As they headed out the door, for what promised to be a joyous and, at the same time, difficult evening, Valerie turned and looked around the room behind her. Her family had been under attack for what felt like an eternity. Bringing Eli home today would be a victory too massive for words to describe.

~

Beau sat staring at his laptop. His unit's deployment was finally over and they were on a layover while waiting to fly back to the United States. Andy didn't say where they were exactly, but Beau assumed it might be Uzbekistan — the same place they'd stopped on the way over. He'd been chatting with Andy for more than an hour. Somehow, even over thousands of miles, he found himself unable to keep things from Andy. Andy Mack had heard all about the issues he was having with his shoulder, his frustration over remaining alone in the hospital, Julia's rapidly growing belly, Ivy's new boyfriend and Eli's broken heart. Beau could feel fatigue and soreness in his right forearm. He cursed under his breath at the fact that even typing seemed to be physically taxing. He reached for his pain pills and shook two into his mouth, swallowing both. He then reached for his Styrofoam cup and took one quick sip of water.

Eli sat in the chair by his bed, changing the channels on the TV, but without really watching anything. In his peripheral vision, he saw his brother pop more pills. It didn't feel like it had been that long since his last dose. He registered the thought and then turned his thoughts back inside himself. Another few minutes passed and the door to their room swung open. Valerie walked through the door first, carrying her bag and Julia's. Joe held the door for Julia as she waddled in toward Beau's bed. Valerie watched Beau light up when he laid eyes on her.

Eli watched as Julia held her belly and bent toward Beau to kiss him. He felt a pang of resentment well up inside himself and he had to look away — he closed his eyes and tried to tell himself that he had no reason to resent Beau and no reason to begrudge him for his relationship with Julia. Without warning, his mind began to turn on him. He wondered how Beau, who had never even tried to walk the straight and narrow, who had made choices he himself would never make, could somehow be in love with a baby on the way, while he stewed in rejection. As his mind started down a dark path, something in his spirit shouted back, reminding him that he was still blessed beyond measure, reminding him that he was a miracle, and that Beau's life was far from charmed. He physically shook his head, as if he were trying to shake the dark thoughts from his mind, and prayed a quick, silent prayer of thanks.

Eli had been discharged for hours, his belongings were packed up and waiting to be carried out. He'd even cut the hospital bracelet from his arm while he waited on his *ride*. "Should we eat now and load up later, or load up now and eat later?" Joe asked, looking around the room.

"Oh my gosh, let's eat now," Julia didn't hesitate. Beau began to laugh immediately, pulling her toward his bed so he could kiss her stomach. It was still awkward for Valerie to see such affection between them, knowing how physical their relationship had become, but somehow, it warmed her heart at the same time. Joe and Val joined Beau in his laugher. Still, no matter how hard they tried to "act casual," Eli's breakup was the silent elephant in the room — everyone felt it, even Eli, who continued flipping channels in vain. It didn't matter though, he preferred the awkwardness to the discussion. He didn't even want to think about it. Heartbreak had robbed him of his excitement about going home. It had robbed him of his appetite, his sleep, his drive and his motivation, and to make matters worse, he saw her face in every commercial and television show he watched.

When dinner was done and the time came for them to leave, leaving Beau there alone, Valerie couldn't stop crying.

Julia had cried every time they left the hospital, but feeding off Val's emotions made this night even worse. Beau wanted to go with them, but he put a smile on his face for their benefit. As Valerie and Julia sobbed their way through hugs and kisses, he reminded them he *had*, in fact, been alone before. "I was in Afghanistan, remember? I think I can handle it." Joe ran down to pull their vehicle close to the hospital doors. Valerie grabbed Eli's suitcase, leaving him to carry his massive duffle bag. He took one more pass around the room to make sure he hadn't forgotten anything. Beau reminded him that he'd still be there and that anything left behind would be confiscated.

Beau decided to walk with his family down to the hospital lobby. As they stood there in front of the sliding glass doors, he contemplated running away — just for a single brief moment. Finally, once all the bags were loaded, he hugged his crying mother tightly. He kissed his crying and very pregnant girlfriend, quietly telling her that she looked beautiful, which only succeeded in making her cry harder. He hugged his father — three times. Lastly, he turned to Eli. He wrapped both arms around him, as best he could under the circumstances, and squeezed. Eli closed his eyes, burying his face in his brother's good shoulder. They stood there, longer than they might have any other time. Beau leaned in to Eli's ear and whispered, "Everything will be okay." Joe, Valerie and Julia climbed into the SUV. Eli trailed along behind them, but before he got in, Beau stopped in his tracks. "Wait, I almost forgot!" He reached into the pocket of his sweats and pulled out a balled up pair of socks — the socks he'd worn to conditioning and rehab that very day. He snapped them into the air, causing them to unroll and wave in the breeze like a foul-smelling flag. He reached out and tucked them under the collar of Eli's shirt, all the while wearing a broad, pride-displaying grin. Eli dryly looked at the socks hanging down the front of his shirt, then looked back at his brother, cocking a sarcastic eyebrow. "Later Eliza," Beau said, smiling. And then, just like that, Eli McKnight went home.

CHAPTER TWENTY-ONE

Three weeks from the day that Eli had left the TIRR Memorial Hermann Rehab Hospital, Beau sat upright in his bed, waiting for his orthopedist and physical therapist to come and talk to him. His new roommate was an elderly man who hadn't spoken two words since they wheeled him in. Beau didn't mind, in fact, he preferred that the old man stayed quiet. He was already dreading living under the same roof as the motor-mouthed Antonne Young, so as for now, he would take all the silence he could get.

He reached for the large bottle of pain pills he'd received before leaving Germany and felt a sense of panic when he heard the sound of a weak rattle. There were only three pills remaining in the bottle, and Beau wanted to take all of them. He felt his heartrate increase and decided to take only one. He then rolled the bottle around in his fingers to inspect the label. No refills. How would he get more? He'd already taken flak from Eli, so he knew he couldn't tell his doctor that he'd taken not only the two doses his nurse delivered every day, but also the entire bottle of pills he'd received just before leaving the hospital in Germany. And he certainly didn't plan to tell *anyone* that he'd secretly used a few of his new roommate's fentanyl patches, especially since his roommate hadn't been in on the plan.

When he heard the door to his room opening, he quickly slid the almost-empty bottle of pills under the covers on his bed. Dr. Daniels, his orthopedist, came in. He walked to Beau's bed and extended his hand. Beau shook it, albeit more weakly than he'd like. "Mr. McKnight, how are we feeling today?" Dr. Daniels was young, fit and looked like he just walked off the set of a medical drama on TV. Beau liked him. He seemed to be a no-nonsense kind of guy.

"Like we're ready to run away from here." Beau had made no secret of his desire to be out of the hospital. The date of his medical evaluation board was fast approaching, and he thought being discharged from the hospital would improve his chances of being found fit for duty. He knew he still had to undergo outpatient physical therapy, but simple physical therapy wouldn't stop him from being a Marine — not as long as he could still perform his duties. The only problem was, Beau knew he couldn't perform his duties. In fact, lately, he felt like he might be getting worse instead of better, and he didn't know if he'd be able to fake it well enough to get by until he really *did* feel strong again. Combat logistics required lots of heavy lifting, and Beau knew it. He also knew he was responsible for manning a mounted weapon during equipment convoys. Falling down on the job was not an option. His only solace came from the fact that he was still a Marine. He was still drawing a paycheck and still receiving the benefits. As long as he was still a Marine, he could deal with being useless. But, if the MEB found him unfit for duty, he didn't know what he'd do.

Dr. Daniels chuckled, but then looked at Beau with a serious expression and sighed, "Well, I'll be honest with you. I don't think your condition is going to improve dramatically without another surgery. You see, scar tissue develops over time, during healing. Your shoulder took such a severe blow and required so much surgical intervention that, as you've been healing, your body is creating an overabundance of scar tissue. Your shoulder joint is almost entirely encapsulated by scar tissue at this point, which is exacerbating your nerve pain, and severely slowing your rate of progression," he hesitated, looking at Beau intently, as if he had something else to say, but wasn't sure if he should say it. "Technically, we have two options. You can choose to do the surgery now, as in..." he paused and looked up in the air, as if pondering his own schedule. "Today's Friday, so, we could even do it Monday," he looked back at Beau, "or, we could send you home and you could proceed with outpatient therapy for a while, see how it goes, and make a decision about surgery before you see me again in a month or so." Beau was dejected. Dr. Daniels could see it on his face. "I know it's not what you wanted to hear, but it's where we are. And you're so young, what are you, twenty-one, twenty-two?"

Beau dropped his head briefly. "I'll be twenty-one in a few months."

Daniels nodded, "You're young, you're fit, you're otherwise totally healthy. You're a great candidate for the surgery, but this is your call." Daniels set down his clipboard and leaned against the small counter behind him. "What are you thinking? Do you have questions?"

Beau wished his mom were with him. All he could focus on was the medical evaluation, but he knew he should ask other things. Val always knew what to ask. "I'm supposed to have a medical review for the Marine Corps in a week," Beau said. Daniels nodded and Beau added, "What does all this do to that process?"

"Well, I'm not in the military and never have been, so I can't give you perfect answers. But, I have had lots of military patients and I've contributed my findings to more of these reviews than I can count. Now, remember, I am not the authority here, but I believe the surgery would almost certainly delay the board. On the other hand, I still have to report this update, so even if you choose to postpone the surgery and continue with outpatient therapy for a while, the board could choose to delay, or they could push through with what they have." He paused and chuckled to himself, "In my experience, they tend to favor the delays over discharging Marines."

Beau sighed again, unsure of himself. "So, let me ask you this, let's say I didn't choose surgery, do you think I could be fit for duty without it?"

Dr. Daniels made an *mmm* sound with his mouth as he thought about Beau's question, "Unfortunately, there's no way for me to know. I really can't say for sure. But, I can say that I think the surgery is your best bet for returning to full active duty." He paused again, "But, even without it, you might be able to remain a Marine, maybe with a different set of duties? It could go both ways."

"If I go through with it, will I be back to one hundred percent, do you think?" Beau asked in earnest.

"I think we can get you close. Much closer than the fifty percent mobility you're at now, and according to your therapy notes, I'm being generous."

Beau nodded, "I've really been trying." Dr. Daniels could tell that Beau seemed to take his comment personally.

Noting his reaction, Dr. Daniels said, "Your therapy has been grueling. The scar tissue makes it all the more difficult, because you physically can't do the things your protocol demands. It's definitely not a matter of your effort, it's a matter of your physiology." He took a breath, "The surgery is arthroscopic. I'll make tiny holes and slowly, carefully, remove the scar tissue and loosen tight ligaments. While you're asleep, we'll take your shoulder through the full range of motion, releasing the other tissue and loosening the joints, allowing you to progress toward total recovery."

Beau did not want another surgery. He didn't want any of this, but he did want to feel strong again. He *needed* to feel strong. His mind raced. He threw his head back against the pillow. "I think I want to do the surgery. I want to complete my full enlistment, but... My girlfriend is about to have a baby. We're talking any day now." His forehead crinkled as he spoke, "Her due date is like a week away and she's three hours from here. I want to be there when my son is born. I don't want to miss it. I'm sick of this dump… no offense." He reached up to his eyes with his left hand and rubbed them with his fingers.

Dr. Daniels smiled and nodded and then fell silent for what seemed like a long time. Finally he spoke, "What about this? Traditionally, with this surgery, we'd keep you for three days. Your baby is due when?"

He raised his eyebrows toward Beau, whose voice was thick with sarcasm when he responded, "She could be going into labor right this minute for all I know. Literally, any freaking second."

"So, what if I discharge you to outpatient therapy but send your records up the chain, including our intent to do the scar removal surgery? I could schedule it for a month out. They may or may not delay your board. That's out of my hands, but you'd be there for the birth of your child. You could go home and get out of this 'dump,'" he smiled. "You would have to continue with therapy in the meantime. Three days per week. Then, in a month, you can come back for the surgery." He raised his eyebrows, "We'll keep your stay as brief as possible, and then go back to regular therapy until you're fully recovered. I can't control the U.S. Marines, but I *can* write some very compelling notes about your prognosis."

Beau didn't even pause, "I think I like the sound of that. If it's the best we got, it's the best we got. So... when can I go home?" he asked, looking hopeful.

Dr. Daniels laughed, "Is today soon enough?"

"Seriously?" Beau sat up in bed like an excited little boy.

"I'll get your discharge documents together and get with your nurse to make it happen. She'll come in and get your pharmacy info and whatnot. We can take care of the referrals, but you'll leave with copies of all your records and your prescriptions. And, for good measure, I'm going to prescribe you a stool softener. Sometimes narcotic medicines can..., you know," he laughed. "Sound good?" Dr. Daniels reached his hand toward Beau again, signaling his satisfaction with the plan.

"Yes, sir!" Beau said, relieved to be going home and relieved to get another prescription. He wrestled with his thoughts and paused again, debating whether or not he should mention the excess pain medication. He could feel his body craving another dose and decided to keep his mouth shut. It wasn't worth the risk. "Thank you."

As soon as Dr. Daniels was out the door, Beau grabbed the pills from under his covers and took one more. Then he reached for his phone to text Julia. After that, he texted his mom and immediately began packing his belongings. His new roommate was snoring loudly as he moved around the room, but Beau didn't care — he was going home!

CHAPTER TWENTY-TWO

Joe had never been so excited to make a three-hour drive in his life! The minute he got word Beau would be coming home, that very day, he dropped everything to hit the road. Valerie had plans to attend a doctor's appointment with Julia, since the baby was due in a week. This appointment would include some preemptive paperwork and planning for the big day. Half the folks in Joe's department took half days on Fridays anyway, so he had no regrets about packing up and walking out the door at ten-thirty in the morning. He took a few minutes to tell some of his coworkers about the big news, but for the most part, it was full steam ahead toward Houston.

When he turned into the gas station parking lot, he felt an immense sense of joy come over him. He pulled up next to the pump, turned off the ignition, and sat behind the wheel, thanking God over and over. After several long moments, he got out of the car, thinking about where they'd been over the last few years — so many big changes, so many big moments. He pulled the nozzle from the pump, mindlessly going through the motions of filling the tank as he considered the impact the accident had had on all their lives. As he leaned against the car, he realized that enduring such tragedy had transformed his connection with God. He had, admittedly, been slower to trust God's goodness than Valerie had. She had experienced a radical transformation of faith almost immediately after the accident, all because of some preacher's podcast and the perfect timing of the Holy Spirit. But after all was said and done, both of them had been ignited with passion for their faith. He remained amazed at his wife's steadfast faith, trusting that Eli would wake up even after years of what looked like no hope. And, wake up he did! That alone was enough to transform their lives, but now — after everything else — nobody would ever be able to convince him that God wasn't real. He knew God was real. He knew God was good. His family had seen miracles. They had experienced the love of God — the power of God. He and Valerie, for the first time in their lives, knew what it meant to have a real relationship with Jesus and to trust Him with every breath.

Joe felt cold chills run across his skin. He'd heard people say it so many times, but now he knew it to be true — what the enemy meant to destroy them, God had indeed used to bless them, to empower them and to set them free from a lifetime of check-the-boxes, lukewarm faith. He couldn't believe his own ears when he heard himself thanking God for not just bringing them through the journey, but for the journey itself.

When he heard the pump handle click, he finished up his task and ran into the gas station quick-mart to grab some snacks for the road. Once he'd made his way back to the car, he reached for his cellphone in the console and texted Valerie, <I LOVE YOU>. He hit send, but decided to add something else, <GOD IS SO GOOD>. After carefully placing his phone back into the console, he started the engine and pulled out, turning toward the interstate — Beau was waiting.

~

Pete had called half a dozen restaurants before finding one that could accommodate reservations for a party of fifteen of their closest friends and family that very night. Valerie had planned to cook, but Pete convinced her that she needed to focus on the celebration, rather than trying to prep a meal for fifteen on short notice. When he suggested dinner out and dessert at home, she was quick to accept, laughingly saying, "You don't have to twist my arm."

Once the reservations were finally confirmed, Pete made his way to Val's favorite local bakery. After flipping through a book of options and grumbling about the prices for ten minutes, he put in a rush order for a large chocolate ganache cake that would read, "Welcome Home Beau and Eli" across the top, in a contrasting white icing. The clerk punched a few keys on her keyboard and finally said, "Okay, sir, we will have that ready for you by three o'clock."

"That will work," Pete responded. He glanced at his phone to get the time. "Plenty of time to go buy milk and lots of coffee." The clerk looked confused, but laughed anyway. She had no way of knowing that, in Pete's mind, serving cake without milk or coffee was a crime against humanity. After a quick stop at the store, he decided to take his haul of groceries to Joe and Valerie's house, instead of toting it home and then back again. Besides, James and his crew would be pulling into town soon. Pete thought he might ask his brother to join him in picking up the cake, and Valerie's house seemed like the perfect place to hang out in the meantime. But, when he turned into the driveway, there was a truck he didn't recognize parked in his usual spot. "What in the world is happening now?" Pete had come to accept the McKnight way of life — their house was a revolving door of friends and family. Their home had always been *the place* to be — ever since Beau and Eli were little. Valerie wouldn't have it any other way, even when things were broken, messy, slimy, sticky or otherwise chaotic.

Pete stood at the front door, trying to figure out how to open it with full arms. He bent down and pressed the doorbell with his nose, hoping he wouldn't have to set his items down only to pick them back up again. He stood waiting. Just as he was about to put his bags down and dig for his key, the door opened. Pete hesitated, staring blankly at the figure on the other side of the door. His confusion must have been apparent, because before he could even ask, the young man behind the door spoke up, "Hi, I'm Andy. I'm a friend of Beau's. Eli just stepped out, so I decided to answer the door."

"Uh, okay. Um. Well, I'm Pete. I'm the uncle. Well, I'm their uncle — one of them anyway. Nice to meet you, uh, Andy was it?" Pete was taken aback, his arms weighted down with gallons of milk and full grocery bags. He was used to strange kids hanging out at Joe and Valerie's house — but he wasn't used to strange kids opening the door. It felt weird.

"Let me help you with those." Andy reached for the bags, ignoring Pete's expression. He moved through the great room and toward the kitchen like he'd been there a thousand times. Pete was putting the gallons of milk into the fridge when Eli came walking down the back stairs and into the kitchen.

"Hey Uncle Pete! I see you've met Andy." Eli leaned against the kitchen island and gestured gallantly toward his newfound friend.

"Yep, in a way, I guess," Pete spoke flatly as he continued with his work. Andy chuckled at his indifference. It was befitting somehow.

"Uncle Pete, this is Andy. You know, An-dy. Beau's Andy?" Eli was astonished that Pete didn't immediately recognize the name and put two and two together.

Pete stopped in his tracks and dropped a pack of coffee filters onto the floor in the process, "Wait, you're Andy? The Andy? Afghanistan Andy?"

"Well," Andy laughed, "nobody's ever called me Afghanistan Andy before, but yeah, I guess that's me." Pete suddenly registered Andy's country twang. He'd heard a lot about Andy, but had pictured him completely differently in his mind.

"What in the Sam Hill are you doing here? Does Beau know?" Pete asked excitedly.

"No!" Eli said emphatically. "Beau has no idea. Andy sent me a letter a few weeks ago because Beau asked him to. So, when he took leave, we cooked up a plan for him to come up and see Beau as a surprise. The fact that Beau gets to come home today is just an accidental bonus. We didn't plan that, but it couldn't have worked out better."

"Eh, I'd call it God's favor more than an accident," Andy winked. "He and I, we're tight like that."

Eli laughed, "Good point."

"The way I see it, God puts me right where I need to be when I need to be there. I just listen to His voice and go where He says — it always works out just perfect." Andy shoved his hands in his pockets. Pete made a well-then face as he looked at Eli. Eli simply smiled and nodded.

As they walked back into the great room, Pete leaned over toward Eli and whispered, "If you'd told me a year ago that Beau's closest friend would be a card carrying faith man, I would have laughed in your face."

Eli chuckled, "Well, since I couldn't say anything a year ago anyway, laughing in my face might be deemed inappropriate old man."

Pete grabbed Eli around the neck and proceeded to noogie him all the way to the couch. He was relieved to hear Eli crack a joke. He hadn't been himself since Ivy ended things between them, and Pete was relieved to see he could still smile.

~

Joe kept turning his head to look at Beau as they made their way down the interstate toward home. His big McKnight grin stretched ear to ear and pure joy bubbled out of every pore in his body.

"Dad! Stop looking at me like that," Beau laughed. "You're starting to creep me out!"

Joe chuckled, "I can't help it! I'm just so happy you're coming home!" He reached out his right hand and gave Beau's good shoulder a tight squeeze.

"Me too, Dad. You have no idea."

"Hey, I need a break — a bathroom break, that is," Joe laughed at his own words. "Let's pull off, get gas, maybe a snack, okay?"

"Sounds good." When Joe pulled their car up to the pump, he put it in park and got out. Beau followed and said, "You go ahead. I'll get the gas."

"You sure?" Joe asked, but nodded in approval of his son's choice. "You need my card?"

"No, Dad. I got it."

"Geez, I just keep forgetting you're a real live grown up these days!" Joe laughed. "Alright. I'll be back. You want anything?"

"Yes! I want a big water and king size candy bar, emphasis on king size. I don't care what kind." Beau grinned the big McKnight smile back at his father. As soon as Joe was across the parking lot, Beau maneuvered the trigger on the gas pump, allowing the gas to flow without human assistance. He moved quickly around to the passenger side of his father's SUV and opened the back door. He unzipped his duffle bag and began digging around. He paused for just a moment and looked toward the market — his father was still in the bathroom. He pulled a large prescription pill bottle from his bag and rattled it in his hands. He looked at the label, Vicodin. He reached into his duffle bag to retrieve his own almost-empty bottle and emptied the contents of the large bottle into his own. When he found that the pills from the large bottle wouldn't all fit, he put a few in his pocket and then quickly poured the rest into his small leather toiletries bag. He then reached down and pulled three fentanyl patches from inside his right sock and shoved them into the same toiletries bag, before zipping it up and tossing it back into his duffle bag. He walked back around to the driver's side of the car, turning toward the market to see who might be watching. His father was in the checkout line, so he moved toward the trash can between the pumps and tossed the large, now empty pill bottle. He hoped his own prescription would be waiting on him at the pharmacy in the morning, but he couldn't take a chance. Besides, that old man probably wouldn't miss them anyway.

CHAPTER TWENTY-THREE

Valerie, Eli, Julia, Pete, James and his wife, Sophia, along with their youngest daughter, Layla, were all gathered around Andy listening to his stories about the Marine Corps, Beau and their experiences in Afghanistan. They'd been sitting together, laughing and sharing stories since Pete had returned with the "overpriced, over-pretty cake," as he'd called it. Hours had passed quickly as they talked. Being the kind of man he was, Andy managed to tell great, true stories and, at the same time, make Beau sound like a hero in every tale. Only Eli had been in on the secret visit, and now he reveled in the fact that everyone was thrilled with the surprise.

Valerie knew Beau and Andy had grown very close, but she also recalled a time when Beau complained about his very existence — insisting he was one of the most chatty, nosy and annoying people he'd ever met. "But, that was before he met Antonne," she thought to herself, laughing under her breath. Now that she was face to face with Andy, she felt like he was already part of the family.

When the front door opened and Joe walked through, toting a large duffle bag, the group was so caught up in Andy's tale about the morning Beau had hidden his boots, forcing him to either go late to formation or show up in his sock feet, that they almost didn't notice the grand entrance. Julia glanced up and saw Beau saunter through the door. She let out a squeal that could have wakened the dead and then quickly jumped to her feet — well, as quickly as a woman can at thirty-nine weeks pregnant. The rest of the group followed, making their way to the door like a herd of elephants. Beau didn't immediately notice Andy's presence, he was too busy getting swarmed by his family giving hugs. Julia was crying before she even made it to the door. She wrapped her arms around Beau's neck, being careful of his shoulder, and buried her face in his chest. He wrapped her up as best he could, pressing his lips against the top of her head. As the group made a collective, boisterous move toward the great room, Beau looked up and saw Andy standing behind the sofa, his hands in his pockets and a big smile on his face. Beau blinked hard. Was he hallucinating? Was that really Andy standing in his house?"

"Mack?" He called out with an obvious blend of confusion and excitement in his voice, "How in the h... How did you... What are you doing here?" Beau's family watched as he made a bee-line toward Andy. He reached up and wrapped his left arm around Andy's neck as Andy pulled him in for the kind of hug that can only be shared between brothers in arms. Valerie was wiping tears from her eyes as Joe slipped his arm around her waist. The room was quiet — good quiet — as they all silently shared in the joy of the moment.

"You can thank your brother for that one." Andy rubbed Beau's head with his hand and said, "Dang. You need a haircut. Maybe I'll start calling you Shaggy Dog instead of Hangdog." Andy laughed as he roughed up Beau's head with his hand.

"Shut up. I've been busy, okay?" Beau retorted. He turned toward Eli, who hadn't stopped grinning since Beau walked through the door. "You," he said quietly as he pointed at Eli.

"What about me?" Eli asked, moving closer to Beau. Beau reached out his left hand and grabbed the back of Eli's neck, pulling him in. He paused, looking Eli in the eyes before finally speaking up, "I missed you." The tone of his voice made it obvious that Beau wasn't just referring to the few weeks he'd been left alone at the hospital — he was referring to the two years Eli had been locked away, somewhere inside his own head. Beau wanted his brother to know that he was thankful, and everyone in the room felt it.

~

Beau and Eli stood together, hugging a line of family as they filed into the restaurant. Thankfully, they were set up at a table fit for sixteen, so Andy fit right in with no problem. Once everyone was seated, Beau excused himself and made his way to the restroom. On his way, he passed by a large, cherry wood divider wall with open railing and floating shelves, each adorned with opulent sculptures. Though it was meant to divide the main dining room to create a more intimate experience, it also served to enhance the ambiance of the restaurant. It was eye catching and Beau couldn't help but look at it as he walked by. As he passed the wall, he casually turned to look over his left shoulder, still somewhat focused on the décor — but what he saw caused his breath to catch in his chest.

Ivy sat at a corner table with, who Beau could only assume was, the other guy. What was his name? Mark? Her parents were seated with them and they all seemed so content, lost in their own conversation. Beau didn't know it, but this night was Ivy's last night in town before she and Mark were off to visit his parents. From there, she would head back to

Zimbabwe for a few more months — and then, after that, who knew?

Beau turned his eyes toward the restroom quickly and pushed open the door with force. He paced back and forth in front of the stalls, at a loss as to what he should do. He walked to the sink and turned on the water, staring at himself in the mirror. He reached into the pocket of his slacks and retrieved two of the loose Vicodin pills he knew he'd need before the night was out. He swallowed them quickly and washed his hands with cold water. After he dried them on a paper towel, he pressed his palms against his face, feeling the coolness of his own hands against his skin. He felt something pop in his shoulder. It didn't hurt, but it startled him back into thinking about his current predicament. Should he tell Eli Ivy was there? Should he walk to their table and bust that guy in the face with his own dinner plate? The way he felt, it could go either way.

As Beau walked slowly back toward the table, he was careful to keep his eyes downward. He didn't want to make eye contact with anyone at Ivy's table. As soon as he was past the partition, he started taking long strides back to his own table. He quickly sat down across from Eli and next to Andy, both of whom could tell by his face that something was wrong.

"What's going on?" Eli asked. "Are you okay? You look... I dunno... weird."

"I'm fine. Just really hungry is all. I need to eat," Beau responded with short, succinct sentences.

"Well, you're at the right place for it," Andy answered. He knew immediately that Beau was lying. He always knew when someone was lying. He could feel it in his spirit. He watched as Eli stared across the table at Beau suspiciously. He began to make small talk, asking what might be good to order, and if they thought an appetizer might be a good idea. The questions succeeded in distracting Eli, who started looking at his menu. Andy leaned closer to Beau and whispered, "Okay — what's up? And don't say dinner."

Beau knew he couldn't lie to Andy. He'd learned that Andy could read people like a book shortly after meeting him. He turned his face toward his right shoulder as best he could and leaned his body toward Andy. "Eli's ex is on the other side of that wall... with her parents *and* the jackwagon," he whispered, giving Andy a look that was unmistakable.

Andy didn't speak immediately, but returned Beau's hard stare with his own wide-eyed expression. He reached for the basket of bread on the table, shoving it toward Beau. "Bread?" Beau took a roll from the basket and Andy leaned close to him and whispered, "Are you going to tell him?"

"I don't know. Should I?" Beau answered. Eli was on the other side of the table, chatting with his Uncle Pete about the factors that contribute to a quality steak, seemingly unaware of the exchange between Andy and Beau.

Andy looked at him. "I would. If he finds out later that you knew and didn't tell him..." Andy's words were interrupted by Eli's voice.

"Be right back," he said, as he stood up from the table. It was obvious he was going to the restroom. He slapped Pete's shoulder as he scooted behind his chair.

"Too late," Andy whispered. "Maybe he won't see them."

"Trust me. He'll see them. You can't miss them — especially on the way back." Beau looked at Andy with concern in his eyes. They sat in silence, eating bread like it was a job, until they saw Eli coming back around the corner.

"Yep. He saw them," Andy said, as they took in the look on Eli's face. He looked like he'd seen a ghost, or like he wanted to fight — a combination of the two, really. He was pale and carried himself with a defensive posture. Valerie noticed immediately.

"Eli, honey, are you okay? You look pale." She leaned toward him from her place down the table.

Eli saw no point in lying. Everyone would find out eventually anyway — if they didn't already know. "Ivy's on the other side of that wall with her new boyfriend," he spoke frankly. He looked dejected. He pressed his lips together and sat down.

The table grew silent. Finally James spoke up, questioning, "What? What do you mean? What new boyfriend?"

Valerie answered in a low voice, "Ivy and Eli broke up, James."

"Let's just call it what it is, Mom. She dumped me for another guy. Some guy she met in Africa. And now, they're on the other side of that wall with her parents." He was angry, but also he was hurt and in pain. Nobody at the table knew what to do. What could they do? What could they say? The tension was palpable and the awkward silence made everyone uncomfortable and sad.

Joe blew a deep breath out through O-shaped lips, "You know what. It doesn't matter, son. We're here to celebrate, so let's celebrate. Forget about them. Let's be thankful for our miracles right here at this table."

Andy nodded emphatically. "Amen," he said aloud. The table slowly returned to light conversation as Eli sat stewing in his seat. He ate his meal in relative silence, his mind preoccupied by thoughts of Ivy and Mark. He *needed* to see Mark's face. He needed Mark to know that his choices had impacted a real, live person. He needed to lay eyes on the guy who had stolen his future. In a different way, he also needed to see Ivy. He missed her face. He was hurt and angry, but he still loved her. Maybe, if she saw him outside the hospital, it would somehow take her back to where they'd once been. Maybe she would remember who they were supposed to become. Maybe she would change her mind, he thought wistfully. He rocked back and forth in is seat, clearly uneasy. The world moved on around him, everyone talking and laughing, and all he could do was think about Ivy. He seethed at the idea of her hand in another guy's hand, her kiss on another guy's lips. His heart was shattered, like blown glass thrown against a concrete wall.

Everyone was finishing their meals when Eli spoke. "Right," he said suddenly, before rising to his feet. It was abrupt and startling. His posture alone was intimidating. He still wasn't the walking muscle he had been before the accident, but he'd gained enough mass in the last few months to be intimidating once again. He stood beside the table briefly, with is hands balled into fists. The expression on his face was strange. It was intense, but not angry. Instead, it reflected a diehard determination. Joe had seen that face a million times — before big games, before shots at the doctor's office, before big tests — he was priming himself to *do* something.

"Oh boy, here we go." Beau wiped his mouth on his napkin and readied himself to stand up.

"Here we go, what?" Andy asked.

"I don't know yet, but we're his back up either way," Beau responded.

Andy had to admit, the look on Eli's face was hard to read. If he was anything like his brother, Eli was about to start a brawl in one of the finest restaurants in Longview. He'd heard Beau threaten to give the "jackwagon" the beating of his life more than once. And even though Andy didn't understand that rationale and had no desire to fight anyone, he would have their backs anyway.

"Wait, why would we give this guy a beating when Ivy was the guilty party?" Andy leaned in and whispered to Beau.

"Because... because one, you can't beat up a girl and two, this guy knew about Eli and his coma and pursued Ivy anyway," Beau whispered back.

Andy nodded slowly, "Oh, okay." He looked at Beau who was staring at Eli, waiting for him to move. When he finally did, Valerie reached out her arm to stop him and spoke firmly to get his attention.

"Eli..." He paused and looked at her with intensity in his eyes. "Think," she said softly, as if to imply he wasn't thinking clearly. It wasn't like Eli to make rash decisions or to act out of emotion, but where Ivy was concerned, all bets were off. Eli didn't respond and simply kept moving. Beau stood as quickly as he could and Andy followed. Joe jumped up behind them, tossing his napkin onto the table, in the hopes of stopping a scene before it started.

Eli made the turn around the partition wall and his entire family watched in stunned, riveted silence. Pete and James were standing now too, ready to engage in... whatever it was they might need to do. Everyone on their side of the dining room could feel the tension in the air, as people from other tables looked on, trying to figure out what might be happening. Beau and Andy hung back, watching Eli as he took long strides across the dining room toward the Zellway's table. Eileen saw him first and reached out her right hand to rest it on Ivy's forearm. Eli moved quickly toward the table. Don and Mark had both turned toward him as he approached. Andy could see that Mark had tensed up, his muscles taut, ready to respond to a fight that was surely coming his way. Joe stepped in behind Beau and Andy. Beau was ready to pounce, bad shoulder and all, come what may. Andy stood with his hands in his pockets. He seemed as calm as ever. He'd fight if he had to, but he didn't appear worried about it — much less ready for it. When Eli reached the Zellway's table, Ivy stood up. Mark followed. Eileen had a mildly panicked look on her face, but she remained seated. Mark's heart was beating in his throat. Even from across the room, Joe could tell his jaw was clenched.

Both Joe and Beau held their breath, each for a different reason. Eli's movements were abrupt, he lifted his fist. Beau readied himself to run into the fray. But, Eli didn't swing. He didn't shout. He didn't do anything to cause a scene. Instead, he was the composed, self-aware Eli that his family knew, that Ivy knew. He extended his arm and opened his palm toward Mark. Mark looked down at Eli's outstretched hand. He reached out and took it in a handshake. Eli squeezed Mark's hand in his own. Mark was no runt, but even in his weaker state, Eli could have crushed him. Mark tried to ignore the strength of Eli's grip.

"I thought we should meet," Eli said, straight-faced and serious. "I'm Eli McKnight."

"Mark Sandoval." Mark was stunned. He didn't know what to say or how to react.

Eli leaned in close to him and spoke into his ear, loudly enough for Ivy and her parents to hear, but not loudly enough to disturb the room, "You will treat her right. She's better than either of us deserve. If you hurt her, so help me, I will hunt you down and teach you a lesson you will never forget." Eli dropped Mark's hand. Mark nodded, because he didn't know what else to do. Eli had already turned to leave when Don stood up. He put a hand on Eli's shoulder to stop him. He grabbed Eli's hand in a handshake and then pulled him in for a quick hug. Eli glanced at Ivy as he walked away. Her eyes were filled with tears. She looked down toward her feet when his eyes met hers and Eli watched as a single tear rolled down her cheek. He turned back toward his family and took long, brisk strides toward Beau and Andy. He put his head down and shoved his hands in his pockets. Joe, Andy and Beau, James and Pete, and now Julia and Valerie, too, all stepped back, like the seas parting, to allow Eli to pass. He stalked past them and moved through the lobby and out the door of the restaurant without a word. He wanted to be anywhere else.

Ivy watched as he walked away. Her heart ached. She made eye contact with Valerie and felt sick to her stomach. She tried to hold her tears, but couldn't. Mark reached for her hand, but she couldn't take it — not while Valerie's eyes were on her. She was ready to leave town, and tomorrow couldn't come soon enough.

CHAPTER TWENTY-FOUR

Eli sat alone on the back porch while his family enjoyed cake and laughter in the kitchen. As he sat on the stairs staring out at the backyard, distracted by his own thoughts of losing Ivy and the harsh reality of seeing her with another guy, Valerie slowly opened one of the French doors and quietly walked outside. She carried a glass of milk and a slice of cake on a small saucer. She sat next to Eli and extended the plate and glass toward him. He looked at her and quietly said, "Thanks." He took the plate and the glass from her hands and set them on the step next to his right foot.

"Want to talk about it?" Valerie asked. She put her arm around Eli's shoulder and he instinctively leaned into her, resting his head on her shoulder like he had since he was a little boy.

"Not really." He took a deep breath.

"Are you sure? I'm a very good listener." Valerie smiled at him.

Eli smiled back, halfheartedly. "What am I supposed to do now, Mom? I want her back. How can I just sit around here while she falls in love with somebody else?"

"You can't. You can't just sit around and pine for her. It will eat you alive. You have to get up, put one foot in front of the other, and get to the business of fulfilling God's purpose for your life. You're a miracle, son. God didn't bring you this far to leave you hanging — I promise. I might not know much, but I know this — I love you very, very much. Your dad loves you, your brother loves you, your uncles love you and your grandparents, but Jesus loves you more. Don't let yourself stop praising God just because your heart is hurting. There is *always* something to be thankful for." Valerie kissed him on the forehead.

"It's just that, well, I thought she was part of my purpose. I really did. I know we're young, but, so were you and Dad — I thought she was the one."

"If she is, she'll find a way back to you." Valerie wanted to reassure him. But, people strayed from God's best for their lives all the time, and she knew it. It was difficult for her to imagine Eli as anything less than the best for Ivy, or anyone else for that matter.

"Thanks Mom," Eli said with a sigh.

"Now, eat your cake. Uncle Pete has been complaining about how expensive it was all afternoon, so we have to eat it, even if we don't want to." Valerie laughed at her own words and drew a chuckle from Eli. He picked up his plate and carefully lifted the fork from underneath the cake. He put a bite into his mouth and nodded his head. "See, chocolate makes everything better," Valerie said. She stood up to walk away and kissed the top of his head. "Remember, one foot in front of the other."

Eli nodded. He reached down for his milk and took a sip. He closed his eyes, doing his best to connect with God — he needed to feel God's peace, and though he knew that the Holy Spirit was dwelling in his heart and was the very author of peace, he found it difficult to fill his heart with praise. Right now, his pain was so deep that he even struggled to thank God for waking him up, so, he decided to focus on giving thanks for the blessings he had right in front of him — and, at the moment, that happened to be cake.

~

After a while, Eli decided to stop thinking about Ivy for a bit and rejoin his family. He walked back into the house and made his way to the great room where everyone was still gathered, having fun and exchanging stories. Beau sat with his feet up and his arm around Julia, who was as curled up as she could be with her big belly in the way. His eyes were glassed over as he rested his hand on her stomach, trying to feel his unborn son kicking. Andy was settled in on the sectional sofa, his legs stretched out on the chaise. The TV was on, but nobody seemed to be watching it. Joe was sitting in his chair and Valerie was on the floor in front of him leaning back against his legs while he twirled her hair through his fingers. Joe and Valerie both seemed to be in a place of perfect contentment. They looked around the room, recognizing their blessings and making note of how far they'd come in such a short time. God had been so good to them. Despite Satan's every effort, despite poor choices and mistakes, despite bad attitudes and everything else they'd been through — there they sat, showered in blessings.

When Eli came in and sat down, Beau could tell he was hurting. After everything Eli had been through — a tragedy that Beau still blamed himself for — he didn't deserve this. After a few minutes of watching Eli brood while everyone else bantered and laughed without a care in the world, Beau just couldn't take it anymore. He had *to do* something. He leaned forward and spoke up, "It's my turn to tell a story!" He looked around the room noting that he had everyone's attention before making eye contact with his brother. He decided, more for his own benefit than anyone else's, to overdramatize his tale — because if he didn't take his experience too seriously, nobody else would either. Something in his mind needed to mask the gravity of his ordeal. Admitting his fear, his proximity to death and his ultimate weakness somehow stripped him of his sense of control, and he didn't think he could make it through life, much less the story, if he didn't at least feel as though he had some control over his future.

"A few months ago, 'ol Big Mack here was chauffeuring me and some other guys and a load of equipment in a convoy headed for a FOB in the Nahri Saraj District of this God forsaken place we call Afghanistan." Beau spoke using grand gestures with his left hand and was casually holding his milk glass in the other. He was performing a one-man show, his mannerisms alone drawing giggles from his family.

"FOB?" Valerie interjected.

"Forward operating base, ma'am," Andy spoke up.

"Oh, okay. Thank you." Valerie smiled. She had decided that she genuinely liked Andy.

"You're very welcome," Andy responded.

"A-hem," Beau interrupted them. "Are you two done? I'm trying to regale you with tales from exotic lands over here." Julia laughed and rolled her eyes.

"Oh yeah, we're regaled alright," she taunted Beau, winking at him when he gave her a sideways glance. The whole room chuckled, Eli included.

"Anyway, as I was saying... wait, where was I?" Beau asked with a smirk.

"I was chauffeuring you across the Afghan desert," Andy answered.

"Oh, right..." Beau cleared his throat. "Anyway, our convoy got bogged down in the desert. We had creeped along at a snail's pace for days and there was nothing we could do but keep going. We were sitting ducks and we knew it. Then, our VC... That's vehicle commander for you, Mom... heard over the radio that there were insurgents in our area. We were on high alert. I was manning a mounted machine gun on our MRAP..."

"Mine resistant, ambush protected," Andy whispered to Val. "It's a truck." She nodded.

"Shhh," Beau said jokingly. "There we were, bogged down in the desert with enemy combatants moving in on our location. No sooner than I could see them on the horizon, a mortar round crashed to the ground in the distance, sending a huge cloud of sand and smoke into the air." As he looked around the room, he could see that, despite his efforts to keep it light, his audience was now invested in the gravity of the tale — they could tell where the story was going. Only Andy seemed nonchalant about the whole thing, but then again, Andy always seemed nonchalant — unless he was on some rant about the problems with modern Christianity. Beau tried to continue on in dramatic fashion, hoping to minimize the heaviness of the events, but as he recounted his experience, he was transported back in time, and it became impossible to keep up the act. He remembered the day vividly, like it had just happened, with the exception of those shards of recollection that had been stripped away by explosions, unconsciousness and pain. "I yelled into the vehicle, 'Incoming!' and no sooner did I yell than another mortar round dropped at about twenty-five meters to the west, and then another at twenty. I yelled again, 'Incoming!'"

The entire room was hanging onto his every word. He hadn't spoken of the day he got hurt to anyone, and no one had expected him to. Valerie leaned forward with her elbows on her knees, coving her mouth with both hands.

"My heart was racing. I aimed my gun toward the direction of the incoming fire. I could see movement on the horizon. It was hot. It was so hot. I remember feeling like I was choking on the heat. I could see it rising off the sand and dirt in waves. I could see the enemy forming a line of vehicles. I could tell they were planning something, but I didn't know what. I felt sick to my stomach."

Joe was leaning forward now, too. Pete had stopped eating mid-plate. Pete never stopped eating in the middle of a meal. Beau didn't look at Eli. He wanted to, but for some reason, he couldn't make himself do it.

"The lead vehicle still hadn't moved. I don't know if they were even trying to move. We'd been bogged down for days, so they might have been giving it everything they had. I couldn't tell. I could hear the radio inside our MRAP, there were muffled voices and commands coming from all directions. I could hear our vehicle commander yelling, 'What are they doing? Why aren't they moving? Push, somebody tell six to push!' Then I heard the gunner in the lead vehicle yelling. I could hear small arms fire in the distance and turned to see dust rising from somewhere near the rear of the convoy." He was lost in thought now. He was still, his eyes fixed on one spot somewhere on the back wall. He was reliving his story. "My heart was beating so, so fast. I remember thinking I was unprepared. I remember wondering why I'd ever signed up in the first place. I was afraid. I was so afraid." Julia had begun to cry quietly. Valerie reached out for her hand and held it as they listened. "I heard the VC yelling again, 'Push, push, push through! Do not stop!' The radio just kept squawking and the chatter wouldn't stop. I wanted to cover my ears. I could hear shots being fired, but from far away — too far away. And then, there was another mortar, so close, ten meters or less. My ears were ringing. I couldn't hear anything. When the ringing began to fade, I could hear my vehicle commander yelling at me, 'Keep your head down!' He sent our dismounts out. Everything was so loud and it was all happening so fast. I remember feeling lost, like I didn't know what to do, but my body sort of moved on its own, even when my mind felt out of control. There was chaos at the back of the convoy, but I couldn't tell what was happening. I was shaking all over. I still don't know what was happening back there, but it felt like it was getting closer. And then, I heard the gunner from the vehicle ahead of me yell out, 'RPG!' But it happened so fast that the flash hit me almost right when the words did. I remember feeling the heat from the explosion burning my face. It was so hot that I had to turn away. But when I looked back, all I could see was flames and smoke."

Beau's face registered his terror. His eyes still fixed on one spot. "I couldn't breathe. I couldn't hear, for what seemed like a long time. Then, I heard screams. The lead vehicle had been hit. I remember knowing they were dead. There was no way they couldn't be." Beau wiped over his mouth with his hand. "The guys on the ground were running around and then another mortar round struck the ground about fifty meters to my right." He turned his head as though he were looking for something. "Through the dust, I could see about a dozen combatants moving toward us. I could hear them celebrating. Literally cheering because of what they'd done. I'd never felt anger like that before — sheer hatred. Out of nowhere, I heard the pinging sound of bullets against armor. They were too close. I didn't know what to do. The dismounts were trying to clear the lead vehicle. There was so much smoke. I couldn't move. I heard my VC screaming at me to wake up and fire. I turned my weapon on the insurgents and fired, three-round bursts. I saw a man fall on my shot and the others ran. I actually shot a man, a person, an actual person and... I was actually happy about it."

Val's mother quietly slipped out and excused herself to the other room, tears in her eyes. She didn't want to hear any more. Everyone else remained glued in place, awestruck. It was hard to believe that Beau McKnight, their Beau, had been there, had experienced such terror. They listened. Most of them still thought of Beau as a little boy, which made the story that much harder to hear. "Off to my right, I heard someone yell, 'Incoming!' and then things start to get hazy. My head pounded. I was deaf, literally deaf. All I could hear was a roaring sound. For a second, I thought I was okay, but there was so much blood. I think I blacked out. I was on my back when I came to again and, the pain... Oh God, the pain was terrible. I thought for sure I was dying. Then I remember..." He gestured to Andy. "I remember 'ol Andy Mack's face, telling me medevac was coming. He kept telling me not to move, but I didn't know I was. And then," he hesitated. Should he go on?

He mustered the will to look at Eli, who was on the edge of his chair with both arms up, his fingers interlaced, squeezing the top of his head, the exact way he had every time they'd gotten into trouble or watched a scary movie for their entire lives. Beau reasoned that Eli's breakup with Ivy was his fault, as much as he wanted to blame Mark or Ivy, he couldn't. He may say he blamed them, but inside, he blamed himself. If he hadn't fallen asleep at the wheel that night and put Eli into a coma, Ivy would never have gone to Africa. She never would have met Mark.

He decided to press on. Maybe Eli needed to hear it. "And then I think I was in and out of consciousness. I only remember pieces, but I remember Andy praying. He started to pray for me, but I stopped him. I begged him to pray for you instead." He turned to Eli. He looked right at him as he went on. "I remember him crying out to God, screaming it out above the noise of all the chaos, but he didn't ask for anything. He was thanking God for taking care of us, of me, of you. He was thanking God, in the middle of all that. And then, I remember him demanding that you wake up. He was yelling." He looked at Andy, calm Andy, who gave him a slight, close-lipped smile and a little nod, as if to encourage his words. "I'd never heard anything like it. He was giving commands — commanding that you wake up, commanding that your mind be restored." Beau shook his head. "I could feel it. I could feel power. I could feel the presence of God all around us. I know that's what it was. I have never felt anything like it. I've never told anyone about it and I still think I might just be crazy. Then I remember things getting calm. I couldn't tell if I was dying or not, but it seemed like I might be."

Joe and Valerie looked at each other. It's the first time Beau had admitted to any form of faith since he was fourteen.

"After that," Beau said, "things went black. I remember a few flashes from the chopper. And Gabriel, I remember Gabriel."

"Gabriel?" Pete's voice sounded reverent. The only Gabriel he knew of came from scripture, so his need for clarification overwhelmed his ability to stay quiet. He sat motionless, still holding his plate and a half-eaten piece of cake.

"Juan Gabriel, a Navy Corpsman. I didn't know that at the time. I just remember all the blood, so much blood, and knowing that it was coming from me. I remember his name from his uniform. He was holding pressure on my neck, talking to me. He kept telling me I'd be okay. I think he might have carried me, or something. Like I said, I didn't know who he was at the time, but he wrote me a card. He sent it to my unit and then Andy sent it to me."

He looked back at Eli, "Then, they took me to Germany and that's where Mom and Dad told me about you. I saw your video." Beau moved close to his brother and bent his knees, squatting down in front of him. "I did the math and I've tried over and over to make it not true because it can't be true. I mean, it's impossible, but it's not — you woke up on *that* day! That same day, maybe even that same minute!"

Eli dropped his hands from his head, letting them slide down his face and cover his mouth briefly. Beau continued, "So, see, the way I figure it is that you're meant for something big. Why would Satan be trying to take you out if you weren't meant for something big? No girl, no coma, no amount of time can change that fact." Eli moved off the edge of his chair and put his arms around his brother, hugging him tightly. To hear Beau mention God in any capacity seemed like a miracle, but this?

The room was silent for a long time. No one moved. Eli appeared to be deep in thought. The only sounds were Julia's sniffles. Nobody knew what to say or do. How do you segue from a moment like that? Andy had a contented look on his face, like he had expected this moment somehow.

Finally, Eli broke the silence, "Did you ever think that maybe it's you who's meant for something great? I mean, the way I see it, your life was changed by the accident just as much as mine was, maybe more. Maybe it's you Satan wants to stop. Maybe it's you."

Beau sat down on the floor, his knees bent in front of him. He finally set his milk glass down on the floor beside him. He hadn't taken a single sip since he started his story. He didn't say a word. He simply dropped his head between his knees before looking back at his brother. Not only had he not considered that possibility, he found it impossible to believe.

Joe and Valerie looked at each other, both locked in the moment, thankful not only for their sons' lives, but for their love for each other. If anyone could get through to Beau where faith was concerned, it was Eli. Pete, James and Sophia silently marveled at the scene that had just unfolded before them. Until this moment, Beau and Eli had remained kids in their minds, little boys with a whole life ahead of them. As they listened and watched, they realized that each of them had grown into men — each of them had come closer to death than most people ever would. Their love for them had never changed, but now that love had become intertwined with respect.

The tension in the room slowly began to melt and Joe finally stood up and stretched, doing his best to absorb the intensity of what he'd just witnessed and, at the same time, move beyond it. He looked around at the faces in the room and felt the need to put everyone at ease. This was a celebration. He wasn't sure what to say, but he knew he needed to say something to lighten the mood. "Well, I personally think you're both meant for great things. And, you can start with the dishes."

CHAPTER TWENTY-FIVE

Beau, Eli and Andy sat alone in the basement, playing video games and laughing. Eli was trying to keep his mind off Ivy. Beau was trying to keep his mind off his medical evaluation and Andy was just enjoying his life. The conversation was effortless and mostly centered around the idea of Antonne Young taking over the basement in a couple of months. As one hour turned into two, Beau was so engrossed in the moment that he mindlessly reached into the pocket of his sweats and pulled out two pain pills. Without a thought, without trying to hide them, he popped them into his mouth and washed them down with the orange juice he had left over from breakfast. Eli stopped dead in his tracks and watched him. Andy was silently watching too. Both of them had seen Beau take, what they believed was his morning dose, no more than three hours before. When Beau turned back around in his seat, he saw the same look on their faces.

"What?" he said, as if they were acting crazy.

"How many of those are you taking?" Eli asked. "I literally watched you take two when we first came down here. That's less than three hours, Beau."

"Don't worry about it," Beau returned dismissively.

"I have to worry about it, you jerk, because you aren't worried about it." Eli's forehead was crinkled with concern.

"Look I need it, okay. It's not a big deal," Beau returned.

Andy looked at Eli and back at Beau. He'd felt like Beau was hiding something from him for weeks now, but he didn't know what. "It kind of is a big deal — whether you want to admit it to yourself or not," Andy said matter-of-factly.

"You're taking way more than you're supposed to. You either do something about it, or I'm going to tell Mom and Dad," Eli was firm.

"You're going to *tell* on me?" Beau tried to sound dismissive and sarcastic, like Eli's threat held no power, but it did. It held lots of power, and Beau knew it.

"You heard me, and I'm serious." Eli stood up to face his brother. "I'm not messing around, Beau."

"Fine!" Beau said. "I'll stop okay. I'll quit doing it." He told Eli what he wanted to hear. He might even try it. But truthfully, he really did need the pills, at least he felt like he did, and it didn't matter what anyone else said. For the moment, peace and order was restored. But Andy could tell that Beau was simply trying to appease his brother. And more importantly, he also knew that if Beau didn't take action soon, he could end up fighting addiction for the rest of his life.

~

Andy's visit was set to last about ten days. Though he knew God had ordained the timing, he was blown away by the number of major life events unfolding during his stay. Beau's evaluation was only a few days away — if they actually went through with it. Even though his doctor had been very clear about a potential delay because of the recommended follow-up surgery, Beau still seemed to be banking on going back to work. It was obvious to everyone he wasn't ready. He couldn't carry a gallon of milk in his right hand, let along do a pushup. But, he'd somehow convinced himself that if he could just get back to work, everything else would eventually work out. Beau had come to define himself by being a Marine. Before the Marines, he defined himself with football and girls. Andy knew he was trying to fill a void that only God could fill, but Beau was hard headed and Andy knew better than to mention it.

Julia's official due date would coincide with Beau's evaluation, but the entire family expected her to go into labor any minute. She was having contractions and moving very slowly. If she lasted past her due date, it would be a miracle. Julia had always heard that first babies come late, but her doctor told her that based on national averages, more first babies are born a few days early than a few days late. It didn't matter to Julia, she was just ready. She was uncomfortable, she couldn't tie her own shoes, she was hungry all the time, she wasn't sleeping well and she was really tired of having to go to the bathroom every half hour. But, she was super thankful that Beau would be there for the birth. Valerie and Joe had been adamant about the rules of their household, and they didn't hesitate to order separate rooms — but they'd also been more supportive and loving than she could have imagined. The baby's room was ready, she had her bag packed, and she'd already planned for her mom, Val and Beau to be in the room during her delivery. She was anxious, and she paused each time she had a pain, hoping it might signal labor.

~

Valerie had cooked a massive Italian meal for dinner — lasagna, garlic bread, caprese salad and green beans with lemon and capers. Julia helped set the table and Eli and Andy were responsible for getting everyone's drinks. Beau was spreading garlic butter on the bread, preparing it for a few more minutes in the oven. Valerie's heart was full. She watched her boys moving around the kitchen, completing everyday tasks, and realized just how blessed she was that the mundane now felt like a miracle. She was so thankful for this everyday moment on an ordinary Tuesday that it almost brought tears to her eyes.

Any minute, Joe would walk through the door, and the six of them would sit down and eat a family meal just like nothing had ever happened. The only signs of a life changed were Eli's slimmer frame, Beau's high and tight haircut and the presence of two new people who would never have come into their lives had it not been for the crash. She took a deep breath and said a silent prayer of thanks.

During the meal, the conversation turned to the soon coming addition to the family. "Have you two settled on a name yet? You're running out of time, you know," Valerie said lightheartedly.

"Well," Julia spoke up, "I keep going back and forth. Nothing seems to fit, and Beau shoots things down faster than I can come up with them!"

"Listen, I don't want my kid to have a name that sets them up for instant ridicule at school. I mean, look at Eliza for example. I came up with that in the first grade!" Beau casually gestured across the table with his fork. Everyone at the table got a good laugh.

"Look here, I seem to remember somebody else who endured a few names. Only, he didn't have a brother who perpetuated the problem. Isn't that right, Little *Beau* Peep? Or maybe you prefer my personal favorite, *Beau*-nana?" Eli raised his eyebrows and ran his tongue over his teeth and made a smacking sound with his mouth after he finished speaking. For some reason, this succeeded in catapulting Joe into a fit of laughter that brought tears to his eyes. Not even he knew why he found the moment so funny, but after about a minute, his reaction had pushed everyone else over the edge too — they were laughing at his laughter and the chain reaction had taken over.

Finally, after Valerie's stomach was sore from laughing at this nonsense, she composed herself and spoke up. "Oh, me... whew, well, I think kids can come up with nicknames for anyone, regardless of what their actual name is. If they want to poke fun at you, they'll find a way. So, what are your favorites?"

"I wish I could say I had one. I kind of liked Blake Aaron, but Beau said it sounds too much like Hank Aaron," Julia answered.

"What?" Valerie said, sounding shocked. She looked at Beau. "No, it does not. Nobody would even think of that if you hadn't mentioned it."

"Maybe, but now that you've heard it, you can't stop thinking it, can you?" Beau responded. "I couldn't either."

"He's right. It's in my head now," Andy admitted.

"Mine, too," Joe added. Eli nodded his agreement. "You know, Joseph is a great name," Joe added.

The two ladies shared a look that spoke volumes about the male mind. Valerie rolled her eyes at her husband and shook her head. "Let's all think on it a bit, pray about it. The perfect name *will* come up," Valerie reassured Julia with her words and a pat on her forearm.

They continued on with their meal, laughing and chatting about other things when, out of nowhere, Beau suddenly spoke up, completely changing the subject. It just came to him out of the blue. "Gabe. Gabriel Andrew McKnight, after the two men who saved my life." He glanced at Andy. "We'll call him Gabe."

He looked across the table at Julia, who began to smile softly. She nodded and looked to her left at Andy. She reached out her hand and squeezed his shoulder. The name fit. It felt right. "Yes! It's perfect!" she said.

~

Julia had been uncomfortable all morning on what felt like the longest Thursday of her life. After a light lunch, she asked Valerie if she could use her bathroom for a soak in the oversized tub. Unsurprisingly, Valerie graciously agreed and even pulled out some of her favorite bath salts and essential oils in the hopes that Julia might find some relief from the nagging back pain she'd complained about since breakfast. Beau, Eli and Andy had gone out for the day. Beau and Eli both needed distractions and Andy thought a movie might be just what the doctor ordered. They planned to go to a matinee and then they'd grab dinner out, before deciding whether or not they were up for a "boys' night."

With Joe at work and Valerie planning to get the grocery shopping done, Julia thought it would be the perfect day to relax and prepare herself for their new arrival. She looked down at her belly, feeling baby Gabe pressing against her ribs as if he already wanted her full attention. She didn't realize it was possible to love someone you'd never met until she became pregnant, but since the day she saw her baby's heartbeat flashing on her first ultrasound, she'd felt an overwhelming sense of love for him. She was beyond excited to meet him, but she was also terrified of how much their lives would change and how little she knew about being a mother. She began to fill the tub, lost in her thoughts of motherhood, when she heard the house phone ringing in Joe and Valerie's bedroom. She decided to ignore it. It was probably a telemarketer. Anyone who really needed to reach them would probably have their cell numbers anyway. She returned to her bathwater and tried to forget the phone call.

She tried to forget her swollen ankles and aching back and she tried to forget about her worries and fears — so many fears. What if she was a terrible mother? What if Beau deployed again? What if he changes his mind? She imagined holding her baby for the first time and watching Beau as he nestled their tiny boy in his big arms. Now that they'd come this far, she couldn't imagine doing this with anyone but Beau. She couldn't imagine life without him. She wondered how she'd ever lived without him. He wasn't exactly the Beau she remembered from childhood, but he was exactly the Beau she needed him to be. But, what if he never found his happiness again?

She felt her heartrate increasing as her fears about the future gripped her. Why couldn't she stop being afraid?

Suddenly, she felt the overwhelming urge to pray, she didn't know why or even how the idea had come to her. She unexpectedly felt an uncontrollable need to know this Jesus Valerie and Joe and Eli and Andy talked about so often. She felt an overwhelming desire to know the God that was there the day Beau's life was spared. She couldn't let another minute pass without Him. She didn't even really know how to pray, but she couldn't ignore the need.

"God? Are you there? I... I don't know what to say, or how to do this, but... but I'm going to be a mother and I'm scared. I'm so scared. But, I believe. I do believe, in You, in Jesus. I do believe, and I'm so sorry for all the things wrong in my life. So, please God. Please, help me. Help me figure it out. Save me. I need you. And... Beau needs you." The words stopped coming because she didn't know what else to say. Tears filled her eyes and she simply cried out from her spirit. She didn't speak, but she could feel her spirit reaching out to God like a beam of light. And then, as if it were raining down from the sky, she felt an overwhelming sense of peace wash over her entire being. She felt a sense of certainty that everything would be okay. She felt hopeful and she felt... free. As she slid into the warm water, tears began to stream down her face. She couldn't process the overwhelming peace and love that surrounded her. She could literally feel God's love like an invisible embrace. Nothing in her circumstances had changed, but *she* had changed. "Thank you," she whispered. "Thank you. I didn't know. I just didn't know what I was missing."

~

Beau could feel his phone vibrating in his pocket over and over during the movie. He knew he had missed at least one call, but decided to check it after the movie ended. As he and Eli and Andy headed out into the lobby, he pulled the phone from his pocket and saw a missed call from a number he didn't recognize. He had a voicemail and two text messages. He decided to check the text messages first. They were from Julia:

<I MET JESUS TODAY.>

<I LOVE YOU.>

Beau stood staring at his phone. What? What did that even mean? He thought he might know what she meant, but, at the same time, he didn't know for sure. He was speechless. Somehow, instead of feeling gladness, he felt abandoned. For some unknown reason, his kneejerk reaction was resentment. He knew he shouldn't feel that way, so he made a concerted effort to adjust his attitude. He held out his phone to Andy. Andy looked down and Beau watched as a huge smile spread across his face. "I knew it! Praise the Lord!" He turned to Eli, "Come check this out!"

Eli finished putting the last of his trash into the bin and walked over to where Beau and Andy were standing. Andy took Beau's phone from his hand and placed it in Eli's hand. "What? Oh, wow! That's so awesome!" Eli reached the phone toward his brother and moved in close to hug him, a hug that wasn't returned. Eli looked at him and back to Andy, "Oh, my gosh, I needed that. I mean, I *know* she needed it, but I needed it, too." Beau said nothing.

As they continued out into the parking lot, Beau hit the button to play his voice messages and put his phone to his ear. Without warning, he took the phone and hurled it as hard as he could. Andy was walking beside him and Eli was about ten paces ahead. The phone flew over Eli's shoulder, flying end over end through the air before it came to rest in the damp mulch in a median about fifty feet from where they stood. Eli stopped in his tracks, ducking instinctively, even though it was too late by the time he saw the phone flying through the air. "What was that?" He turned toward Andy and Beau with a shocked expression on his face.

"That would be Beau's phone," Andy answered, his hands in his pockets and his face serene as always. But he looked at Beau from the corner of his eye and pursed his lips, as if to suggest an overreaction on Beau's part.

"What? Why? Are you crazy?" Eli asked emphatically.

"They're delaying my med board," Beau said, flatly. Didn't they understand that he needed to get back to being a Marine? He didn't know how to define himself without it. He needed to be good at something and make it the very fiber of who he was as a person. Without it, he felt like he had no value.

No one said anything for a moment. Andy and Eli had both expected it, at least to a certain degree. They didn't exactly understand why he had his heart set on it, but they knew he did, which meant this news was very, very bad.

"Oh, no. I'm sorry, Beau," Eli said. It was clear he meant it — it wasn't a pacifying 'I'm sorry,' it was heartfelt. "But, maybe it's for the best. I mean, you have a better chance of going back to full duty if you're fully healthy, right? I mean, you get this last surgery, get back in the gym, you'll be back to work in no time!" Eli tried to sound hopeful.

"When did they delay until?" Andy asked. He knew that the longer Beau was away, the more difficult it would be to step back into his normal duties.

"They'll 'reassess my case' and let me know, but I'm probably looking at four more months, minimum, before they even look at it. I mean, my next surgery is in like a month, then there's six to eight weeks recovery and another month of rehab after that." Beau reached up with his hands and pressed against his eyes with his palms. Andy and Eli could hear the frustration in his voice.

"Dude," Andy said, "that will fly by. You're going to have a new baby to take care of. You probably won't even notice." He, too, kept his voice light.

As the three young men walked the rest of the way to the truck, Beau thought about their words. He knew, logically, they were right. He was still a Marine. It just didn't feel like it. But, he couldn't help feeling lost somehow. He didn't want his son to be born to a useless man. He felt like something was missing, something was off. He felt… empty. He looked at Eli and then at Andy, "You're right. I know you're right, it's just that…" He stopped short and changed course, "You know what, you all go on ahead. I just need some time, okay?"

"What? No," Eli said. "We're going to eat. You don't have a way home. I don't want to drive back up here tonight."

"Don't worry about me. I just need to walk around and clear my head." He turned to walk away. Eli called after him, but he kept walking. Andy watched him go, an uneasy feeling coming over him, but he kept it to himself.

"C'mon. Let him go cool off," Andy said. He knew there would be no deterring Beau at this point. His hard-headedness was in control.

"Really?" Eli said. He didn't want to leave his brother behind. Andy nodded. They got into the truck and Eli started it up. He started to pull up behind his brother, but something about Beau's posture told him not to. As Beau made his way toward the adjacent strip mall, Eli and Andy pulled out of the parking lot. Eli watched Beau closely as he trudged across the parking lot with his hands in his pockets and his head down.

"You think he'll be okay?" he asked Andy.

Andy still felt uneasy, but he answered honestly, "As long as he doesn't do something stupid."

As Eli and Andy pulled away, Beau turned and watched them over his shoulder. He didn't know where he was going, or what he planned to do, but he needed an outlet. He reached into his pocket and fiddled with the loose pills rolling around inside. He pulled out three and swallowed them all at once. He felt a pang of guilt, knowing he'd promised Eli that he'd stop, but he *needed* them, now more than ever.

CHAPTER TWENTY-SIX

When Andy and Eli walked through the front door, they were engaged in casual conversation, getting to know each other and becoming fast friends. They were very different but seemed to have a lot in common, and Eli found Andy to be hilarious, which definitely aided in their fast-growing "like" for one another. They'd exchanged "Beau stories" all afternoon and into the evening, and since Beau had returned a text confirming that he was okay and would be catching a ride home with one of his old buddies, they'd let themselves move past the hard news of the afternoon. When they walked into the great room together, Julia was pacing the floor, breathing heavily, and Valerie was sitting nearby staring at her watch.

"They're getting closer together, but they're still far enough apart that you might not want to go just yet. Still, I think this might be it," Valerie said. "Maybe you should get back into the tub for a while?" she suggested.

Julia looked up at the boys, her face was flushed and her hair was pulled back, but she smiled. "I'm so glad you all are back," she said. Eli and Andy looked at each other, knowing it wasn't *them* she was glad about. Julia saw the look they exchanged. "What's happening? Where's Beau?" she asked, urgency building in her voice.

"You mean he didn't call you?" Eli asked.

"What do you mean, 'call me'? No," she answered.

"Well," Eli began, "he got a call about his medical evaluation. They delayed it. He was pretty upset and wanted to be by himself for a while. He left before we went to dinner."

"But he texted and said he was getting a ride home with one of his buddies. Some guy he knew from the gym or something," Andy added.

As Julia's contraction subsided, so did the urgency in her voice. "Okay." She appeared relieved. "We need to get him back here, though."

Valerie closed her eyes. She knew which buddies he was referring to. She grabbed her phone and dialed Joe's number. As she filled him in on what was happening, both Eli and Andy began texting away, trying to reach Beau. Julia reached for her phone and decided to skip a text and just call. She dialed Beau's number quickly and waited, after four rings it went straight to voicemail.

Eli and Andy listened as she spoke, "Hiya handsome, give me a call quick, okay? I think we're having a baby!" Her voice was soft and sweet. She didn't sound agitated and seemed to be at peace.

"Wait," Andy remarked, "didn't you share some news with Beau earlier?" He spoke excitedly. For some reason, it felt like weeks had passed since the afternoon, instead of mere hours.

"That's right!" Eli added. He walked over to hug her and Andy followed. Andy barely even knew her, but he felt like a hug was appropriate.

"What is happening?" Valerie asked, seemingly confused by the scene. She walked over to the trio of huggers as they stood in the middle of the great room. Julia was beaming, and Andy and Eli along with her. "Somebody tell me!" she exclaimed. Valerie was smiling along with them, but she didn't know why.

"I met Jesus today Ms. Valerie. I gave my life to Him." She smiled at Val, who immediately burst into tears. She'd been praying for Julia for months and months, and to know that she'd step into motherhood as the daughter of the King gave her such joy, and such relief, that she couldn't put it into words. The celebration was short lived however, because Julia felt another contraction coming on.

"That wasn't very long at all." She looked at Julia and back at the boys. "I think it might be a good idea if we went on to the hospital, just in case."

Julia nodded emphatically. She couldn't speak, but wanted Valerie to know that the hospital would be a welcomed destination.

"Alright, you two need to find Beau. This is a big deal now, so maybe go to the gym and start asking questions. We'll all keep calling him, surely one of us will reach him. I'm going to text Joe. Julia, honey, when this one passes, you need to call your mom."

"Yes ma'am," Eli said. Julia just nodded.

"Maybe we should take my truck and your dad's truck, just in case. I mean, it feels like we should. I don't know why," Andy spoke up.

"Dude, if I'm going with anybody's gut feeling, it's yours. Mom, can we use the truck again?"

"Yes, yes. Just be careful." It hadn't dawned on Valerie until that moment that neither of her boys had a vehicle on hand. She'd fought Joe on the need for an extra truck that she didn't think they'd use often enough, but right now, she was glad she'd lost that battle.

~

Andy and Beau had followed breadcrumbs all over Longview searching for Beau. Hours had passed and Julia was in full blown labor. When Valerie called, Eli could tell that they were getting dangerously close to baby time. He could hear Julia asking for Beau in the background, "Is he here yet?"

"Not yet, but he's coming," Valerie answered.

"They're hopefully coming to give her an epidural soon. The anesthesiologist has been tied up and Julia's growing impatient." In a hushed voice, she added, "If they don't hurry, she'll be too far gone to have one, but I'm not going to tell her that."

"We're trying, Mom."

"I know. Just, hurry," Val said. "Love you."

"Love you," Eli returned.

Andy felt his phone buzz in his pocket. He pulled it out and noticed a text from a number he didn't recognize.

<HEY, IT'S JON AT GYMBOX. THERE'S A HOUSE PARTY HAPPENING ON MAHLOW, HEARD YOUR BOY WAS THERE.> He held the phone out to Eli and let him read the text.

"Let's go," Eli said, plugging the street name into his GPS.

"Right behind you," Andy added.

Ten minutes later, they were driving slowly down Mahlow Street, making their way to the house hosting the party. It was hard to miss. There were dozens of cars parked on the lawn and the curb. Eli and Andy parked a good distance away and got out of their respective vehicles at the same time. They looked at each other, hesitant to walk to the door, but determined to do so anyway. "Well, let's do this," Eli said as he took the first few strides toward the house. Andy followed right behind him.

Andy rang the doorbell. They stood for several minutes before deciding that no one would be coming. Eli knocked with all the force he could muster, beating his hand on the door like a gorilla beating the ground. A young woman with jet black hair, dressed in a T-shirt and cut-off shorts and black combat boots and sporting a rather impressive nose ring answered the door. "Yeah?" she said, dismissively.

"Uh, we're looking for Beau McKnight. Is he here?" Eli asked.

"Um. Maybe. You can come in and see for yourself, I guess. You're not cops are ya?"

"Not cops," Andy added.

The girl moved out of their way and they passed through the door into a loud, smoky room full of people they'd never seen before. Music blared and there was barely room to move. Most of the crowd ignored them completely. Two people asked if they wanted drinks and a third swore she knew Andy from high school, though he was certain she did not. Eli and Andy looked room to room, face to face, hoping to find Beau. Finally, Andy spotted a muscular guy in a GymBox T-shirt standing in the kitchen. He held a beer in one hand and a slice of pizza in the other. He was laughing loudly and seemed like the kind of guy who really liked attention. Andy pointed in his direction for Eli's benefit, the music was so loud it was impossible to speak over it.

Eli made his way across the room and Andy followed. "Hey, man," Eli yelled. "I'm looking for Beau McKnight."

"What the… Dude, I know your face!" the guy screamed back at Eli.

"I'm Eli. Beau is my brother."

"No way. Dude, we thought you were dead!" The big guy laughed at his own joke and seemed totally oblivious to the fact that Eli and Andy didn't join in.

"Yeah, yeah. Is he here?" Eli shouted, getting to the point.

"What?"

"Beau, is he here?"

"Oh, yeah. He's here. He passed out, man. He's in the back bedroom." Eli gestured down the hallway, silently asking which way to go.

"Yeah, bro. Last door on your left," the big guy yelled and then turned away from them as they moved slowly through the crowd and down the hallway. Andy opened the door to the last room on the left and slowly stepped inside. Except for the glow from a digital clock, it was pitch black.

"I can't see anything," Eli whispered.

"It stinks," Andy added. Andy flipped the switch on the wall but nothing happened. "Great."

Eli got his phone out and used its light to create a faint glow on the floor. There appeared to be stuff laying everywhere. He moved cautiously through the mess until he came to a desk. "A lamp," he whispered. He flipped the button on the small desk lamp and light filled the room. Andy blinked against the light and began looking around. There was a person sprawled out face down on the bed, but it most definitely wasn't Beau.

"There," he said in a hushed voice, pointing to a grungy plaid sofa that was pushed up against the back wall. They each carefully stepped over cans and clothes and papers and all manner of trash scattered on the ground as they made their way toward the sofa.

When they found Beau, he was lying with his back toward the room, on his left side. He had one shoe on and one off and his head was cocked awkwardly toward his left shoulder. Eli walked over and put a hand on his brother's arm. He didn't budge. In fact, he didn't move at all. "Beau," Eli whisper-shouted. "Beau, wake up." He shook him again. Nothing.

"Let's roll him over," Andy suggested. Together, they managed to roll Beau onto his back, the right half of his body was off the couch. His wounded arm fell backward toward the floor and stuck out, stiff, in the air. His face showed obvious signs of pallor. "Eli, check him. Is he breathing?" Andy's hushed voice rang out with urgency.

Eli moved close to Beau. He put his ear almost on his brother's mouth, feeling for breath. He watched for his chest to rise and fall. He held his own breath in suspense. "He's breathing! Thank God!" He moved his ear to Beau's chest and listened for his heartbeat. As he did this, the big guy from the kitchen stepped through the door.

"Wow. He's worse for wares, ain't he?" he chuckled.

"How much did he have to drink?" Eli asked.

"Did he take something?" Andy added immediately.

"Whoa, whoa now. I don't know how much he drank, but he was already kinda messed up when I picked him up at that strip mall by the theater."

Eli felt anger wash over him like hot lava. He abruptly reached toward Beau's pockets, patting them with his hands like a police officer frisking a suspect. "He's taken too many of those pills, I'd bet anything. I don't know how, but I know it. He took those pills and then came over here to drink and now, this." He stood up and gestured toward his brother angrily.

"We need to get him out of here," Andy said. Eli nodded and working together they put his shoe on and hoisted him up to a seated position. His head flopped forward like a rag doll. Andy sighed. "What were you thinking, you big idiot?" he spoke to Beau under his breath. Beau's right arm wouldn't extend enough to raise over Eli's shoulder, but with Andy on his left side and Eli holding the weight of his body at his beltline, they managed to get him up. He hung between them, lifelessly. "Let's get him outside." They slowly and clumsily pulled him toward the door, his feet dragging behind him and his shoes scrubbing the floor beneath his toes. When the crowds of people saw them coming, dragging Beau's flopping body, they instinctively made a path. It was slow going, and none of the other party guests offered to help or even get the door. Once they finally got him outside, they knew they'd have to carry him the rest of the way to where they'd parked.

"What are we going to do?" Eli asked. "He can't go see Julia like this." No sooner than the words were out of his mouth, Beau began to retch. He threw up all down the front of his shirt and jeans and Eli gagged at the sight of it. "Are you kidding me right now?" he yelled into the night. "Do we need to take him to the emergency room?"

"I don't know," Andy answered. Let's get him into the back of my truck. He can lay back there until we figure out what to do." Together, they worked to pull Beau's solid frame into the back of Andy's truck. "Let's roll him over. What if he pukes again?" Andy asked.

Just as they began to roll him over, Eli felt his phone buzzing in his pocket. He quickly pulled it out and saw a text from his mother, <DILATED TO TEN. IT'S TIME. WHERE ARE YOU?!???!!> "No!" Eli said emphatically. "He's missing it. He's going to miss it. We're all missing it!" Eli was angry, but he was also worried. Andy could hear disappointment and regret in his voice. "What an idiot!" Eli rubbed his face hard. "Why did I let him walk off like that? What was I thinking?"

"This is *not* your fault." Andy also bore his own regret. He recalled his uneasy feeling — the Holy Spirit trying to guide him — but he'd dismissed it and now, this. Beau retched again. "You go to the hospital. I'll try to get him cleaned up. If we take him to the ER, it could ruin his life. He's still under 21."

"Look at him, Andy. He's ruining his life all on his own!" Eli was so angry he couldn't muster the ability to feel sorry for Beau.

"You go. Get to the hospital. Maybe you can make it before the baby gets here. I'll deal with Beau. I'll figure it out."

"What do I tell Julia when I get there? What do I tell Mom?" Eli's arms were up, his fingers interlaced on top of his head, in the same posture Andy had seen during Beau's battle story. "I mean, this should be the best day of her life — first, her faith and now the baby — but, what...? I'm supposed to rush into the room while her child is being born and say 'Guess what, your baby's father is passed out in the back of a truck, drugged out of his mind'?" He paced back and forth quickly. "I just can't do that, man!"

"Then don't..." Andy felt pressed for time. Normally, he'd try to slow down and wait for the spirit to give him *something* to go on, but this circumstance didn't lend itself to anything he considered *normal*. "Just, well, just tell them I found him and that we'll be there as fast as we can. At least we know where he is. Maybe that will help." Andy looked at Eli, "Now go, hurry!"

"Are you sure? Is that the right thing? Is that what you want to do?" Eli asked.

"Go! I'm sure!" Andy said again, with some force this time. Eli moved slowly toward his dad's truck, watching Andy in the back of his own, staring down at Beau from under a crinkled brow. As Eli pulled out, he could see Andy kneeling over Beau, one hand on his forehead and the other extended toward Heaven. He watched in his rearview mirror as Andy and Beau grew smaller and smaller until they'd faded out of sight.

Andy looked up toward his outstretched hand and began to call out to God. Two words into his prayer, Beau began to shake. Without warning, he began to jolt violently against the truck's abrasive bed liner. He was on his stomach and his face jerked roughly against the bed beneath him. Andy fell to both knees and moved toward Beau's head. His typical level of confidence and certainty seemed to evaporate as he watched his friend seizing beneath him. He did his best to gently create a barrier between the skin of Beau's face and the bed of his truck. He'd never seen a seizure before, but somehow, he knew what it was immediately. He held Beau's head in his hands as the consequences of his choices wreaked havoc on his body. As he postured himself to call on God for a second time, he found himself feeling uncertain for the first time in a long time, so he paused. He felt the icy chill of fear creep up his spine and did his best to reject it, but he struggled. Should he rush Beau to the hospital? Should he call 911? Andy's mind raced. He knew God had brought him and Beau together for a reason, but what if he didn't have enough faith to help him? What if he wasn't strong enough? "Beau made this storm all by himself," he thought. "What if I don't have enough faith to protect him from the rain?"

~

Eli sprinted through the sliding doors of the emergency entrance at Longview Regional. He huffed and puffed, trying to fill his lungs with oxygen. As he made his way to the directory of floors hanging on the wall, he realized he hadn't run like that since, well since before the coma, and he tried to slow his breathing to calm himself. His eyes skimmed over the long list of names and floors mounted on the wood-toned panel in front of him. He wasn't exactly sure what he was looking for until he saw it. "Maternity care," he whispered to himself. He tore off around the corner toward the elevators.

A short woman in scrubs was heading down the adjacent hall toward the elevators and saw Eli's uncertainty. "Can I help you out?"

"Labor and delivery?" Eli asked, clearly frazzled.

"Third floor, hon," she responded with a smile. "Congratulations!" Given his level of stress, she incorrectly assumed Eli was an expecting father. He knew what she was thinking, but didn't bother to correct her.

"Thank you," he said, as the elevator doors closed behind him. When he finally found labor and delivery, he was directed to Julia's room and stopped outside the door. Should he knock? The nurse at the nurse's station saw him.

"Can I help you?"

"Um, I don't know. I'm the uncle, but my brother isn't here yet and I know she's anxious about it. I just want her to know that we found him and he'll be here as soon as he can."

"Okay. Sit tight. I'll let them know you're here." She stood up from her spot and walked around the desk. Eli stepped back and put his back to the wall outside the room. The nurse opened the door just enough to fit her body through and was gone for about a minute before she stepped back out into the hall. "It won't be long and you'll be an uncle! I told her you were here and your brother was coming as fast as he could. She's doing great."

"Thank you," Eli said, letting out a breath he felt like he'd been holding for an hour.

The nurse pointed him to the waiting room and vending machines. "In fact," she said, "I think that might be your dad in there... Joe, I think it was?"

"Yes ma'am, thank you." Eli nodded his thanks. "But, I think I'm just going to sit here for a minute, if that's okay?" Eli knew there was no way he'd be able to sit in a room with his father and not give Beau's secret away. He knew he couldn't look his dad in the eye and pretend everything was fine, when he knew in his heart they were anything but fine. His father would see right through him. He slid down the wall to the floor, his knees bent in front of him. He propped his forearms on his knees and lowered his head toward his chest. He whispered, "We could really use your help now, Lord." Though he still felt stressed, Eli gave his worry over to God and grabbed on to His promise of peace. He lifted his head, leaned it back against the wall, and waited.

~

"You're doing great, honey!" Valerie called out.

"Yes, baby, you got this!" Julia's mom stood on one side of the bed and Valerie stood on the other. Julia was focused on her doctor. She was exhausted, but calm. She had thanked God for epidurals several times since her anesthesiologist showed up, and now, she was moments away from meeting her son. As baby Gabe made his way into the world, Valerie burst into tears. Julia's mother cheered and Julia gave herself over to a love that would change her life forever. Tears rolled down her face as she gave thanks to her newfound Savior for her newborn baby.

The nurses and her doctor were all smiling and laughing. In the hallway, Eli heard the laughter and the cheering. He climbed to his feet quickly. A smile spread across his face as he listened to the sounds of new life pouring from the room behind him. He blinked against the tears forming in his eyes and allowed himself to focus on nothing but the miracle of the new baby's cries.

"He looks perfect!" Julia's doctor said, as Gabe let out his first sweet cries. "Ten fingers and ten toes!"

"Wow, Mama!" one of the nurses said. "He's a big little bundle!" Valerie laughed and gave Julia a look that spoke volumes.

"You should see his father," Julia added with a laugh.

"Who's going to cut this cord?" Julia's doctor was sweet and patient, but he also had a commanding presence and remained very focused. He had a job to do.

Julia looked at her mom, and then at Valerie. Beau should have been there — they all felt it — but he wasn't, and Julia had a decision to make. "What about Eli?" she asked excitedly. "Maybe his uncle would want to do it? If it's not too... you know... uncomfortable." The nurse moved toward the door. "I think Beau would like that. Don't you?" Julia looked toward Val.

Valerie smiled and said, "Absolutely!"

When the nurse asked Eli if he wanted to cut the umbilical cord for his nephew, he paused, "Really?" he asked. The nurse nodded, she was smiling and he couldn't help but smile back. He followed her into the room. Julia's nurses had worked quickly to make sure she could preserve at least some of her modesty before Eli came in. Baby Gabe was loosely wrapped up, resting on his mother's chest — mere seconds old. Julia watched as Eli quickly wiped a tear from his eye while he listened to the doctor's instructions. He seemed entirely unfazed by the scene and engrossed in the majesty of the moment. Eli did exactly as he was told and watched as a nurse moved Gabe from Julia's chest to a small tray across the room. He watched them as they worked, weighing, measuring and wrapping this delicate, tiny person. He put his hands in his pockets and did his best to stay out of the way.

"Nine pounds, two ounces!" Julia's nurse called out from her spot at the scale.

"Holy moly!" Julia's mom chuckled.

"Yep, that's a ballplayer," Valerie added, as they all laughed together.

Eli couldn't stop staring at his nephew, taking in the sight of his tiny hands and feet as they stretched and kicked against the cold air and bright light of the real world. The nurse looked over her shoulder at Julia. The doctor was still tending to her. Valerie was already taking pictures and Julia's mother was already sending joy-filled messages to the world.

The nurse lifted little Gabe into her arms and walked toward Eli, who was caught off guard, but quickly pulled his hands from his pockets. He held out his arms and Gabe's nurse placed him gently into them. Eli stared down at him, smiling, and then he turned toward Valerie with a look of sheer awe on his face. Valerie sniffed against her tears and snapped the first of many photos of Uncle Eli and baby Gabe. As the doctor finished with Julia's post-delivery care, Eli walked slowly and carefully toward her, his eyes locked on his new nephew's perfect face. He knew, in that moment, that none of life's circumstances could outdo God's blessings. Even if Ivy never came back to him... even if he never got through to Beau — God would always be good and he would always be blessed. As Eli nestled the baby into his mother's arms, there was no question, no doubt in anyone's mind that love had bonded them for life.

The Hangdog Trilogy Continues in Book Three,
~Hangdog III — The Absolution~

AUTHOR'S NOTE

Thus far in my life, I have yet to do anything one hundred percent flawlessly. This book is no exception. I have done my best to present accuracy and continuity in every line, but if you search for mistakes, you'll likely find them.

I should also add that this is a work of fiction. Names, characters, events and incidents are either the products of my imagination or used in a fictitious manner. Any resemblance to actual persons, living or dead, or actual events is purely coincidental.

WHAT I BELIEVE

As this is a work of *Christian* fiction, I would be remiss not to share the greatest news I've ever received – Christ. I believe in the One living God, and Jesus Christ as God in the flesh. I believe Christ died on the cross at the hands of sinful man to redeem me (all of us) from our sin and to restore our perfect relationship with the Father. I believe in *every* promise of Scripture. I believe in miracles – I've lived them. I believe God wants to bless us – I walk in it. I believe He wants us to live lives full of joy. I believe He wants the best for us. And I believe loving others means sharing this news, come what may.

THE PLAN OF SALVATION

Accepting this gift is simple – Once you've chosen to trust Christ as your Savior, and you truly believe in your heart that God loves you, that He sent His son, Jesus, to die as redemption for your sins, and that Christ rose again to conquer the grave, all you have to do is confess that belief.

"9 If you declare with your mouth, "Jesus is Lord," and believe in your heart that God raised him from the dead, you will be saved. 10 For it is with your heart that you believe and are justified, and it is with your mouth that you profess your faith and are saved." Romans 10:9-10

Once you've done these things, it's time to live as a Christ follower. It's challenging, but it's the most amazing, rewarding adventure I've ever been on. Get into the Bible, find like-minded people, and take active steps to resist sin and to grow in your faith. Once you see what God has in store for your life, you, too, will want to shout it from the rooftops – I guarantee it.

Made in the USA
Middletown, DE
29 October 2023

41504876R00183